長崎真珠

Also by Jill Vedebrand

TWO SAILORS
(Fiction)
Adventure/Sea Story

Six years in the early lives of Swedish Leif and Brazilian Georgio who run away to sea when they are sixteen and fourteen, meet in a dramatic shipwreck, become friends and professional sailors, share adventures, discover women, dangerous men and the world. A dramatic adventure set in the 1950's and located in Scandinavia, South America, West Africa and the Amazon.

TRAVELS WITH MY SEA CAPTAIN
(Non fiction)

A wonderfully funny and personal account of Jill Vedebrand's life on board a modern cargo ship with her sea captain husband and on their farm in a glen in Scotland. No shortage of drama, drunken cooks, surly engineers, violent weather and the fiery sea captain. True stories from thirty five different ports all over the world.

THE NAGASAKI PEARLS

Jill Vedebrand

Order this book online at www.trafford.com
or email orders@trafford.com
Most Trafford titles are also available at major online book retailers.

This is a work of fiction. All of the characters, names, organizations, and dialogue in this novel are
either the products of the author's imagination or are used fictitiously.
Printed in Victoria, BC, Canada.

ISBN: 978-1-4269-2416-3 (sc)
ISBN: 978-1-4269-2417-0 (dj)

Library of Congress Control Number: 2009914052

*Our mission is to efficiently provide the world's finest, most comprehensive book publishing service,
enabling every author to experience success. To find out how to publish your book, your way, and have it
available worldwide, visit us online at www.trafford.com*

Trafford rev. 1/14/2010

 www.trafford.com

North America & international
toll-free: 1 888 232 4444 (USA & Canada)
phone: 250 383 6864 ♦ fax: 812 355 4082

For Claire, Nicola and Peter

INTRODUCTION

For more than three hundred years, the daughters of the Takahashi family have cared for Yumiko's precious pearls, but after the war, the pearls disappeared. The year is now 1977. The recently retired chairman of the Takahashi Shipping company, Taru Takahashi, can now fulfil his ambition at last. No matter what the cost, he is prepared to travel the world and go to any lengths to find the family pearls. His seventeen year old granddaughter, Mariko, will travel with him.

In Sweden, Leif Hansson, the owner of a cargo ship, is a worried man. Strikes and violence are affecting the port in Gothenburg, he suspects his captain of stealing cargo, and his family is under threat. In Brazil, Georgia Silva is about to lose his licence. His fishing boats need serious repairs before they are allowed to put to sea again, his wife is expecting their sixth child, and he has very little money.

Twenty years ago, when Leif and Georgio were young sailors, the pearls were given to them by a Japanese captain they had rescued from the sea. Without knowing their significance, they sold them and the money they received changed their lives. When Taru discovers what happened, Leif and Georgio find themselves drawn into his obsession. Taru Takahashi is a very rich man with influence in the shipping business and they are ambitious men, but as the story unfolds, the search brings the three families closer together and their relationships change. As they begin to unravel the continuing story of the pearls and trace where they have gone they discover that money and influence will not be enough. The final step will take courage.

Chapter 1

There had been an accident on the exit road that led down to the docks from the bridge and traffic was at a standstill. Ships continued to sail into port or down to the sea, but on the bridge overhead, the traffic didn't move. Leif Hansson looked at the cars behind him. There was no space for anyone to turn around. They had nosed along behind each other, anxious to gain every inch and now they were stuck like lemmings with only one way to go. He stared through the windscreen at the flashing lights of the police cars and ambulance, several cars ahead of him in the line. Almost an hour had gone by.

He lit a cigarette, blew the smoke out of the open window into the icy rain and tried to stop thinking about everything he had meant to achieve that afternoon. The bank would be closing soon. He could use the time to visit the STELLA, if she was in port. The last message from the pilot station said she would be late getting in, but when he stepped out of the car for a moment, he could see her funnel among the other ships at Frihamnen far below.

Kurt would be packing up his cabin ready to go ashore for six weeks. It would be an idea to be there to meet Pettersson, the relief captain, when he arrived. Kurt had been a good captain for the STELLA until the last few months when his paperwork had begun to go astray. Kurt had apologized many times, but there had been serious problems with the lading bills on the last voyage and it had cost Leif a lot of money. Leif had gone back and forth in his mind about it. He was reluctant to tell an old friend that he was thinking of letting him go, but something was wrong, and he knew he had to make a decision soon.

The STELLA was a 12,000 ton general cargo ship and Leif's one and only vessel in his company. Gothenburg was her home port and Leif the sole owner. It gave him independence up to a point, but he couldn't control everything.

Leif had felt the tension at the docks growing month by month. Each time the ship owners agreed to new conditions with the stevedores, it was only a matter of time before more proposals would be presented. Negotiating with the unions was not the only problem. The long accepted case of whisky or box of oranges that went missing now and then, had started to become a noticeable percentage of the cargo. Leif suspected that like others, he was becoming a victim of a more assured and organized gang. Honest workers, afraid of losing their jobs, were threatened into silence. Leif was not planning to be silent. There were days when he was burning with anger, ready to confront them, even if he lost everything in the fight. At other times he thought of the consequences for his family.

He had poured everything he had into buying the STELLA, even taking out a second mortgage on the house, something he had kept from Ella. It niggled at him every day, but he didn't want to have to discuss the risk to their security each time the ship was delayed, or they lost an assignment to another company.

After he had bought the ship, he'd decided to stay ashore in the office, to keep control of his investment. He had hired Kurt and two relief captains and accepted that he would no longer go to sea himself, but it wasn't long before Leif became bored. He had thought of a new plan, to take over himself as a relief captain now and then, but by that time the threat of strikes at the port and problems with the stevedores had begun in earnest.

He thought about Kurt. He had seemed very nervous lately. He was remembering the young shipmate he had known years ago, leaning out from the cabin door with a broad smile, the day Leif had joined the BUENOS AIRES, and later, the dangerous voyage they had shared when they brought the ELISE back across the Atlantic, just the two of them, with no other crew and no proper sleep for days. Kurt's uncomplaining cheery nature had brought them through, standing at the helm with his red curly hair sticking up in all directions. Leif smiled as he thought of Kurt's hair as it was now, reduced to a few carefully arranged strands across his head.

You had a lot of courage when you were young, Leif was thinking. Was it courage, or the belief that nothing could possibly happen to you - only to other people. Would he attempt such a crossing today? Someone had said to him once that adventure was something that happened when you didn't have a proper plan but you went ahead anyway, and if you came out of it alive, you would say you had had an adventure, just as if you had planned it that way, all along. He remembered who it was now; it was his father, a man who had worked hard all his life on their small farm and never left Sweden. After he died, Leif discovered a box of travel books, maps, and tales of the sea that his father had collected over the years. Their farm was on the shores of Lake Vanern, a lake like an inland sea, where ships would come and go from the Göta canal and where his father must have looked up from the ploughing, or herding in the cows, to watch the ships pass by on their way to Gothenburg and the world.

It had been an adventure, that voyage back from the Amazon with Kurt on the ELISE. The boat had been his passion at the time. Now she stayed tied up at Lundbykajen and had been there all the previous summer without leaving the harbour once. If only Jörgen was interested, it would have been something. The few times he and Jörgen had taken her out in previous years had been a failure and they had arrived back irritable with each other, and Jörgen's resentment had lasted for days. Leif had quarreled with Ella about it. "How can you teach anyone to sail without giving orders?" he had asked her. "The ELISE is not a fancy yacht but an old cargo sailing ship and she's heavy to manouevre, you have to watch what you're doing". Ella had accused him of trying to force Jörgen to be interested in sailing when it was obvious that he wasn't and Leif had reminded her that he had made a promise to Georgio, Jörgen's father. "That was years ago", Ella had said "Things have changed."

Leif looked at himself in the mirror. A couple of years to go and I will be forty, he said to himself. He still had a good head of hair but he didn't always like the look in his eyes reflected in the mirror. He was preoccupied, ambitious, and he was already thinking about a second ship. He must be mad, he told himself. There were not many moments these days when he had time like this to reflect. It was true what Ella had said that morning, that the company was taking over his life and he had no time for his family. He thought of his fifteen year old daughter, Helen. Helen seemed to be getting along alright at school but what did he know? At least she was interested in ships and the sea. She had shown herself to be a good sailor, and had an instinct for it. He was remembering her the last time they had gone sailing on the ELISE, she must have been about thirteen. Why hadn't he thought about Helen learning to sail? He hadn't even talked about it to her. After he had bought the STELLA, the ship and the cargo business was all he had had time for. There was always something to worry about and he was swamped by the paperwork and tired out from the telephone calls at all hours. He had hired someone for the office but as everything required his decision and signature anyway, he was never free.

It was almost spring now. He must find time for the ELISE this summer and he would take Helen with him. He wouldn't bother Jörgen again, but he would have to think of something to help him take an interest in his future. Jörgen had been very moody since he had graduated last summer, hanging around the house and not putting much effort into looking for a job.

"When is this traffic going to be able to move again?" he yelled out of the window at a policeman walking by between the cars.

"When we have removed the two who are dead" the policeman replied with significance, reaching for his radio as he hurried by.

Leif looked down at the port. How bleak and uninviting it looked in the rain, not like a sunny port in Argentina with the warm smell of the tropics and tango playing on the radio all day.

The STELLA was leaving for Rio de Janeiro tomorrow. It made Leif think of Georgio, who had a fishing business now of his own to run, and four, or was it five children? Leif hadn't spoken to Georgio in a year. Their friendship was just another thing that had been pushed aside. The last time Georgio had seen his son was when Jörgen was ten years old. Why not ask Captain Pettersson to take Jörgen on board for the trip? Jörgen could see his father and get some experience on board. He would be surprised if Pettersson didn't persuade Jörgen to go. He had a powerful personality and teenage sons of his own. Leif decided to be clever about it. He would ask Jörgen to take a message to the ship tonight and let Captain Pettersson present it as his own idea. The thought cheered him, but as the traffic started to move forward again, he realized that it was what he would have chosen for himself at eighteen, and not what Jörgen would want to do at all.

Chapter 2

It was a Tullverket car and a container truck that had been involved in the accident. The Customs and Excise car had taken the worst of the impact, the front of the car was almost gone. There was a great deal of blood across the two front seats and blood ran with the rain down the side of the road. A man was standing by the cab door of the truck, smoking and talking to two policemen.

It was the back of the container truck that had collided with the car. One corner of the steel container was crushed in and the container was halfway off the truck, sloping at an odd angle, where the crane had pulled it away from the car. At a glance, it seemed to Leif that the truck had swerved, and the container had then broken loose and sliced across the car, but he couldn't understand how that could happen.

Leif wondered if he had known the men who were killed. Could have been anyone, could have been him, if he had been there earlier. He drove slowly down to the dock area, watching out for trucks and fork lifts that were always sweeping around, roaring back and forth between the dockside and the warehouses on the other side. He parked and sat with his hands on the wheel. He was shaken by the image of the accident. He probably did know the two men who were killed, and he had been thinking of himself, of being delayed, while they were dying in that mangled car.

He had no close friends among the Customs men, but they were all familiar faces. Sometimes they talked about personal things but it was not often. They were like the police, needing to stick to their official business. It was obviously an accident, but Leif felt uneasy. It was only two weeks ago that a Customs man had been found beaten up behind one of the warehouses.

The rain had now stopped and a soft light appeared through an opening in the grey clouds. Leif got out of the car and stood looking up at his ship, taking a moment to look along the white hull and read the name. The bridge and accommodation were at midship and it gave the STELLA a balanced look, as if the ship was a large motor yacht. Leif was glad he had arranged a repaint when the ship was delayed on the last voyage. It was only paint but it did impress people into thinking a ship was well maintained inside and out. It wasn't necessarily true, but Leif did keep the STELLA up to a high standard. Too high, others had said.

Now she was back in her home port again and Leif could look her over. When the ship was away he worried and felt disconnected. There was the telex, the VHF or the radio telephone when an agent in a dusty port thousands of miles away would manage to have a conversation with the captain on board, and then phone Leif at the office, but he felt out of control if he was not on board himself. He hoped the engineer had nothing new to report.

As he approached the ship he saw that one of the cranes on board was unloading at hatch number one and he was puzzled. The STELLA's last port was Hamburg where all cargo should have been unloaded. The gantry crane on the dock was loading containers onto the starboard side as he had expected but what was happening at hatch number one? He crossed the crane tramlines as the massive machine slid along the tracks behind him.

At the bottom of the gangway, three welders were leaning against their parked truck, smoking and reading newspapers. Leif had arranged that they should meet the ship when it came into port, to make repairs to hatch number one. He didn't have to ask them why they were not at work. One of the welders looked up and shrugged, indicating the activity at the hatch on board with a jerk of his head. They would have been there since the ship came in and Leif would still have to pay for their time and they hadn't even started. What was Kurt thinking? Why hadn't he put them to work? He had sent a telex yesterday.

Leif went up the gangway swiftly and made his way to the ship's office. Kurt was not there. Leif went over to the desk and looked around among the scattered papers. He took the stairs to the bridge and crossed to the chart table, found the log book and flipped it open. The binder where the telexes were filed was tucked away under a shelf. He went through the last few copies, turned a page or two on the log book and then went back down the stairs.

The door to the captain's cabin was slightly open and Leif could hear voices. There was a thick set man standing in the doorway, his back turned away and Leif didn't immediately recognise who it was. He could see Kurt over by the bed, bent over a suitcase, packing.

"I tell you I have had enough" Kurt was saying.

"That's for us to decide. We know all about you, don't forget that and don't think we.. " the man's voice was harsh, threatening. He stopped when he saw Leif. It was Jan, the foreman from ashore. What was he doing up here, in the captain's cabin."Captain Hansson" said Jan in greeting, his voice changing.

Leif looked across the room at Kurt's white face. "I

want to speak to you Kurt. Right away. Upstairs." He turned to the foreman who was still half blocking the doorway. "I suggest you continue this discussion by making an appointment to come to the ship's office.. The new captain is arriving this afternoon. You can take up any problems you may have with him."

The foreman almost smiled, but his eyes were hard. "Is that so? Then perhaps we shall do that" He glanced at Kurt and walked away up the passage.

Leif called after him "And first you make an appointment through the Chief Officer anytime you want to speak to the captain on board this ship."

The foreman raised a hand without turning around and went out on deck.

Kurt followed Leif up the stairs to the bridge. Leif closed the door and locked it.

"What's going on at number one?" Leif asked angrily. "I have three welders cooling their heels on the dock. I see you got my telex. What happened in Hamburg?"

"The hatch. We had a problem discharging number one. We couldn't discharge everything" said Kurt, avoiding his eyes and moving restlessly about.

"Couldn't.. Kurt you are talking to me, not a deck boy. It's not a reason and you know it." Leif opened the log book. "And what happened to the last few entries? Don't you believe in keeping a log book anymore?"

Kurt reached out to examine the log book and Leif saw that his hand was trembling. Kurt turned the pages back and forth as if he expected it to be in order. Through the bridge windows the arm of the crane could be seen swinging away to trucks waiting below, the net bulging with sacks of coffee. Leif went out on the bridge wing and looked down, then back at Kurt. He went in again, sliding the door closed with a crash.

"Are you stealing from me Kurt? I don't recognize

those trucks. What was Jan doing in your room, paying a visit?"

Kurt glared at him. Leif never alluded to Kurt's personal life and preferred to believe that it didn't exist. Sometimes he would ask after Bob, the steward that they had all sailed with years ago and he knew lived with Kurt in Dalarna, but Bob had been ill for sometime and was now permanently ashore. Kurt was away a long time when he was on the South American run, well, he had to have a life, perhaps it was that.

Kurt was pacing around opening cupboard doors as if he was looking for something, then he seemed to remember and reached into one of the pigeon holes where the flags were stored.

"It's the lens for Helen's camera. She left it behind when she was on board last month" Kurt gave it to Leif with a half smile, but Leif was not to be distracted. He put the lens cap in his pocket and took Kurt firmly by the arm.

"Well ... ?"

"I can't tell you now Leif"

"Can't?!" Leif cried. He looked into Kurt's eyes and saw how afraid he was. Did he guess Leif was thinking of replacing him? No, it was more than that. "Something is going on with you and this ship and you have to tell me. Right now Kurt."

"Leif, can you wait here and hand over for me? I have to leave. Captain Pettersson was delayed but he should be here within the hour. I want to talk to you, but not now, not here on board. I'll come to the house in the morning."

"You want me to sign you off and hand over the ship to Pettersson without giving me an explanation? First you can tell me why they are unloading coffee from number one. All of it should have been discharged in Hamburg, you know that. Never mind the problem with the hatch, that would not have been a concern. Are you in trouble Kurt? Because if you are, that means trouble for me, for the STELLA and for the company. That coffee has been deliberately overcarried, hasn't it? Good God Kurt, what are you doing? What have you involved yourself with? I can't believe this of you."

"They'll be finished soon. It wasn't more than a quarter of the cargo and just from number one. Don't do anything now Leif. They are dangerous and organised and they have the union in their pocket. The loading for Brazil is going well. They could even finish all the containers tonight, but if you interfere they'll make sure the ship is delayed. It would cost you more than a few tons of coffee."

"Interfere!?" Leif yelled "This is my damn ship, not theirs!" He let go of Kurt's arm and stormed around the room. This explained the missing cargo on the last two voyages, and the appointment Leif had arranged with the inspector from the insurance company concerning 'damaged cargo'. That had been changed at the last minute to a time when the ship had already sailed.

"Customs and Excise. They'll know how to deal with this" said Leif reaching for the VHF.

Kurt grabbed his hand. "No! They'll know I've been talking."

"This is stealing Kurt. From the supplier, from the ship, you, me and the crew. It affects us all. We can't afford it. Are you part of it? Are you getting a share? Is that it?"

Leif didn't believe it of Kurt but he wanted to provoke him, to give him courage to get out of whatever mess he was in. He had always known Kurt was vulnerable. He really liked him, liked his jokes over the telex, valued his friendship, the support Kurt had given them in the beginning when he and Ella had started to live together, the really good job he had been doing as captain on the Stella but it had always been a nag at the back of his mind that Kurt's private life would make a problem one day. They were probably blackmailing him.

"OK" said Leif, replacing the receiver, "but you can't expect me not to put a stop to this. You come to the house tomorrow and tell me everything. OK?"

As Kurt went down the stairs to get his bags, Leif called after him. "Don't worry Kurt, we'll see these devils in jail." He didn't see that Jan was standing on the next level by the open door.

Leif went back to the bridge and stared out across the port. He wasn't as confident as he had tried to sound. It would be a long road to get to that point and what was going to happen to his ship in the meantime, to the goodwill and the trade he had built up so carefully over the years?

He thought about the accident that afternoon. They wouldn't go that far would they? If they were prepared to be that violent he would have to worry for his family. How could he fight this and keep the ship running? His margins were so small, they could strike or just go slow and ruin his business.

Kurt hurried back to his cabin, picked up his suitcases and made for the gangway. Out on deck, Jan saw him appear at the top of the steps and signalled to the crane driver seated in the cab high above the ship. The crane began to move along the tramlines, carrying one of the steel containers that it had picked up from the dockside.

The container was swinging and turning a little. Instead of being lowered onto the deck of the ship, it was being carried further along the tracks.

Kurt was so eager to get away that he allowed himself only a moment of confusion that his car was parked on the dock close to the ships side. One of the seamen must have brought it from the car park. He felt in his pocket for the keys. Had he left them on his desk? He looked inside the car. No, there they were, in the ignition. He put his suitcases in the back and jumped into the driver's seat.

Leif was out on the bridge wing waiting for him to leave. As soon as Kurt was on his way he would start to sort the papers out and put what he could in order before Captain Pettersson arrived.

Down on the dockside, Kurt was turning the key in the ignition but the car was refusing to start. Out of the corner of his eye Leif saw the huge container travelling in mid air along the side of the ship. What was the driver doing? Leif shouted at him, but the noise of the crane drowned him out. He could see the driver through the cab windows. The crane driver's concentration was not on the ship but on the dockside below. The container was being lowered very slowly, to a position just above Kurt's car. Leif went to the rail and shouted again, then he ran down to the ship's office, to the drawer he knew would be locked, scrabbling for the master key on the chain of keys attached to his belt and grabbing a walkie-talkie from the shelf. Then across to the ship's safe and back up to the bridge wing, the ship's revolver in hand.

The container was now touching the roof of Kurt's car. There was a screech of metal on metal above the roar of the crane's machinery as the container swung gently to and fro, scraping the roof. Inside the car it had become as dark as night and Leif saw Kurt's terrified face at the window. Why doesn't he just get out of the car and run for it thought Leif. The car roof was beginning to buckle.

"This is Captain Hansson on the STELLA!" Leif roared into the walkie-talkie. "Stop what you are doing or I'll fire!" He unclipped a hailer from the wall and repeated the command.

The crane driver's walkie-talkie had to be on the same frequency. Leif watched him react and turn his head to look at the ship. Leif fired at the edge of the cab windows shattering one of the panes of glass.

"BACK UP! BACK UP I SAY OR YOU'LL BE NEXT!" Leif shouted into the walkie-talkie. The driver reacted immediately, working the levers. The container was raised up and the crane started to reverse back along the tramlines.

Leif raced down the stairs and onto the dockside, gun in hand. Sailors working on deck were already at the rail. Two of the crew followed Leif down the gangway carrying metal bars. The workers on the dockside backed away, then stood around in groups talking and watching.

Kurt climbed unsteadily out of the car. He stared up at the container as it swung away, then he pulled the bonnet of his car open and began to look inside. When the stevedores saw that Leif was advancing on Jan, they came forward, crowding around. Leif pushed the gun up against Jan's chest

"I could shoot you right here and now" said Leif, shrugging off the arms that were trying to pull him back. The two crew from the STELLA took a position either side of him.

"What is your problem Captain Hansson?" asked Jan with a smile. "A mistake, a joke. What do you want from this? No harm done except for damage to the crane windows."

"Don't you lie to me you fat pig" Leif replied. They all

turned their heads at the sound of Kurt's car starting up. Kurt jumped in and sped away.

"You see?" said Jan, pushing the barrel of the gun to one side. "All is well. If you want to make a problem there are many witnesses here to say you are threatening me with a gun and you have been shooting at our crane driver. Maybe they think you are not well, or crazy or something, but they could arrest you. That is a possibility."

"You are dealing with me now, not Captain Kurt. You can think of me as a lousy ship owner, a paper pusher, but you don't know anything about me and I can be capable of anything. You should watch yourself I can tell you." said Leif. "If anything happens to my ship I shall know just where to come and I won't be needing the police. When you have finished unloading number one you will see those two trucks stay right where they are. As you know well, that's part of a shipment for Hamburg and you will see that it gets loaded onto the next ship bound for there. You can fix that I'm sure and at no expense to me. When the STELLA is loaded with her new cargo you will see that she leaves on time."

"You are making accusations Captain Hansson and we may become angry at that we may not guarantee…"

A taxi was pulling up at the end of the dock. The driver opened the passenger door and a tall slim man in uniform got out.

"I think you will. The overloaded cargo and all loading completed on time. No delays. This is Captain Pettersson arriving and you won't find him such a pushover either. There will be an enquiry about the accident at the bridge this afternoon. Perhaps you and your men have been going too far this time. It might pay you not to make any more trouble"

Leif thought he may have gone too far himself, but he saw the nervous looks that the men exchanged with each other and he was sickened at the idea that he might be right. "You get the Customs and Excise on your back and I won't have to worry about you anymore"

Leif slipped the gun into his belt. Captain Pettersson stopped at the gangway, waiting for him.

"Problems?" the captain asked as they climbed the stairs to the ship's office. "In other ports too. Biting the hand that feeds us all and it's spreading. They come not to work but to have meetings. They have no respect for the employer anymore. They think all ship owners are rich and just out to exploit them"

Leif placed the revolver on the desk. "You might want to keep that close to you instead of locked away" He took a bottle from behind the bookshelf and poured two whiskies.

Captain Pettersson leant back in the chair. "I told you about my company. Strikes, work to rule, stealing cargo, then bankruptcy. If it helps at all, you know I am one step ahead of the game because of what I went through myself. When you have three ships, if they fail to hold up one then they'll get you on the next. Having the one ship could give you an advantage"

"And everything to lose" said Leif looking down at the dockside through the office windows. The whisky glass shook in his hand and he set it down. The men on the dock appeared to be going back to work, he heard the crane starting up on deck.

He thought about the madness of the past half hour. He couldn't have open warfare. There had to be another way. He hoped Kurt was not too afraid to meet him at the house in the morning, but suspected that he had just kept on driving and was now on his way home to Dalarna.

Chapter 3

Helen Hansson was trying to take photographs of her friends outside the school gates but they were not co-operating. They jostled each other, making jokes and wouldn't keep still. Helen was beginning to think it was deliberate. She lowered the camera in exasperation, tucked her blonde hair behind her ears again and waited for them to settle down.

"Hey Helen! Take one of me!" said a boy passing by. He stopped and stood very close, directly in front of her, hands on hips. She looked at him in what she hoped was a critical, professional way and started to fiddle with the adjustments on the camera to change the focus, wishing she had paid more attention to the instruction book. The camera was an expensive Nikon and more complicated than her old box camera and the results so far had been disappointing.

"Need some help?"

Helen turned to see who was speaking to her and was a little surprised to see it was a policeman.

"I'm just getting the hang of it" she said.

The boy gave up his pose and went on his way.

"Can I see ?" the policeman asked, smiling and holding out his hand.

She hesitated, then gave him the camera.

"I got it for my birthday" she said proudly.

The policeman was turning it over in his hands.

"And how old were you then? Fifteen? Is that a good guess?" He held the camera up, took a picture of her and smiled "My daughter is in your class"

"Can I have my camera back now" said Helen slightly annoyed.

"Present from your family?" the policeman asked, still holding on to it.

Helen face grew warm. Her friends gathered round.

"My uncle, well, a friend of my Dad's, he gave it to me" Helen said, sensing a change in the policeman's attitude. "Can I have it back now?"

The policeman slung the camera strap on his shoulder and took out his notebook.

"I'll give you a receipt" he said, starting to write in the book.

Helen was outraged. All eyes were fixed on her.

"Give it back!" Helen demanded angrily. She not only looked like her father with her clear blue eyes and slightly pointed nose, but had many of his characteristics. The policeman stared back at her.

"Can you give me your name and address"

"Why"?

"I have reason to believe this camera was stolen"

"Of course it wasn't stolen! What are you saying! My father will be furious if you take it away from me. How do I know you're a proper policeman anyway!"

Her friends goggled at her in amazement but Helen was more angry than confident. Something had to be wrong. This was Kurt's fault. What was he doing giving her a stolen camera?

"Your family name?" asked the policeman.

"My father is Captain Hansson" said Helen with a challenging look in her eye.

"Keillers Park. Your father owns the STELLA doesn't he?"

"Why did you ask me my name when you seem to know all about me?"

Her friends started to drift away. She was glad to see them go.

"And what's your name?" said Helen crossly.

The policeman took out his identification and pointed to his name on his uniform.

"Eliasson" said Helen "I shall remember that" she continued defiantly.

"And my father will telephone the police station tonight so you can apologise and return my camera!" she shouted back at him as she walked away.

Helen marched up the hill towards her home, digging her nails into her hands to stop the tears. How humiliating. In front of her friends too, and especially that Lisa, who she remembered now had been smiling through the whole thing. When she reached the driveway she stopped to get her breath. There were no cars. She was glad no one was home. She looked up at the house and then away down the hill across the harbour to the sea. The storm had passed and a strip of sunlight was spreading along the distant horizon. She could see a tiny sailing ship skipping along in the wind, passing the lighthouse and heading out to sea and she wished she were on board. 'But not with any of my so called friends,' she thought as she crunched up the drive. '.. especially not that Lisa. Just.. by.. myself'

Ella was humming to herself as she walked into the office. She placed the brochure and completed forms on the manager's desk and waited for him to finish talking on the telephone. "Sold" she said as he turned and looked up at her.

"Oh? Well done" said Mike Worchek as if he didn't quite believe her. "A solid deal? All signed? And the price?"

"Six hundred and twenty thousand kronor" Ella said and placed the check on the desk.

"Well, well. You are a surprise Ella."

"Am I?" said Ella in a softer tone than she felt.

Why should you be surprised? Because I am a woman? Because I am attractive? Ella's success in real estate sales had been increasing every week, and she was thinking it was about time Worchek got over his surprise. He hadn't asked her to sit down, so she took a chair for herself and sat looking at him as he studied the completed forms. She was enjoying the moment, the look on his face, the widening of his bloodshot eyes as he tried to focus through what Ella had first described to Leif as his 'spectacularly unattractive spectacles.'

"They have made a note here that you have promised to advise them on the colour scheme and the arrangement of the office furniture and equipment."

"That's right. I will do that in my spare time as I always do. It won't cost you anything Mr. Worchek."

"Is this a side business?"

"You could say so. Any fee I get I declare to the tax authorities. We have had this discussion before."

"Mmm" said Worchek, sucking his teeth.

Ella had passed her exams a year ago. She hadn't expected to be given the prime properties to sell in the beginning but was disappointed to receive the difficult commercial side of the business, the properties that had been on the books for weeks, usually located in run down parts of the city where the price and commission were low. When she was studying for the exam she had been motivated by the idea of introducing people to their new homes. Ella's hobby had always been looking at houses. Before she had decided on this new career she would annoy Leif by asking him to stop at 'for sale' signs when they were driving somewhere.

Five years ago, when the STELLA started to make a small profit, Leif had bought the villa at Keillers Park. Built in the 1920's it was a solid but charming house with a mature garden and Ella loved it, and for Leif, it was high enough on the hill to give a good view of the harbour. He couldn't understand why Ella still liked window shopping for houses when they had no plans to move. "Don't you like our house?" he asked her one day and she had laughed. "Of course. But I like my new dress and that won't stop me looking at others."

Her answer had irritated him. He was always conscious of Ella's background, the estate at Lidingö, the apartment on Strandvägen overlooking Stockholm harbour, and he had worked hard to provide her with the comfort she had known before. He didn't like her going to work and to his relief she had not been successful at the two jobs she had taken at first, in quick succession. 'That's the end of that then' he had thought. Then she had decided to work in real estate and he remembered all those 'for sale' signs that used to attract her like a magnet. He had been surprised at how hard she had studied for her certificate. When he saw that she had found something she loved to do, he tried to stop complaining when he came home and found her not there. Leif was too proud to admit to her what was really troubling him. They were the same age, thirty seven, but to Leif, Ella was still as beautiful as she was seventeen years ago when Leif had seen her for the first time, when she came on board the BUENOS AIRES. He hated the idea of other men being around her when he wasn't there.

When Ella had started to work for Worchek and was given the lists and photographs of unattractive office blocks and run down stores she was bitterly disappointed. She was not used to getting the least attractive side of a situation or of finding a man who took an instant dislike to her. She was surprised he hired her at all. Sitting in his functional but uninspiring office she had started to plan her strategy.

When a company made an enquiry she wouldn't rush to show them all the properties that might be suitable. First she would spend a little time finding out more about the client, their trade, the previous location and why they wanted to move. By the time she met a client at a property that might be suitable she had already made sketches for inexpensive improvements including colour schemes and with her enthusiasm the client would be swept along into seeing beyond what was usually a dull and boring space. She would have suggestions on how to have more light and comfort and she never showed a completely empty office. There would be flowers, a painting, even an exceptional table and chair brought temporarily from home. The clients began by asking price per square meter but quickly found themselves discussing curtains.

"Think how charming this room could be for your staff if..." Ella would begin.

It was hard work with the addition of the side business of 'interior design consultant'. It was a high flying title for someone who improved run down office spaces Leif had said at first, but when it was clear that it worked, he had no argument and Ella was in her element, always coming and going and so much on the telephone they had had to put in a second line.

They were both exhausted when they came home and had hardly seen each other recently. Leif had tried to slow her down by explaining that most of the extra money was simply going in tax and if she worked a little less it would make no difference to their economy, but it was not the money, it was the achievement, and Leif, in spite of his own ambitious nature could not understand why Ella was so fired up by her success.

Born into a rich family, there had been neither the expectation or the need to do anything more than make a good marriage and raise a family. It was not surprising that when Ella discovered that she had ability she was full of such enthusiasm.

Chapter 4

Jörgen was standing on the deck of the ELISE. It was early in the evening but it was getting dark and cold. Someone must have started the generator as the lights came on around the ship. He couldn't hear anything except the music and the noise from the party. He wondered who knew how to do that and what they might do next - try to take the ship out to sea? He swore at himself for allowing Kristian to persuade him to have a party on the ship as they all wanted to smoke. Lundbykajen was close to the commercial port. Kristian had said there would not be many people about after seven but Jörgen couldn't relax.

He could see some of his friends crammed into the wheelhouse behind him and hoped they wouldn't put their cigarettes or joints out on the floor. As it was he knew he would have to be up at dawn the next day to clean up in case Leif decided to check on the ELISE in the next few days. He had heard Leif say he had a busy day ahead so it wasn't likely Leif would come down to the ELISE that night, but Jörgen had been a bit unnerved to see that the STELLA was in port as they had passed by on the way to the party. Leif would certainly have been to visit the STELLA that day. There were several ships in port and Jörgen was relieved when he arrived to discover that he couldn't see the STELLA from where the ELISE was moored.

Jörgen had never liked being on board the ELISE; too much hard work. They never had any fun on board. Leif was so concerned about doing everything the right way and wanting to keep everything in perfect order. It was as if the ship was a person, almost a religion, and not some old cargo boat. Now Jörgen had put himself in the position of having to worry that something would happen to her. He had to smile.

In his own way Jörgen did care about the ELISE, but only for Leif's sake. He was bored with Leif telling the same stories about how he came to own the ELISE. He understood the part the ship had played in their history, but there was too much significance attached to it all, it had become a burden. It was history, and to Jörgen, that meant it was a long time ago.

"Jörgen!" someone shouted and Rune put his head out of the wheelhouse door. "Get your arse over here. Why the fuck are you freezing out on deck?"

"I'm waiting for the pizza!" Jörgen yelled back. He didn't want the pizza man to come onto the ship looking for them. The air was pungent even up on deck. Part of him didn't care. He was tired of caring he said to himself. Everyone wanting answers. His future. He had no idea. No idea at all.

A girl with wild red hair came up from below. It was Lisa. For sometime Jörgen had been tempted to ask Lisa out but had never got around to it. She had arrived at the party with someone else and he cursed himself for not phoning her before. She strolled across the deck and his eyes slid over her breasts as she leant back against the rail.

"I'm starving" she announced. "When's the food coming?"

Jörgen shrugged. Lisa pulled a face at him. She walked across to the other side of the ship and looked out into the night in the direction of the side road that led down to the port. Then she suddenly turned around and looked up at the main mast, stretching up her arms towards the light at the top. Her yellow mini skirt rose to the top of her thighs. Jörgen couldn't take his eyes away and she smiled a small knowing smile at him before returning to the rail.

The beat from the music thumped around the ship and out across the water. Someone will turn up to complain, Jörgen was thinking. He had been the one to collect the money for food. Maybe he would get a chance to turn the music down a bit without looking like a jerk, once everyone was eating. Lisa was leaning over the rail to look down into the water, displaying tiny underpants and curves. Jörgen turned his head away and took a breath, rolling and crushing the kronor bills in his fist.

"I see lights!" Lisa shouted suddenly. "And it's a van. Coming down the side road!" She ran to the gangway."Got the money?" she asked, turning on the steps to look up at him. Jörgen passed her the handful of crumpled notes.

"Don't let him come near .. " he began..

Lisa shrugged her shoulders. "As if... " she said. She jumped down onto the dockside and ran to position herself in the middle of the road. The van came around the corner, and Lisa was illuminated in the headlights. The van stopped at a distance from the ship but Jörgen waited at the bottom of the gangway.

The pizza delivery driver, a tired looking youth in a soiled hat, put his arm out of the window and Lisa handed over the money. There was a discussion as he tried to smooth and unfold the notes. Lisa lent in at the cab window. The driver said something to her that Jörgen couldn't hear but the way Lisa laughed at him and then looked back at Jörgen was annoying. The driver got out and they both went out of sight behind the back of the van but a moment later Lisa put her head around the corner and called out.

"Come on Jörgen! Wake up!" she yelled. "Come and help me carry this stuff."

The pizza smelt greasy and was almost cold but Jörgen was hungry and he hung on to the last box. He walked up the deck and sat down by himself to eat. He could see Lisa and her boy friend feeding slices of pizza to each other and he turned his back on them. Kristian was walking towards him from the other direction, snapping open a couple of cans of beer. Some of the beer spilt onto the deck as he bent down to give Jörgen one of the cans. Jörgen looked up at him and then at the pool of beer on the polished deck. "Here" said Kristian handing him a joint. "Get into the party mood."

Jörgen took a couple of draws on the joint and passed it back. He leant against the rail and looked around. He didn't know most of the people at the party and wondered where they had all came from. More seemed to be arriving all the time. They clambered up the gangway and swirled up and down the deck, clattering about in their high heeled boots, shouting over the music, calling to each other to dance. The girls were wearing a strip of mini skirt, or a long skirt reaching down to their ankles. Their breasts moved under their brilliantly coloured shirts, nipples pointing and swinging along with the music and the strings of beads around their necks. The men all had long hair and beards and wore large hats with feathers, or leather head bands and were as colourful as the girls. Jörgen admired their brocade waistcoats, embroidered shirts and flared trousers. He had let his hair grow a bit longer in the last few months, ignoring Leif's reminders to get it cut, but now he felt like an alien in his plain white shirt and jeans, a 'square'. He hadn't wanted to draw attention to himself when he had left home that evening, to give anyone the idea he was going to a party. There was also the ELISE, the responsibility of that, like an albatross around his neck. How was he supposed to enjoy himself?

A tall thin figure dressed in black was drawing a crowd. He was wearing a top hat and sunglasses and telling a funny story that he kept repeating. Jörgen couldn't get the point of it but everyone else was screaming with laughter. He heard someone say that they had seen him last week on the television.

"What kind of an idiot wears sunglasses in the middle of the night?" Jörgen said, but Kristian had gone. He saw him at a distance moving among the crowd, stopping to talk, kissing girls on the cheek. He seemed to know everybody, including the man in black.

Empty pizza boxes and left over food were scattered around the deck and being trampled under the dancing feet. Half empty beer cans got left and overturned. It suddenly struck Jörgen as funny. It was too much. He saw someone crush a lighted cigarette out on the rail. Leif's precious ship. He could just imagine the state of the cabins and toilets down below. 'What the hell' thought Jörgen, laughing aloud.

"Hey!" someone shouted "Darky got himself stoned at last. Hey Darky!" Strange, thought Jörgen, he didn't feel the usual rush of resentment. He could guess it was Ulf who had called out as he could see him grinning over at him in that way that he had. Ulf of the oh so blue eyes and bright blonde hair.

"I just love your look" a girl was saying, slipping down on the deck to sit beside him. Jörgen looked at her. It was Petra, or Pia, something like that. Her black eye makeup was blotched around her eyes. Your look? What did that mean? "And your lovely curly black hair" she continued reaching out to touch him.

"You're drunk" Jörgen said rudely. He didn't know who he hated more, Ulf or her, whoever she was, with her stupid compliments.

"No. I mean it" she continued, drawing heavily on her cigarette. "But you don't look at all like your sister" she said suddenly. "Helen, you know. She goes to my dance class".

"My father is from Brazil" he said proudly, thinking how exotic she would find that to be; then angry with himself for having bothered to give her an explanation, he stood up and walked away.

"That's so .." the girl called after him but her words were lost to the Bee Gees as 'Night fever, Night fever' boomed out from the speakers and Jörgen found himself dancing, singing along with the music, smiling at everyone in the crowd.

Lisa was dancing nearby. She waved to him and suddenly he wanted to do something to impress her. Something entertaining, like a firework display or something. That would have been a great idea. He wished he had thought to bring some. Then he remembered the box of distress signals. He had never sent one off before, but he remembered something of Leif's instructions. He tapped Lisa on the shoulder.

"Come with me. I want to show you something" he said. "You can come too if you like" he added, returning the boy friend's cold stare.

The rocket shot up into the night in a spectacular fashion and lit up the port for miles around. There was a stampede as everyone rushed up on deck to see. Jörgen was in shock. He couldn't believe the effect. When the bright orange flare had died away, Lisa leant on his arm. "Go on. Light another one."

Leif was still on board the STELLA. The coffee had been unloaded, the welders had completed the repair to the hatch but there was a delay in loading the rest of the containers. The union representative had been on board, complaining about the danger to one of it's members driving the gantry crane with limited vision on the portside window. It was the shattered glass from the bullet of course and the discussion had become heated. Leif was direct about why he had fired at the cab window but without Kurt as a witness there was no proof as to why, and whether Kurt had been in danger. It would only stir up trouble if he called any of the men up from the dock and so Leif had grown weary of the argument. Time was all that mattered and the longer the debate went on, the more the ship would be delayed. In the end he had sent for a company to repair the window. There were six containers left to be loaded containing expensive machinery parts and Leif knew the ship could not leave without them. It would be letting his clients down in Sweden and Brazil and threaten future contracts.

Now he was sitting up on the bridge where he liked to be, finishing up the documents from the last voyage that Kurt had left behind. He was reaching for his coffee cup when the sky lit up in an orange glow. He reached instead for the VHF and tuned in to the emergency frequency. "What was that?" asked the third mate who was at the chart table. "Here in the harbour I'd say." They slid the doors to the bridge wing open and stepped outside. Crews on other ships alongside them were doing the same.

"In the port" said Leif. "Came from the direction of Lundbykajen."

They were scanning the sky. A second rocket went up. They could hear the sirens now. "Can't imagine anyone is sinking in the dock on a calm night like this" said Leif, "Must be someone fooling around." They could see two police cars sweeping across the Götaälvbron, lights flashing.

"Someone's going to get it" said the third mate returning to the chart table.

There was nothing on the VHF. Leif changed channels

but it was only port control giving instructions to an incoming ship. He went back outside. He was thinking what he always did every time he came on board. He wished he was at sea again. He could take a turn on the STELLA himself, his license was up to date, but he knew he was dreaming. He couldn't leave. But what a simple life it was compared to dealing with these sharks ashore.

Captain Pettersson came up from the lower deck.

"Window's repaired. They'll start loading again in ten minutes. What was that with the distress signals?"

Leif looked around in the sky above the ships.

"No fire anywhere. Nothing on the radio. Some idiot who should be locked up. I have my yacht moored down there in that direction. I'm going to take a look at her when I leave."

Pettersson cleared his throat. "I'm thinking of bunkering out on the estuary to save time and get away from the port before they find something else to delay us"

"I'll wait until the agent comes" said Leif. He sat down and rubbed his eyes. God he was tired.

"No need Captain. I think we are on the home stretch" said Pettersson folding his hands behind his back. Leif understood that tone. He had used it himself when he was a serving captain. The Captain wanted to take charge of the ship. He stood up and reached for his briefcase.

"I'll take a drive along to see my yacht" he said, holding out his hand.

"I look forward to your telex once you are underway. Safe voyage then Captain."

Leif was thinking about the whisky he had had as he approached his car. Well, it was hours ago and the police seemed to have other interests tonight. He could hear more police cars approaching the port in the distance. He walked all around his car. It wouldn't have surprised him to see his tires slashed. He threw the briefcase in the back and climbed in. He looked up at the STELLA with all her lights shining, waiting for the sweep of pride he usually felt to know she was off again on another voyage but he could only feel discouraged and tired. He would close his eyes before driving off, just for a moment.

Chapter 5

It was the rattle from the anchor chain that woke Leif up. He looked up at the ship. All the containers seemed to be loaded and the crew were about to cast off. He must have been asleep for at least two hours. He hoped Captain Pettersson had not noticed his car and thought he had been sitting there to check up on him.

As he drove out of the port and back across the bridge he remembered he was going to look in on the ELISE and now he was heading directly home. It was a clear night and there was a good view of the port as he crossed over. All seemed to be quiet. He could see the masts of the ELISE and it reassured him. He was too tired to go back now, his head ached and there was a car behind him driving too close. He touched his brakes but the car continued to drive right behind him, dazzling him with its headlights. He was thinking to jam on his brakes, jump out and ask them what the hell they were doing but he had had enough of confrontations for the day. The car continued behind him, up the hill and all the way to his house where a police car parked in the driveway caused Leif to stop suddenly. The car behind him swerved to one side, turned and went back down the hill.

Ella must have heard his car. She opened the door as he approached the house. There was a policeman standing in the hall. He knew his face. Ella looked strained.

"What's happened?" Leif asked her.

"It's alright. Everyone is alright" she said, but her hands were trembling as she took his briefcase from him and placed it on the hall table.

"Good evening Leif" said the policeman. "Can we go somewhere to talk?"

Leif? Of course, he recognized him now. It was Olofsson, one of the policemen who used to be on duty at the port. He would come on board the ELISE and have coffee at the time Leif was running her to and from the Faroe Islands. He used to live at Klippan. They were the same age. He could even remember playing football in the park with him years ago. He didn't want Ella to hear about him firing the gun, if she didn't know already, and it seemed that Olofsson was thinking the same way. It was probably the union representative who had reported him.

"Can you make us some coffee"? He asked her, with a reassuring smile.

They went into the dining room and Leif closed the door. In a way he was glad to see him. He could tell him about the incident with Kurt, get his advice. He hadn't thought about going to the police but it made sense.

"It might be good if I came down to the station and made a statement" Leif started to say, "but I am a bit tired. Perhaps in the .. "

"Statement? What about?"

"The trouble on the STELLA this afternoon."

Olofsson looked puzzled. "Haven't heard about that one yet. This is not about the STELLA. This is about the ELISE and your son, Jörgen."

Leif sat down, his mind racing. The distress rockets. Had Jörgen set fire to the ship? Did he hate it so much that ..

"He was holding a party on board" Olofsson was saying.

Party? On the ELISE? That explained the rockets.

"Without my permission I can tell you" said Leif angrily."They let off the rockets I suppose. I saw the flares. I was on board the STELLA."

"Yes. He admits to that, but it's not the only problem." Olofsson sat across from him at the table.

"There were drugs at the party."

"Drugs?" This was all he needed. Ella came in with the coffee. He stared at her but she avoided looking at him and went out, closing the door behind her.

"Marijuana. We took quite a few people down to the station and booked them. Didn't find anything on Jörgen you might be glad to know but I thought you might have a word with him before he gets himself arrested next time. He'll have to answer the charge of setting off an unnecessary emergency distress signal in a built up area. No damage as far as we know, but a serious waste of police time. Coastguard was involved as well as you would expect. It did alert us to the drugs though. That in a way is in Jörgen's favor. It's not exactly what someone would do if they wanted to avoid attention" said Olofsson ironically.

"He's not too popular with his friends right now. They came to the same conclusion when they realized why we had turned up."

Leif was stunned."Where is he now?" Half of his brain was telling him that it was no more than what the average eighteen year old would do, the other half was telling him to thrash Jörgen the minute he saw him.

"Oh he's here" said Olofsson pouring himself a coffee."Brought him home myself."

"Kind of you."

"But you were saying you had trouble in the port?"

What do I say now, thought Leif, that while Jörgen was having a party, sending up flares and smoking marijuana his father was shooting at crane drivers and drove home after a double whisky? He went to the sideboard and poured himself a shot before Olofsson could detect his breath. For a moment he wanted to laugh, as if he was Jörgen's co-conspirator cocking a nose at the law.

"The discrepancies in the cargo are getting out of hand and the unions are in on it, I'm sure. It's going to make the difference between whether we make a

profit or go under. What are the police doing about it?"
He hadn't meant to sound so aggressive.

"Sorry. Not been a good day."

"I can see that."

"Well we can't turn a blind eye anymore. They're getting greedy. They want the lions share. It's going to get violent before it gets better."

"What did you mean about a statement?"

"I'll think about it. Maybe it is time to do just that. All the owners are worried. If we complain, they have many ways to hold up the ship. Blackmail. That's what it is. Jävla pack!"

"We're only too aware of it. This is a political situation as you know Leif, and the solution lies right there, but, if there is anything I can do to help in the meantime." Olofsson gave him his card.

"Ever play football these days?"

"Never. No time. And I'd probably break my leg if I tried." said Leif, seeing him to the door. "I appreciate what you did tonight. You must hear it all the time, but I can assure you .."

"Not easy to have teenagers these days. I have two boys myself. Different to when we were young Leif."

Well, thought Leif, as he closed the door, Olofsson would have been surprised if he had known the half of what he had got up to.

Leif snapped on the light. Jörgen was rolled up in a duvet, still wearing his tee shirt and jeans.

"Get up."

"What for?"

"You're coming with me."

Jörgen rolled himself off the bed and sat up on the floor. Leif took his arm and pulled him to his feet. He picked up a sports bag from the corner of the room and threw it onto the bed.

"Pack some clothes."

"Why?"

"Just do it. I'll be back in a few minutes and you had better be ready."

The telephone was ringing downstairs. Leif went to answer it, taking the call in the study.

"Leif? It's Sven Olofsson again."

Leif kicked the door shut behind him.

Ella came out of the bedroom as Leif was propelling Jörgen down the stairs.

"What's going on? What are you doing?"

"I'm taking Jörgen down to the ELISE."

"In the middle of the night?"

They stopped in the hall. Jörgen looked up at his mother in appeal. Leif took his shoulder and turned him towards the front door.

"That's why he has a bag. He'll stay there until the ship is completely cleaned up."

"By himself?"

"That's the deal. I'll be back in half an hour"

It was partly true and his original idea, but since the phone call from Olofsson, things had changed.

There were no lights on at the house when Leif returned. It was now one o'clock in the morning. Leif let himself in very quietly and was surprised to see Ella sitting in the hall in the dark. She went to him immediately.

"You have to go back and get Jörgen" she whispered

"What's the matter?"

"There was a phone call after you left .."

It was already starting. He was more certain than ever about his decision, but he had to calm Ella down first ..

"Everything seems to be OK on the ship, but my God you should see the mess .."

"Ssshh. Don't wake Helen" She put her lips against his ear. "There's someone in the garden."

"What do you mean? In the garden?" Leif went to the window, then to the door.

"Don't open the door! They asked for you and .."

"Did you say where I was?"

"Of course not. Why should that matter anyway! What is this about? Is it because of the drugs at the party?"

Leif checked the bolt on the door, pointed up the stairs. He didn't want to wake Helen either, not yet. They went through into the kitchen.

As it was Helen was awake, standing on the landing in the dark listening. And she hadn't even told them about the camera yet. Why did that idiot brother of hers have to have a party on the ELISE of all places. She had seen him come back in the police car and caught some of the conversation the policeman had had with her mother in the hall. Worried that the next subject would be the camera, she had disappeared back into her room. When no one came, she put on some music. Later she heard her father come up and wake Jörgen and then the car drive away. Now there was a tension in her mother's voice and although Helen couldn't hear what they were saying it frightened her, as if something worse was about to happen. She went back into her room, put on her earphones and lay down on the bed. Perhaps everything would be alright in the morning.

Leif checked the back doors, drew the curtains and switched on the light. He filled the kettle and took down two mugs from the shelf.

"What was the phone call?

"When I said you were not home they said they would wait in the garden."

"Did they. Well they didn't show themselves when I came in just now. Sounds like someone was trying to be funny."

"Not funny. Trying to frighten me"

Leif thought so too. "What else did they say?" he asked, trying to sound calm.

"They said I was a beautiful woman .. but not in a nice way, a horrible way and they asked about Jörgen. They even mentioned Helen and where she went to school ..."

Leif put his arms around her. He said nothing and went to make the coffee. He took the cooking brandy from the shelf and poured some into one of mugs and handed it to her.

"Drink this. I have something to tell you. You know there have been serious problems at the port for some time now. Olofsson, the policeman who was here tonight? He telephoned before Jörgen and I went out. Something big is going on. Olofsson is risking his job to tell me but he heard some things after he left here and he thought I should know. There's going to be a raid on the port at dawn. Police, customs. They're bringing in extra forces from other areas, maybe the army."

"What has that got to do with us?"

"There was an incident this afternoon. They tried to frighten Kurt, they could have killed him. I fired a shot ..no wait, this is not the first time I have had a confrontation with some of them and they know I am on the edge of going to the police. Coming home from the port tonight I was followed. When they saw the police car here .."

"You see, the police can.."

"The police are going to be too busy to look after us and seeing the police car in our driveway will make them think that I have informed on them. Olofsson has insider information and he thinks we are better out of it for a few days. Trying to scare you tonight is just the beginning"

"You're the one who is frightening me .."

"First thing I expect is that now the STELLA has left port they will turn to the ELISE, try to scuttle her, damage her, as a kind of warning."

"And you left Jörgen on his own? You must go back for him. Now!"

"He knows. And he's not asleep. He's alert and he's waiting for us"

"Waiting..what?"

"We're going to put to sea for a few days, just down the coast a way.."

"We?! You mean all of us? You and your bloody ships!" Ella cried, jumping up and pacing around, "This is all about ships and shipping that we have to listen to day and night .."

Leif caught her arm and held her. "Wake Helen and start her off packing a few things. Dress in some warm clothes. Pack a bag for both of us. I have to go out again but I'll be back soon."

"Where are you going now?"

"To the office. To pick up some files and check the telex" He didn't add that he would also be bringing dollars and the revolver from the safe. Who knew how long they would have to be away. He hated the idea of running off, hiding, but protecting the family had to come before his pride.

On the ELISE Jörgen was sitting in the wheelhouse as Leif had instructed him, the old Mauser rifle that Leif kept hidden on the ship was now balanced across his thighs. He was sitting in the dark but he had the pen light that was used for reading the charts at night in his pocket. He took it out and switched it on for a few seconds to check that the safety catch on the rifle was on. He didn't want to make any mistakes. Leif had warned him about getting too jumpy. He was still feeling a bit numb, thinking about the things Leif had told him on the drive down to the ship. Jörgen had groaned when he saw the mess on the deck when they arrived, and below decks was even worse, but Leif had hardly seemed to notice it, going straight to get the rifle from its hiding place.

"You can deal with the clean up another day" was all he had said. "We have more important things to worry about right now."

Leif had switched off all the lights before he left but Jörgen could see the rest of the ship quite well in the light from the street lamps along the road. He saw something move between the storage buildings on the jetty. He lifted the rifle, his heart pounding, but it was only a stray dog sniffing around. He checked the safety catch again. He would hate to shoot a dog or anything at all for that matter. He was tired and afraid. He hoped Leif would not be too long.

Leif was back from the office and now loading up the car. Ella and Helen were sitting in the back in angry silence. They had been fuming at him as they left the house, Ella about her job and Helen about an exam she had the next day but he had turned a deaf ear to it all. It did make him doubt what he was doing for a moment, dragging them both off in the middle of the night, but he had always followed his instincts and everything was telling him to leave.

Chapter 6

Jörgen was getting sleepy. He jerked himself awake as his head touched the window. His stomach ached as it always did when he was nervous and he couldn't rid himself of the thought that somehow he was responsible for everything. Here he was sitting in the place he never wanted to be, defending it even. He began to think about the next few days. It was probably going to be hell, with Leif barking orders at him and losing his temper if he did the wrong thing or wasn't quick enough. He could imagine what his mother was thinking, and Helen, well Helen always liked to go sailing. She had a knack for it and was strong enough now to help haul up the sails and he hoped it would save him from having to do too much himself. But it was always Jörgen that Leif concentrated on when they were on board. Something to do with a promise Leif had made to his father.

Well he hadn't seen him since he was ten years old when they sent him on that holiday. He had been excited to go to Rio, the flight was boring, endless, but his friends at school had been amazed at how far away he was going. The teacher had made a lesson about it with maps on the wall and everything. He had felt uncomfortable when Georgio met him at the airport. There was the father thing and the strange experience of looking at an older version of yourself but it was later, trying to adjust to the idea of Georgio's huge extended family, and his half brothers and sisters, that were somehow his family as well, that was the most difficult. He didn't speak Portuguese and except for Georgio, no one spoke English. He didn't feel he belonged at all. At home he felt Swedish most of the time when they didn't call him 'darky' and other so called jokes that made him feel different. Well he was Swedish. He was born in Sweden after all. He was uneasy when he remembered the way they had looked at him in the police station. Kristian had called him stupid. Someone else had sworn at him but he just hadn't realized what the rockets do. When he thought about them going up, the whole sky lit up and Lisa's admiring face he felt better, except she was probably mad with him as well now. Maybe it was good to be away for awhile.

Jan and Rolf had let the car free wheel slowly down to the jetty with the lights off. They were now parked at the side of the buildings close to the ELISE. They were being cautious and sat quietly in the car looking out for any signs of life. Jan lived near the port and had seen the rockets from his window. He had called Rolf, a security guard and sometime drinking buddy of his, and they had watched the police arrive and board the ELISE from his house. Rolf was far from happy. He thrust his hands into his pockets and slumped in the seat.

"Can't see anyone's coming back tonight. Silent as the grave" said Jan. "And if anyone sees us, so what? Checking on those flares that got let off, that's what. Safety and security, safety and security, that's your job, see?" He laughed softly.

"Why don't you just use petrol and set fire to it" said Rolf, but he was being sarcastic.

"No. If we open up the sea locker they will just think those idiots on board did it and they overlooked it, see? They weren't exactly looking at the maintenance were they? Boy have I got that Hansson where I want him with his kid in trouble he will have something else to worry about, especially when he finds his old schooner sunk in the port."

"Nice boat. Got to be over fifty years old but she's in good condition" said Rolf.

"You changing your mind?" said Jan glaring at him

in the half light. "I have to remind you that you owe me one? People like this Leif Hansson are trouble. Got to scare these kind of people otherwise they'll walk all over us."

"Shame to sink her" Rolf continued.

"Well she won't be really sunk in just a couple of meters of water will she. Give him something to do until the STELLA gets back. Take his mind off coffee. Come on looks deserted." They stepped out of the car and Rolf accidently slammed the door. Jan was carrying the tool box and gave Rolf an angry push forward. By the time they reached the ELISE, Jörgen was waiting for them at the top of the gangway.

"It's the black kid" said Jan. "Been thrown out of the house have you? Spending the night here?"

"What do you want?" said Jörgen. He held the rifle but pointed away from them.

"Pigeon shooting at night are you?" Jan continued "They allow black boys like you to play with guns?"

Jörgen's knees were trembling but he held the rifle in a firm grip. "I'm Swedish and I have a license" he said, allowing himself to be distracted into an argument.

"Now how can you possibly be Swedish" Jan laughed turning to Rolf "Does he look Swedish to you?" He placed his boot on the bottom step of the gangway. Jörgen pointed the gun directly at him.

"Well now" said Jan "You are going to stop us making a security check? Aren't you in enough trouble?"

"I know who you are. Make another step and I'll shoot" said Jörgen, his voice shaking.

"Come on Jan" said Rolf, taking his arm, but Jan was angry at the threat and wanted to win. He knocked Rolf aside and moved fast, running up the gangway to make a grab for the rifle, but Jörgen jumped backwards. Jan lost his balance and slipped down the steps. What had been almost a joke, a little sabotage, was going to turn into violence if that was what the boy wanted. He dropped back onto the jetty, reached into the tool box and took out a large hammer.

"What do you think of that eh!?" Jan cried striking at the hull. "And that! How about you will be next eh?!" Jan swung the hammer menacingly as climbed the gangway again.

"You get off this ship!" Jörgen shouted, fear making him brave. He raised the rifle, slipped the safety catch, took careful aim and fired to one side as Jan advanced. The bullet nearly hit Rolf standing on the jetty and he ducked. It had passed some distance from Jan but it frightened him almost to death. He stopped on the last step breathing heavily.

Jörgen was suddenly aware of Leif running out of the shadows. Leif grabbed Rolf and knocked him down. Jan turned, leapt down the gangway and now advanced on Leif, the hammer swinging.

"Not wise Jan" said Leif, standing his ground. "He may not miss this time."

Leif and Jörgen escorted them back to their car, Jan screaming abuse all the way at Jörgen who was still holding the rifle. They watched the car drive away and turn onto the highway.

"Well they're going to get a big surprise in the morning" said Leif. He put his arm around Jörgen's shoulders. "Helen and your mother are up at the side road, waiting in the car. If you can find a kettle and some clean cups you can make us all some tea and put all the lights back on. We're going to load up and take off as soon as we can."

Leif turned to go, then deciding to take the rifle, took hold of the strap and swung the gun over his own shoulder. They looked at each other for a moment, then Leif reached out and held him.

"You reminded me of your father. He was never one

to back down either. You have his blood alright" Leif gave him a friendly punch on the arm.

Jörgen watched him walking away. It's you who have been my father, he said to himself as he went back on board.

Chapter 7

The KISHIWADA II dipped and lurched from side to side in the swell as it approached Montevideo, but they were sheltered by the Uruguay coast now and out of the wind. The storm had tired them all out on board. The crew were moody and short tempered with each other, from battling with the weather and only too conscious of the poor result from their two months out at sea. Georgio had decided to raise the crew's spirits and let them spend a day ashore while he was bunkering, but he was anxious to return to Rio. He couldn't wait to see Garcia the wholesaler and tell him what he thought of his big talk and stories that the tuna had come back to the area three hundred miles off the coast of Argentina. He should have listened to his old Uncle Souza who shook his head when he told him where they were going.

"Overfished. Almost gone by the late sixties" Souza had said "It will take more than a few years to bring them back as they were before."

But Garcia had been enthusiastic, reporting that boats had come in loaded with tuna, and blue fin as well as skipjack. Now Georgio suspected that he had made a fool of him. That he had sent him off on a wild goose chase and other boats who had paid him for the right advice, were sent in another direction. Georgio hadn't thought about giving Garcia money for what he believed was something that would benefit them both in the end. They had known each other for some time, several years, since Georgio had started his own business, although it wasn't a friendship. Georgio had always found him to be tricky, especially when it came to money. He would talk to Ed about it when the KATO came in. The KATO was half a day behind and had taken more of the storm than the KISHIWADA II.

Ed had hinted over the radio that some repairs were required.

"We'll make it OK to Montevideo" he had said in his laconic way. The radio was full of static and Georgio gave up trying to get any detail but he understood that they had had a problem with the steering. Georgio was thinking it would be cheaper to repair in their home port where they knew everyone. They could stay close to the coastline on their journey back to Rio, and in sight of each other, unless it was serious and had to be fixed right away. He groaned at the thought. He was going to lose a lot of money on this trip as it was.

Ed Bates had known Georgio since Georgio was a stowaway cabin boy on board the first KISHIWADA and Kato had been the captain and Ed the fishing captain. Twenty years ago, in 1957, Ed had joined the KISHIWADA off the coast of Sierra Leone and as a black American had had to work hard to prove himself. As the only crew on board who were not Japanese, Ed and Georgio had quickly developed a bond. It was Ed who had taught Georgio to speak English, introduced him to American music. He had told him all he knew about tuna fishing and they had had fun on board, as they found someone who could share their jokes. The Japanese crew rarely laughed, even when they were off duty, and Captain Kato never smiled. It was time before Georgio understood why.

When Kato died and left the pearls to Georgio and Leif, Georgio had bought the two tuna fishing boats they were operating today, and Leif had bought the ELISE. At first Ed had gone to work with Leif on the ELISE in Sweden, when it was still operating as a working cargo ship, but when he found himself back in Brazil again, he had decided to stay. Ed had a cheerful personality, but he had become subdued and withdrawn working in Europe, where he often found himself in trouble because he was a black man. In Brazil it was more important to laugh and to dance than to point a finger and judge someone by the color of their skin.

The KATO was only making five knots as it approached Montevideo. "These boats are getting old, like me" Ed said to the mate as he wrestled with the steering, but he didn't really believe it of himself. Ed was over forty but as fit and strong as he was when the boats were new. When he was ashore he kept himself slim by dancing, and what he called sardonically, 'that other thing'. Ed had never married. He had many admirers waiting for him up and down the coast.

Ed found a place alongside the KISHIWADA II and they tied up with some relief. He looked across at the other boat. It seemed deserted. Then Georgio appeared from below rubbing his head and frowning.

"What did you do man?" Ed called "I know. You were so eager to see me you sat up too fast in your bunk and cracked your head."

"First sleep in twenty four" said Georgio climbing on board the KATO. "Good to see you made it"

"You let the crew go ashore? I was thinking the same, only thing is old Montevideo don't do you no favours. Too many casinos."

"They think they have money to throw around after this voyage?" said Georgio as they went into the wheelhouse. "Let them go. Get ourselves a bit of peace to talk." They had only screamed at each other across the sea or over the radio for the last two months.

They went down into Ed's cabin. Ed slammed a bottle of Bacardi on the table. "Been nursing that one since we left Rio" he said, pouring a few shots into each glass.

"That Garcia. A crook don't you think?"

"We didn't have to take his advice.." Ed began but he didn't want to remind Georgio of the row they had had before they left. Georgio was only too aware that Ed had been against it, and had wanted to go to their usual area off the northern coast of Brazil.

"Didn't even get to dance the tango" Ed laughed "What those Argentinean dames have missed, they'll never know" He took a large gulp of rum. "And would you believe it, I'm not going ashore even now! Like you, got to bunker up, then sleep, and then listen to what they say about that steering."

"I haven't called anyone yet Ed." Georgia said, looking defensive. "We should try to make it to Rio first."

"OK" said Ed as if he didn't accept it. "If that's your decision. But you can take her and I'll take your boat. When you see how way off the steering is yourself, you might change your mind."

"You think I don't believe you? It's all about money Ed."

"Yeh. And my balls on the line."

Georgio woke up after only one hour more of sleep. The bunkering was going on, but it wasn't the whine from the refueling that had woken him but the nagging memory of violently arguing with Ed after they had finished the bottle of rum. Tired and drunk they had refused to agree on anything except that Georgio would take Ed's boat and risk the journey home. Georgio really wanted a sympathetic ear but Ed was not about to give him one and the argument they had had in Rio before they left was rehashed, rephrased and got nowhere, especially as Ed put it, the almost empty cargo holds were all the argument he needed to prove he had been right.

Georgio got up and went ashore to the agent's office. The agent was out but he was glad of that.

He only wanted to use the telephone. The secretary was eating her lunch at the table outside the door. He pointed to the phone and she nodded, barely looking up from her magazine. He was no longer looking for sympathy but information, and he hoped Souza would also be at home having his lunch.

The lines to Rio were busy and Georgio kept looking out of the window while he was waiting, but there was no sign of the agent. He wanted to talk to Souza in private. The phone rang and he ignored it until it stopped, as did the secretary outside who simply turned to another page of her magazine. It was lunchtime after all.

"It's Georgio"

"You are back! So how did it go vaqueiro?"

"Not good. We have just under ten tons between us so I am checking the prices. I need some good news. I am in Montevideo right now, bunkering up and my credit is not so hot as you can expect. Can you give me something to tell the agent?"

"Montevideo!" Souza exclaimed. "Wait a minute, wait a minute" Georgio could hear him shuffling around for a cigarette. The lighter clicked in the background.

"Have you seen the DOMINGO?" Souza asked.

Georgio held on to his patience. "No, should I?"

"Is refrigerator cargo ship carrying pure gold, my gold, boy-o, and I cannot believe you are there in Montevideo. But we have to act quickly."

"Gold?"

"Gold!" Souza snorted. "But almost. Bacalao! I have contract but this ship DOMINGO she have now to go to Chile for a much bigger cargo, so they tell me. They were delayed by a storm. You have storm in last two days? I think they lie. Now they make me an offer to unload the bacalao in Montevideo and for me to sell it in Uruguay! Uruguay! Where it is worth less than half what I can get in Rio! I fight with the agent since yesterday.

You can bring the cargo Georgio! Your boats can take twenty tons each! There is twenty ton of bacaloa my God! They are screaming for it here. After Lent there is not one kilo of bacaloa left in the city."

Georgio was thinking fast. Bacalao. Salted Cod. It couldn't be frozen, but Souza was already answering the questions forming in his mind.

"Sell your tuna in Montevideo, you get better price for that then here. Do it now. You need to bring the temperature up in the holds as soon as you can"

"Why would I get a better price for tuna here than in Rio? Don't tell me, Garcia has ..."

"Piss about Garcia! You no listen to him again eh? You listen to your uncle and we make money."

Georgio looked up at the blackboard over the desk where the ships were written up with times of arrival and departure.

"I see the DOMINGO on the board, but looks like she is due to leave tonight."

"You get that agent on the telephone to me and I fix everything. I know wholesaler there and he will come down to check the tuna. Stay awake and keep busy. You sound a little drunk."

"Tired" Georgio explained, smiling. You couldn't fool Souza about anything.

He met the agent on his way back and gave him the plan. The agent had found the whole DOMINGO problem a headache and he was delighted that he could fix the deal. Georgio asked him to send a mechanic as soon as possible to fix the steering on the KATO and almost ran back to the jetty. He couldn't wait to tell Ed. They would be able to pay the crew, the repair and the bunkering. Perhaps they would at least break even. It was better than nothing and far better than the situation an hour ago.

Chapter 8

They had motored out down the estuary within the hour, Leif at the helm. Everyone else was below, sleeping among the rubbish left from the party and their own unopened suitcases. It was now three in the morning. Leif was tired but elated. He stripped off his jacket and tie and threw his old sailing jacket around his shoulders. It was as if he had stepped off the planet. He had forgotten the feeling. A hundred memories came flooding back as the gentle swell slapped against the hull, and as she eased along he thought again of the men who had built her. How proud they would be to see that she was still going strong.

When he left the estuary he turned north and some hours later, on a pale yellow morning, he docked at an inlet close to Andalen and went below to wake them.

"You look terrible" said Ella, emerging from a blanket. She was still fully dressed.

"Do I? I don't feel it."

"Where are we?"

"Andalen."

"That's north. I thought you said we were going down the coast."

"Can you go ashore for groceries and supplies? I doubt if there is any toilet paper left on board and we need cleaning stuff, things like that. Get enough food for a couple of weeks.".

"Two weeks? Why two weeks?" Ella protested, reaching for her shoes. Leif took his boots off and fell onto the bed.

"Take a taxi. Money up in my jacket in the wheelhouse" he yawned, turning on his side. "Tell Jörgen and Helen to go with you."

"God it smells terrible in here" said Ella from the toilet.

"Jörgen has to clean up, but he needs ..."

"Cleaning supplies. So you said" said Ella, emerging from the toilet and adjusting her skirt.

"Leif you are not really thinking of staying away for two weeks are you? Leif?" But Leif was asleep.

Another smell woke him."Prinskorv" he said aloud. He was surprised to see that it was dark outside. He must have slept all day. He padded out into the passageway in his socks. He could see Helen through the open door of the galley, cooking at the stove. He was overwhelmed at how happy he felt.

"Where's everybody?" he leant over her shoulder and took a hot sausage from the pan. "Ouch."

"You should wait, as you would say to me."

"Did you get a taxi?"

"Three times. Jörgen has been to the laundry place and back twice with all the sheets and towels. Mum is checking the supplies up on deck. I had to clean this place before I could start cooking and Mum won't put anything away until Jörgen has washed the cupboards, so she's listing everything."

"Very efficient. Why the three taxis?" Leif was thinking of how much cash he had had in his wallet but he still had the dollars from the safe.

"Phone calls. Mum shopping."

"Phone calls? Who to?"

"To my school Dad. What do you think. And Mum's office and Britt. Jörgen didn't have any calls to make as he doesn't have anyone expecting him so he spent the time while he was waiting for the laundry to flirt with a terrible looking hippy girl at the counter."

"Britt? Who's Britt?"

"The lady who comes to clean on Wednesdays. You may be on your own agenda Dad but .."

"Did you tell Britt where we were?"

"Mum spoke to her. Have some sausages. There's bread over there in the bag" She held up a coffee pot and poured some into a mug as Leif sat down at the table. Ella came in, carrying a large box.

"For the galley. You can put this away. I'm exhausted. Pour me some coffee Helen."

"What's the time?" Leif asked.

"About six."

"I slept for twelve hours. You phoned Britt?"

"She has her own key so I phoned her at the house. There was a message from Kurt. Gone home, and the phone number. I wrote it down."

Ella looked upset. Leif put his hand on hers but she withdrew it and picked up her coffee.

"What's up?"

Helen sat down with her plate "Mum got fired."

"Yes, yes" said Ella.

"Why?" said Leif "For being away for a couple of days? You're on an independent contract .."

"At Mr. Worchek's discretion. I was supposed to meet the client today about designing the office and when I didn't turn up he cancelled the check."

"Worchek was just waiting for an excuse."

"Exactly."

"You were great at your job. You'll get another job with a better company."

"With a wonderful recommendation from Worchek no doubt."

"I'll go and see him."

"No you won't. This is nothing to do with you."

"Oh, and what did they say at my school Dad?" said Helen, helping herself to a bottle of beer. "That I can take the exam at anytime I choose?"

Leif reached over and exchanged the beer for a soft drink and opened the beer for himself. Don't they both understand that we could have had worse problems?

thought Leif, getting angry. He looked across the table at Helen as she bent over her plate. He would kill anyone who tried to hurt her. He used to regret that she hadn't taken after her mother but she had her own kind of beauty and he enjoyed people saying she was like him. It must make Jörgen feel left out though, he realized with sudden insight.

He was tempted to tell them what had happened with Jörgen and Jan. Jörgen hadn't mentioned it and neither had Leif. Ella and Helen had apparently not heard anything as they waited in the car up by the road, so it hadn't been necessary. Leif recognized Jörgen's restraint and admired him for it. Someone else would have been boasting for hours.

"You know I was going to ask Captain Pettersson to take Jörgen on for a voyage or two" he said trying to change the subject. "The problems at the port took it out of my mind."
"That would have been popular" said Helen without looking up "You don't give up do you Dad?"
"And you are getting too damn rude."
"She's just telling the truth" said Ella
"Where is he?"
"In the storeroom."
Leif took up his plate, loaded it with more sausages and bread and picked up another beer.

Jörgen was sitting on the floor surrounded by boxes. Leif placed the plate of sausages and beer in front of him. "Have something to eat" he said, starting to stack things up on the shelves himself.
"We should lash this stuff. Otherwise it'll fly around" Leif continued, picking up a line. He looped it through the hooks on the shelves, made an expert knot and pulled it tight.

"I was going to do that" said Jörgen. "When I had finished putting it all away" he added pointedly.

Leif sat down on the floor and took up his beer, annoyed with himself. He shouldn't have interfered. The danger they had shared before they left had given them a kind of bond that they hadn't had for years, and here he was again, forgetting that Jörgen was almost nineteen. Would he have liked to be told how to do everything when he was nineteen? He had been on the BUENOS AIRES at Jörgen's age and had been treated like a man, expected to be a man. That's what I have to do, he thought, I have to treat Jörgen the same.

"Ever think about going to see your father again?" he asked, thinking of the idea he had had about Jörgen joining the STELLA. Jörgen shook his head. It wasn't the time to talk about that anyway, Leif decided. It would be weeks before the STELLA was back in Gothenburg and the opportunity came up again. Better to talk about it then.

"I'm going up top to see if I can reach Kurt" he said. "You're doing a great job here" he called down to him as he reached the top of the stairs.

Doing a great job? What did he say that for?

Leif woke Jörgen up the next morning at dawn and Helen heard them pass her door. She pulled on her sailing clothes and followed. She had felt in her sleep that they were underway. When she arrived on deck she saw they were some distance from shore.

"You'll have to move quicker than that if you don't want her to go over" Leif called to Jörgen. Helen moved swiftly to help. Jörgen gave her a smile, glad to see her. There was a good stiff breeze. They were already making seven knots.

"She's powerful" Helen said "Watch the pennants and keep them flying like that. I'll be back" She went into the wheelhouse and looked at the compass. "You're going west" she said to Leif.

"That's right."

"Where are we going?"

"Somewhere warm. Look at the chart on the wall"

Leif had pinned up the north Atlantic chart. Helen looked at the end of the course line.

"Canary Islands? But that will take days."

"That's right It's a surprise."

"It certainly is."

She immediately went below. Leif knew she would be telling Ella but she had to know sooner or later. Helen came back out on deck carrying a waterproof jacket. She handed it to Jörgen and Leif watched his face as she gave him the news but Jörgen wasn't giving much away. Ella came running up the steps.

"Leif you can just stop this, this joke. You can't be serious about the Canary Islands."

"I spoke to Kurt last night. It'll be a couple of weeks before the port is back to normal. I sent a telex to the STELLA and a reply came this morning. I'm changing one or two ports of call but I can do that from the ELISE. Pettersson's a good man. Everything will work out." He looked at her and smiled. Ella was furious.

"You may have straightened out your problems but what about us? As long as your damn ships are alright then never mind anything else."

"It will be a holiday" said Leif. "It will be good for all of us. Jörgen can learn to sail.."

"For God's sake Leif! He is not you. He is not his father either. He doesn't want to be a sailor. You're so selfish! I'll never forgive you for this Leif. Nobody wants to be on this bloody ship! Only you!" She ran back down the stairs. Leif turned away and went pacing up the deck. Helen came and linked her arm with his.

"She's upset about her job."

"I know" Leif said, but he was depressed.

"It's all a bit of an adventure now isn't it?" Helen said. "Mum doesn't understand how serious all that stuff at the docks is."

"And you do?"

"We live in the port Dad. I go to school close to the port. The kids talk about it. Some of their fathers work at the docks. What do you think?"

Leif kept walking. Both of my kids are more grown up than I realize. Just as well, the way things are going. Kurt had said more on the phone. Leif's office had had a break in. His house could be next. Ella had many things there that she treasured. If she knew, she would want to turn back. If someone did break into his house when he was there and threaten his family, he'd end up in prison as well, he knew it.

Chapter 9

In the city of Kobe, on the island of Honshu, the network of freight and commuter train lines criss crossed the city from the mountains to the sea. From the steel works that rose up along the coastline to the ship yards and the port, trains came and went day and night. In 1977 the city was booming. Ship building had taken off in Japan and Kobe and Osaka to the east were at the center of it all. Dozens of ships in various stages of construction could be seen in all directions, some no more than a framework or part of a hull, others getting near to completion and swarming with welders, carpenters and engineers. Cranes were moving to and fro, carrying girders, plates of steel and parts of machinery. Oil tankers were the main industry, built to a system that Henry Ford would have admired, simple, uniform and spartan.

There were one or two among the executives who thought it was sad that Taru Takahashi, Chairman and Chief Executive of the Takahashi Shipping Corporation was going to retire at such an exciting time, but Taru did not share that view. As he had said to his man servant that morning, "Better on a winning note."

Privately he had found the pressure and the drive for so much expansion in such a short time completely unnecessary. The calm considered meetings with the board had become hours, even days of conflict, and he became increasingly more irritated by the other members and their ambitions. They wanted to rush things along when caution had served the company so well over the years under his leadership. Investment was excellent, they were making a lot of money, but when did anyone have any time to enjoy it? I am getting old, he thought after the last meeting, and on his sixty fifth birthday he announced his retirement.

The Takahashi Building was one of the tallest in the central business district with an unsurpassed view over the harbour. On the top floor, a formal lunch had been set out in the board room. The day was warm and humid and as everyone was familiar with the view, delicate silk curtain blinds had been lowered across the great windows to let in the light and as little as possible of the heat. The air conditioning whirred softly in the background. On either side of the great table, sat a row of men, indistinguishable from each other somewhat, in almost identical dark business suits. They stared into space, not at each other, and carefully not at the speaker at the head of the table. The flower arrangements down the center of the table were understated masterpieces, the pastel silk napkins fanned precisely, their colours carefully chosen to complement the flowers. A champagne glass, on the most fragile of stems, gleamed at the side of each place. The effect was delicately feminine, except there were no women present. The waiters, standing to attention against the walls holding the champagne in silver buckets, were all men.

Everyone was listening to the familiar voice of the man who had been the head of the company for the past seventeen years. Taru had decided to make his speech short and optimistic. He spoke quietly as if to friends. Japan had cut itself off from the world with its militancy and arrogance. Humiliated, broken and almost destroyed, it had not only survived but had been reborn. A new era had dawned. Now in peace and democracy Japan was becoming prosperous again. He was leaving the company at the dawn of a new age and in the most capable of hands.

Not everyone at the table agreed with the politics, and familiar with the chairman's views on progress on so many weary occasions, many did not believe he meant what he said, but they all clapped politely as the waiters stepped forward to serve the champagne. Taru's concession to a progressive Japan, French Champagne, not sake. The popping of the corks changed the atmosphere, and there was an exchange of good wishes as each glass was raised for the toast. Taru raised his glass to the men at the table and then to the rows of model ships in their glass cases that lined the walls.

"To our ships".

"What will you do now you are no longer coming to the office each day?" asked his successor as they walked to the lift.

"Something I have wanted to do for a long time"

"Travel the World?"

"If I have to" Taru replied.

North of Kobe, in the Inland Sea of the National Park, seventeen year old Mariko Suzuki was exercising her horse, but she had been thinking all morning about her grandfather. She had ridden almost as far as the foothills of the Rokko Mountains when a glance at her watch made her turn back towards the golf course. A cool breeze was sweeping over the green slopes from the sea and her dark hair flew behind her. When she galloped up to the stables, she gave the reins to the first stablehand she saw and within minutes she was driving down the mountain road towards the city.

Akira had been Taru's man servant for twenty years and knew his employer's routine in every detail. He was wondering what Taru's retirement would mean, what changes it would bring to the household. He would not have the apartment to himself all day and he hoped that this would not bring conflict. His employer was set in his ways, but Akira, a man of fifty two now himself, was set in his.

Today was already a different day. Akira was not sure what food he should prepare as Taru would be coming home in the middle of the afternoon. Taru would have had lunch as usual, perhaps a special lunch and would not be hungry. He may not have felt like eating at all, as it was the kind of occasion that could affect the stomach. Akira took pride in anticipating what may be required and so he decided he would only place three decorative bowls of dried fish and some rice cakes on the low mahogany table. If Taru was hungry, it was there, if not, nothing would go to waste. He filled a crystal jug with water, removed the lemon from his apron pocket and a sharp knife from his belt. A few twirls of the blade and the lemon became a chrysanthemum which he dropped in to the jug of water. He straightened the cushions and the rice mats and stopped at the window to adjust the blind.

The apartment, like Taru's office, was at the top of a tall building, but closer to the sea with a view of the bay. Akira stepped out onto the balcony. It was one of his little pleasures to sit out there when his tasks were done. He looked wistfully at the seat where he always sat and sighed. This would not be possible in the future.

He went back inside, crossed the dining room and went into the kitchen to check the yasenabe soup that was simmering on the stove. It was Taru's favourite and Akira always made a considerable amount so that he could enjoy a bowl or two himself the next day. Perhaps Taru would not notice, or care what he was eating, but Akira did not feel he would be able to give himself that freedom anymore.

He went to the sitting room. This was the only room in the apartment that was furnished in western style. Akira disliked it, especially the modern art on the walls and the bar at one end. Akira was constantly checking to see if the bar was fully stocked. He never knew when to expect visitors. Taru would entertain businessmen from abroad in this room and they would always ask for something different. If there was a party, Taru would hire extra staff, and a barman, but most of the time it was Akira trying to understand from his cocktail book what a 'Tom Collins' or a 'White Lady' was. This would be a positive change, Akira decided, as the sitting room may not be used so much in the future. Taru had a private sitting room off the master bedroom where he preferred to be, when there were no guests.

Akira continued his rounds along the passageway to Taru's private suite. The bedroom was simple, almost bare, with futon and a small hard pillow stored to one side, a carved chest with drawers, paper screens and fitted cupboards that merged into the walls. Akira slid the hidden wardrobe door aside, selected a grey silk robe and hung it at the open window to catch the breeze. He unwrapped a new bar of soap in the bathroom, placed it on the low wash stand, positioned the wooden stool and was checking the steam room when he heard the door bell.

"Forgot my key" said Mariko, breathless at the door. She was still wearing her riding habit. Akira raised his eyebrows and then bowed. Mariko was now hopping about on one foot, trying to remove her riding boots. "Grandfather home yet?" she asked. Almost immediately Akira heard the lift descending again to the ground floor. He pointed to the door of Mariko's room, picked up her boots with thumb and forefinger and hid them in the hall closet.

In her room, Mariko stripped off her clothes and went into the shower. When she came out, she heard her grandfather's voice in the hall. She quickly selected a simple pale blue dress and a flowered cotton yukata and tied her hair back with a ribbon.

By the time she was dressed Taru was already sitting out on the balcony, wearing the grey silk robe and looking out to sea.

"So now you are free, Grandfather" said Mariko, making a small bow and seating herself on a cushion at his feet.

"Not so" said Taru, "I have always had a goal, something to drive me on. I am not going to sit around like an old man yet."

"But you are free from worry. No one to argue with now" said Mariko, looking up into his face.

"Is that so? I am still the biggest shareholder in the company. I have responsibilities. I shall attend meetings now and then."

"As a surprise."

Taru shook his head. She was amusing and pretty like her mother was, and just as disrespectful, but unlike her mother, he knew Mariko cared for him. Akira came out on the balcony, poured two glasses of water, set them on the small table and then stood back at the open doorway.

"And how was the lecture at University today?" Taru asked, gazing once more out to sea.

Mariko widened her eyes "There was a lecture."

"And did your horse enjoy the lecture?"

"Akira!" Mariko cried "You told him" Akira opened and closed his mouth, bowed and then retreated back into the dining room.

"Do not raise your voice to Akira. He did not tell me.

You left mud in the lift and in the hall. I do not think Akira has been ploughing fields today."

"Oh Grandfather, it was such a beautiful day and the winter has been so long. I am doing well at University and it was not so important to go to the lecture. I knew everything he was going to say."

"Perhaps your friends are not a good influence on you Mariko. I am thinking you should stay here permanently now I am retired and give up your student apartment" In the dining room, Akira drew in his breath and began to rearrange the bowls on the table. Taru smiled as he heard the nervous clinking of china.

"I was not with my friends, I was alone. I make my own decisions" said Mariko indignantly.

"You see? You express yourself without respect."

"But I do respect you Grandfather. I am staying here this weekend because I know this is an important time for you. I wanted to be here, but it would be tiring for you if I was here all the time" Akira was listening avidly to the conversation but withdrew when he remembered the soup on the stove.

"I have been speaking to the University today. This is how I also know you were not there."

"Today? On this day of all days?"

"I am quite used to doing many things in one day. Yes, I know you are a bright student and you are expected to pass your exams but I had another reason for the call. Come to the sitting room. I have something to show you."

In the sitting room, Taru pressed a hidden latch behind the Matisse and the painting swung to one side to expose the safe. Taru worked the combination and the safe swung open. Inside were many files and papers. Mariko had been expecting something more dramatic.

Taru took a pair of white gloves from the top shelf, and then reached inside for a scroll.

"You see the seal? From the time of the Tokugawa Shogunate, when Tokyo was known as Edo. Too delicate to open, but I have had a copy made" Taru took a thick piece of paper from the safe and gave it to her.

"To honor Yumiko Suzuki Takahashi, for her brave deed" Mariko read aloud "To honor her, her daughter and all daughters who may follow, on this day, April 7 1638, we present this box of pearls that they may be passed on from generation to generation in recognition of her sacrifice'. Sacrifice? What did she do?"

"Her husband was a samurai who was killed trying to save his lord. The lord was very old, almost blind and could not defend himself. Yumiko picked up her husband's sword and stood in his place, but her small daughter came running between them and the assassin took the child and held a knife to her throat. He ordered Yumiko to throw down the sword. Yumiko killed the assassin, but not before he had killed her daughter"

"How terrible."

"In this time of the Tokugawa Shogunate, there was an uprising against the government. The poor had suffered high taxes and cruel treatment for many years. You have heard of the Shimabara Rebellion. It is said that more than two hundred thousand people were executed. Christian missionaries were blamed and were among the many victims, and any countrymen who had converted to Christianity. After that, the time of sakoku began. For the following two hundred years, Japan shut itself off from the rest of the world. They banned all foreigners from entering the country. But, during this long time of seclusion, the economy and the arts flourished, cities developed and there was stability."

"Are you saying they were right to do this, grandfather?"

"Of course it cannot be right to kill thousands of people. I have lived through a war, Mariko. Your reaction is understandable, but your question is too simple. It is all too easy to make judgments about events in the past. Situations are always more complex than they appear to be in books."

"But this is something to do with the pearls, with Yumiko?"

"The date, Mariko. The date on the scroll. You are studying history, are you not? April 1638, when the last battle between the government forces and the rebels took place. Over thirty five thousand men, women and children, had taken refuge in an abandoned castle. They were led by a sixteen year old boy, Amakusa Shiro, a Christian convert, who was said to be able to perform miracles. They fought for many weeks. In the end, all were believed to have been killed."

"I know of this grandfather. The castle was Hara. Was Yumiko there? Was she one of the rebels?"

"If she was, she must have escaped, or how were the pearls and the scroll passed on to the family? You can see why this significant date has interested me. We know that she was awarded for her bravery. I believe, by the date, that it was at Hara, in that last battle."

Taru took Mariko's hand. "I have not talked about this before and there is a reason. You are the next daughter. The pearls should have been in your care long ago, but our family has been dishonoured, Mariko. The pearls have been sold."

"They have been sold?"

"Yes. I fear so. We have a duty to that brave woman to find them. The pearls are unique. I could buy pearls to replace them, but it would be difficult to find fifty natural pearls, of equal size. How would it be the same, mean the same? Collected over many years, centuries. Think of the divers who risked their lives searching for a pearl that would match the others. No artificial pearls were made at that time. They are beautiful. Such a luster."

"You have seen them?"

"My sister. She was the last to have the pearls."

Mariko knew that Taru's sister and her children were killed in the bomb on Nagasaki. They had spoken about it, but only once.

"Her husband was Kato. He was a battle ship commander in the war. I don't think I told you. He was away, of course, but the war was quickly over after that, and he went home. There was no one to be buried. There was only chaos, and the safe, half buried I imagine, in the ruins of his home".

"The pearls. They were in the safe. And he sold them? How could he do that?"

"Wait Mariko. We will sit here and Akira can bring us some tea. I have a long story to tell you" He was excited and seemed disturbed.

"This isn't good for you grandfather."

"But I have yet to tell you what I have planned. We are going to look for the pearls Mariko. You and I together. For family honour we will return them to the family. We begin our search in Rio de Janeiro."

Mariko had lived with her grandfather since she was ten years old, when her parents were killed in a car accident. The shipping company had taken so much of Taru's attention that he had arranged that tutors would come to the apartment after Mariko came home from school, to occupy her when he was not there. A housekeeper came each day in the morning and evening to see her to school, to care for her clothes and food and to see her into bed each night. There was little in Mariko's life except to study, and her horse, and when she proved herself to be an exceptional pupil, far in advance of the others, she was accepted by the University, and, for the first time, she lived away from home. She had now enjoyed a year of independence. She was not the only one who had welcomed the new arrangement. Akira, who had kept himself apart from tutors and housekeepers as much as he could, was relieved to have the apartment to himself again, as it had been in the very beginning as Taru's wife had died long before he came.

Mariko was touched by the story of Yumiko and the pearls but she was not happy to have her independence taken away from her. Of course the University had agreed that she could take off and go travelling with her grandfather, she thought rebelliously, he was a prominent member of the board and contributed a great deal of money to the University. She did not want to go to Rio de Janeiro and resented the idea.

Akira came in with the tea and Taru asked him to stay for a few minutes and explained that they would be travelling to Brazil, the day after tomorrow, and Akira was to accompany them. Akira almost dropped the tray. He had expected change but not this. He looked at Mariko and they exchanged the same look of reluctance and resignation. Akira received the news without comment, bowed and left, but on the other side of the door, his expression changed.

Taru sipped his tea. He was now talking about ancestry, honour and reputation and Mariko was barely listening. Then he began to talk about Kato, his brother in law, and how he had found out what happened to the pearls, and she became interested again.

"I had a letter many years ago concerning a box of papers that Kato had left behind. The letter was from the shipping company that had employed him as a captain on a fishing boat, the KISHIWADA. When the KISHIWADA was lost and it had been confirmed that Kato had died, they opened the box that he had left in their safekeeping. It contained legal papers, documents concerning ownership of his house and letters that he had saved. It also contained the scroll, the one you have seen, and it was the name, Takahashi on the scroll, that prompted them to write to me. I had started to get a reputation in the shipping business and they recognized the name. The company was jointly owned by Brazilians and Japanese who had invested in the tuna fishing business to supply their restaurants in Brazil. There were many Japanese people living in Rio before and after the war. When they sent the box to me and I saw the scroll, it became a delicate situation. I believed the papers to be the contents of Kato's safe, probably rescued from his house in Nagasaki, but the pearls were not there. Had the pearls been stolen by someone at the shipping company? Or had Kato taken them with him? They were lost, that was all I could conclude, and I could not accuse anyone. I tried to forget about it."

"But you know where they are now?"

"No. But there is more. A year ago our company took part in a shipping conference. It was held in Tokyo and many people in the profession came. One of the speakers, a Captain Wennström, a retired Swedish sea captain, was sitting in the hotel bar. I was at a table nearby and could hear what he was saying as he was speaking in a loud and excitable way to his companions. He was describing a rescue that had happened on board his ship and how they had buried the Japanese captain with honour at sea. I went over to the table and asked if he knew the name of the captain. When he told me,

Captain Isami, and I told him it was my brother in law, you can imagine his surprise."

"So Kato had the pearls with him and gave them to this Captain Wennström"

"Kato did have the pearls, you are right, but he gave them to the two young sailors who rescued him. What were they going to do with such a gift? Wennström's ship was a cargo passenger ship. He had a friend on board who was a jeweller who offered to sell the pearls on their behalf, and that is what happened. Captain Wennström said they were sold at an auction in Stockholm, he was sure of that as his friend, Mr. Jörgensen, had sent the two sailors the money from the sale."

"You can find out who bought them. There would be a record of the sale."

"Of course, but I have not been able to reach Erik Jörgensen. Wennström gave me his telephone number, but the people at the house will not disclose any information. They tell me he is retired and travelling abroad."

"He is in Rio de Janeiro?"

"I don't know. It would be fortunate if he was, because I have found one of the young sailors and this is why we are going there. Looking in the ship's registry one day, I found the name KISHIWADA II."

"The company used the name again."

"Not the company. This ship is privately owned. One of the young sailors who took part in the rescue was a Brazilian. This boat is registered in Rio de Janeiro. It was purchased the year after Kato died. This ship has been bought with the money from the sale of the pearls! It is not right they were sold to buy a fishing boat!"

"Oh grandfather, how was he to know what they meant? What can you do about it now?"

"A great deal. A great deal. I am going to start our search in Brazil. I intend to find the pearls Mariko. Is this not important? You must be excited and share this. Think of our family honor. You will be the one to hold the pearls in your possession when they are returned to us."

"Grandfather, I want to ask you something. Why were you not speaking to your brother in law Kato when he came home? Why did you not talk about this? Your sister had been killed. Did you not see each other? Was there not a funeral?"

Taru finished his tea and sat in silence for a few minutes. Mariko understood she had asked him something he didn't want to talk about, but then he took her hand.

"Mariko, you were born in 1960 and you are part of the new Japan. It is good that you know our history, all of it, but I, who lived through many things, do not wish to visit painful times again, but, I will tell you, briefly. I had moved to the north, to Hokkaido, with my wife and my daughter, your mother, at the beginning of the war. During the war I became a prisoner of the Russians and I did not see my family for years. When the war was over, I was not released for another two years and my wife believed I was dead. They were living with friends in Tokyo. It took a long time to find them. Kato would not have known where to find us, if he had tried. Perhaps he tried. It must be difficult for you to imagine how our country was after Hiroshima, and Nagasaki. We were demilitarized and the country was under an American administration. I had been a regular soldier. Many Japanese people were horrified when they learnt of the brutality of the Japanese army. I was ashamed. It was a lonely time. I changed my profession and I have had a new life. I have been honoured and privileged to have had success."

"But you were not a soldier like that. You told me you were a translator."

"A translator has to take part in interrogation Mariko. I do not wish to speak of this again."

Mariko took both of his hands in her own. "I will help you find the pearls, grandfather. It will be an adventure, won't it."

Chapter 10

Leif drifted up out of his dream, conscious of the warmth of Ella's thigh against his hand. They had made love for the first time in weeks, glorious sensual love that had happened because of a joke he had made, the atmosphere had changed between them and they had found each other again.

The journey had been difficult through the Dover Straits, they had had fog, but when they reached Brixham on the Devonshire coast they had been able to wait for good weather before taking off into the Atlantic. They took on fuel and provisions in Brixham and the ELISE had drawn a lot of attention. An old Swedish cargo sailing ship was not something that came into port every day. Fishermen and pilots from the port asked to come on board to be shown around and Leif was pleased that even Jörgen took pride in telling them about the ship, that it had been built in the 1930's and how far it had travelled since. Leif was surprised that he knew so much. So he had taken an interest in the ship after all. "Look at the timber" one old retired sailor had said "Nothing like that today" and Jörgen had agreed, looking up and catching Leif's eye and smiling across the deck at him.

When they turned south into the wild north Atlantic, they had no time for conversation as they were on deck day and night, even Ella was called on to help. Leif tried to be patient with everyone but it was not easy when he knew more than the family, knew how quickly they could make a mistake and all be gone.

He thought of himself and Georgio, taking the ELISE from Africa to Rio and then that insane voyage up the Amazon. How strong you were when you were twenty. When he watched Helen and Jörgen hauling on the sails, he saw himself at that age, working with conviction and without fear. Too much knowledge can be a handicap, thought Leif, I see a disaster around every corner. But I haven't changed so much if I can decide to take off like this and bring the family so far away. He blamed it on the ELISE. She had always seduced him into doing something extreme.

His arms were still sore from the trip and his back ached but he was remembering how the mood had changed after they had gone through the Bay of Biscay. The days had started to get warmer, the wind less threatening and patches of blue had begun to open up in the sky. They had continued to edge south until one magical evening the islands appeared on the horizon, purple against the setting sun. Everyone sent up a cheer and then became spellbound as they sailed over the calm shimmering water towards them. They had anchored off a reef for the night not to break the spell, shed all of their clothes and swam out from the ship in the dark, the lights from the ELISE guiding them back across the warm rippling water. After supper Helen had begun to sing an old Swedish song.

Leif began to sing the song again and Ella turned over and laid her arm gently across his chest. It was the middle of the afternoon. Jörgen and Helen had gone ashore for the third day running. Helen, tanned and relaxed in her new straw hat and sandals, Jörgen in a white baseball cap and shorts, they had strolled off arm in arm that morning and Ella, watching them go, had arranged to meet them for lunch, but she hadn't got that far. Leif was surprised that they hadn't returned to see what had happened. The restaurant was within walking distance and feeling suddenly tense with concern, he swung his legs over the bed.

"Where are you going?" Ella said sleepily.

"I remembered you arranged to meet them for lunch."

Ella looked at her watch on the shelf. "Well it's too late now. Why don't you come back to bed?"

"I'd better see if I can find them" said Leif pulling on his trousers.

"They'll be OK. They have each other."

"But why didn't they come back when you didn't turn up? It's almost three" He was hurrying now. He grabbed a shirt from the chair. Ella pushed the sheet away from her with her feet and Leif was aroused again. How lovely she was. He sat down on the bed and touched her. "I'll be back soon. I just want to check they are alright."

"They'll be at the beach now" she said reaching up to kiss him.

"But they didn't come back to ..." he tried to say.

Her mouth was so warm.

"Oh yes they did" said Ella, laughing at Leif's expression. "But they went away again."

"They came in here?"

Ella fell back on the pillow, laughing at Leif's red face. "No of course they didn't but I heard them come on board and then whispering outside the door. What's the matter? You're not ashamed are you? They're not exactly children you know."

Leif slowly removed his clothes and laid down. How could he expect Jörgen to be more responsible when he was controlling him all the time, and Helen, he shouldn't keep insisting that she was back at the ship at seven every evening, not when Jörgen was with her.

"What are you thinking" said Ella, propping herself up on her elbow and smiling at him.

"That I'm not always right."

"Well that's an admission I don't hear very often."

Jörgen couldn't remember feeling as good as he did now, except perhaps when they had all dived off the ship the evening they had arrived. He was sitting on the beach after a swim and the temperature was just right. He could hear his favourite band playing on someone's radio further up the beach and he was surrounded by people all trying to get as brown as he was and he was way ahead of them. He could see the two girls who had arrived on the same strip of beach the day before in their bikinis, their bodies very white, almost luminous, and had watched out of the corner of his eye as they had smothered each other in cream. Today they were turning rather pink and he worried for them that they would suffer later. For the first time he felt proud of his dark brown body that was so comfortable in the sun.

He and Helen had spent the lunchtime at the open market, eating sandwiches and strolling around listening to the Spanish stall holders, enjoying the easy way they joked with their customers and each other, shouting out the price of their fish or vegetables, stopping to take a gulp of wine from a bottle hung up on string. It was very different to a market in Sweden.

There were many tourists. Helen and Jörgen were interested in the languages, catching bits of conversation here and there. An Englishman in a floral shirt was speaking in Spanish in a very quiet voice to a man selling fruit and vegetables. The stall holder kept saying "No entiendo" over and over again and had decided to ignore him when six other English people arrived in a noisy group. One of the men, red faced, bare chested and loud, managed to buy what he wanted and help the other Englishman without bothering to speak Spanish at all. "There you are mate" said the man, breathing beer. "Thank you so much" said the one in the floral shirt, raising his hat. Then a Frenchman arrived, very exact as to the number of tomatoes and onions he required, pointing to be helpful, speaking about everything, the good weather, how he was going to cook the vegetables he was buying, but only in French. The stallholder smiled, money was exchanged. "Adios" called the stallholder "Au Revoir" said the Frenchman.

A man and a woman were looking at china nearby and Jörgen got excited when he heard them talking.

"Are you from Brazil?" he asked them but they had not understood. "Brazil? Rio de Janeiro?" A light of understanding appeared in the man's eyes. "Desculpe. Sinto muito. No Brazil. Portugal" said the man smiling at him expectantly but Jörgen could only smile back.

Helen had wanted to look around the shops instead of going for a swim, so they had arranged to meet on the corner by the taxi stand. Jörgen was not surprised to see that she was wearing something new, a bright tee shirt that had a palm tree and TENERIFE printed on the front. They stopped to look at view cards at a stand on the corner but Helen said they couldn't send any as no one was supposed to know where they were. "I'd love to send a card to friends at school, like this, with the beach and palm trees."

"Just so they can get jealous eh?" Jörgen said but his mind was elsewhere. He was thinking about his father, Georgio, and that he didn't even know his address and had never bothered to find out. He would have liked to send him a card, remembering the silent moody boy he had been when they met. There were postcards with cartoons. He could have sent one of those.

"Where's Jörgen?" Leif asked automatically as Helen appeared at the galley door. "Forget that I said that" He turned the fish over in the pan.

Helen gave him one of those smiles "He's dancing at the club on the beach and I came back at seven if you notice, to ask if I can go."

"We could all go" said Ella, putting her head round the door.

"You must be joking" said Helen and stomped back up the stairs. Ella smiled at Leif and then followed.

"Tell her she can go for a couple of hours" Leif called after her .. "But I'm bringing the plates up. Let's eat on deck." He tucked a bottle of wine under one arm and arrived on deck in time to see Helen running off down the jetty. He put the two plates of fish on the table and was just arranging the chairs when Helen returned.

"I thought so" said Leif reaching into his pocket, "but this is the last for awhile" Helen kissed him on the cheek and set off again.

"Nice Tee shirt" he called after her. She said something and ran on.

"What did she say?" asked Ella.

"Something about lovebirds" he said, pouring the wine. Ella laughed. She was taking a sip from her wine when the radio telex started up and she groaned as it went chattering on at length.

"You should turn that thing off in the evening"

"Problem is, it isn't evening everywhere else" He came back carrying the telex. "See? It was good news. The agent with more cargo for the STELLA and another" He placed the second telex on the table and Ella read it aloud.

GOT THE KEY FROM BRITT. SETTLING IN NICELY. BROUGHT SAMSON SO STOP WORRYING. KURT

"What's this about?"

"Well it's from Kurt obviously and he is now at the house, taking care of things."

"You asked him to do this? Why didn't you discuss this with me?"

"I wanted to fix it first and Kurt volunteered. Thought we shouldn't leave the house empty, all things considered."

"All things considered" Ella repeated angrily "And who is Samson? One of Kurt's boyfriends?"

Leif laughed "It's his dog."

"His dog!" Ella cried, thinking of her rugs and furniture.

"It's a very small dog but it makes a lot of noise" said Leif laughing.

Chapter 11

By the time Georgio had marched along Rua de Carioca, the conversation he was going to have with Garcia, the wholesale fish merchant, complete with counter arguments, insults and a triumphant conclusion, had been rehearsed many times. When he stepped into Garcia's office, there was Garcia alright, but sitting next to him, with their guns stuck into their trouser belts, were two capanga. One of the reasons for the hired security was immediately obvious. Garcia laughed at Georgio's angry face and pointed to the leg that was encased in plaster to the top of his thigh.

"You want to break the other leg?" Garcia asked "I see it on your face. 'Para que nossas mulheres nao fiquem viuva!'" He was drinking cachaca and he poured a glass for Georgio. "Have a drink. You can tell me all that is on your mind. I understand that the bacalao was a very good price, eh? Smart that Souza. So you are OK now eh?"

"Someone pay you to give the wrong information Garcia, because after many years in the business you don't seem to know shit."

The guards shifted their positions.

"Now. Don't make my friends here mad eh? I give advice, not information. I give opinion, and see what it does for me. No advice no more."

"You have never been out there. Weather is one thing. Days going by and nothing to show for it and men to pay is another. You call it advice, you were begging me to go to that area and you know Ed gave you good reasons why he was against it. I think you gave the same 'advice' to someone else" Georgio tapped the bottom of his glass on the plastered leg.

"No. This was my wife. She catch me with another

woman" Garcia roared. Georgio knew Garcia's wife, a shy, tiny woman who rarely spoke to anyone.

"That so? What did she use? A tank?"

Garcia held up his hand. "Wait Georgio my friend, I will give you some advice that is true. You want to catch fish these days? You need helicopter. Yes, that is what they are using today, to see where the fish are. You have to be more up to date. You don't know this?" Garcia lit a cigar "And your boats are getting old Georgio, you need new boats or a refit of the ones you got already. I have seen your boats don't look so good these days."

"A helicopter" Georgio snorted. "Three hundred miles off the coast of Argentina?"

"You have a landing place on the boat, of course. Not boat like your boat, but one that is built with a helicopter pad, you know? This is the modern way Georgio. If you had had a modern boat with a helicopter you would have come back full of tuna. You can ask Ed if he like to train to be a helicopter pilot" laughed Garcia, rolling his head back, his mouth wide. Georgio looked at the display of black fillings along his teeth and would have liked to knock out everyone of them.

Georgio was taking the long drive home. Years ago he had bought his mother a house at Ubatuba, on the shoreline of the northern Sao Paulo coast, with the money he had received for his share of the pearls. When his mother died, he had moved his wife Ceyla and their two children from the apartment they were renting in Rio and in to the beach house. It was an inconvenient place for business, far away from the city and the port, but a good place for his children to grow up and he felt secure. He owned the property. He never forgot the misery his parents had endured, with a landlord who was always threatening to take their tiny home away from them.

His brothers Paulo and Chico had moved out long ago. Both married and moved to Brasilia to work in the construction business, but they found they had to live over thirty kilometres outside of the city. Brasilia was too expensive, except for government officials and wealthy businessmen, but the building work kept them in the area. They had both made Georgio an uncle several times over but the family could only afford to get together once a year and they did this at Christmas and New Year. Then the beach house overflowed and all the cousins stayed together in tents on the beach and Ceyla was happy all day long.

Their house at Ubatuba was now full of children of their own, as the two had grown into five. Daniela, Georgio, Roberto, Maria, and one year old Carla. The last time he was home Ceyla told him that there could be number six on the way and Georgio had forced himself to appear happy at the news. He loved his children. It was the money.

Ten, even twenty, OK! he said to himself as he drove along, if they can just run barefoot on the beach. Ceyla took the bus once a week to Sao Paulo to the cathedral with all the children and she insisted that they were dressed in their best for the occasion. Sao Paulo was four hours away and the bus fares and the necessary clothes and shoes were expensive and they kept growing out of everything. Ceyla went to a small church nearby for confession but she would not discuss her weekly trip to Sao Paulo, only saying that it was essential to go to the Cathedral if the children were to grow up to be good Catholics. He had stopped trying to change her mind long ago; he was often away at sea and it was something she looked forward to do each week. He knew that the visit to the Cathedral was not the only reason, and that the crowded city with its many shops and cafes was an important part of the day. It was the window shopping and perhaps a coffee and ice cream for the children as well. He liked to tease her about it, pretending it was something neither of them knew. The children would love to tell him about what they had seen in the big city and he would quiz them in a teasing way, within Ceyla's hearing. "Oh, is that so? What were you doing there?" he would ask, his eye on Ceyla through the open door as she stood cooking at the stove.

He wished his brothers lived close by. Ceyla was from Ouro Preto, far north of Rio de Janeiro and she did not see her family very often either and she had few friends in the area. The houses that had been built in recent years were expensive holiday villas for wealthy people from Sao Paulo who only came at the weekends. Georgio had been thinking for sometime that he should sell the house, he would get a good price, more than he paid for it. They could move to Rio de Janeiro closer to his business, but he was afraid for his children. They would not have to live in the poorest part of town but it would not be the best either and he would worry about them more when he was away. The children would miss their life on the beach, but Ceyla would be happier. He often thought of it, but he was a long way from deciding, and as he turned down the beach road and smelt the fresh breeze from the sea, the idea went out of his mind again.

Akira had sat alert and upright for the entire four hour journey in the hot and crowded bus, thinking something might happen, he did not know what, but something, if he fell asleep. He was alarmed by the noisy chatter around him but it helped to keep him awake. When he arrived at Ubatuba, he had walked up and down the dusty beach road several times before he found Georgio's house. He looked so tired when he arrived that Ceyla had settled him in an armchair out on the porch. When she went back a few minutes later with a glass of cold tea, he was fast asleep. They had had a difficult, halting conversation that morning on the telephone, but Ceyla had managed to explain that Georgio would be coming home, late that afternoon, but that he had been at sea for two months and perhaps it would be better if Akira came the next day? Akira had simply replied, "I come today". She had tried to describe the house but finding it impossible for anyone not used to the area she suggested that she would tie a red scarf to the door, but unfortunately it had blown away.

Now the older children were back from school and all four were sitting lined up on the steps, whispering to each other and giggling each time Akira muttered in his sleep or started to snore. Ceyla had said they could wait for their father outside as long as they were very quiet, but when they saw Georgio's car coming along the road they made such a noise that Akira nearly fell out of the chair. Ceyla came to the door, baby Carla in her arms and ran down the steps. They all crowded around the car, the children shouting and jumping up and down and Georgio smiling and smiling inside the car but locking all the doors and pretending he wasn't going to get out. He reached in the back and held up five large lollipops on sticks at the car window and the screaming increased. Akira was unsure what to do. His instinct was to run into the house to get away from the noise but that would not do at all, he had yet to be invited inside, so he stood stiffly to attention. As Georgia got out of the car and gave the children their sweets he noticed the small grey haired Japanese man standing on the porch and looked at Ceyla. She shrugged her shoulders. "I only know his name is Akira... and he came from Rio today to see you."

"Konnichiwa" said Georgio and bowed.
"Konnichiwa" said Akira, and also bowed.
The children stared in silence, their mouths busy with their sweets. Georgio turned the handle on the front door and gestured for Akira to step inside. "No, no." said Georgio turning to the children "I will see you soon. I have to do business."
Ceyla sat down in the old armchair "I will come in a moment."

Ceyla had so little company except her children or Georgio when he was home that she had become unsure of herself over the years, especially with strangers. Sometimes there were still moments when the talkative, exuberant, twenty year old Ceyla and the happy go lucky Georgio could be heard, but the insecurity of the fishing business came to dominate most of the moods. Each time Georgio set off to sea again, Ceyla would be afraid she would never see him again, but Georgio was only too anxious to leave after he had been home a week or two. It was the pressure to make money, but it was also the sailor in him, anxious to be at sea and away from the shore. They had their children, and were closer as friends and occasional lovers than many others, but their exciting days were fifteen years in the past.

Taru, Mariko and Akira had been in Brazil a week. It had taken them some time to find out that Georgio was out at sea and did not even live in Rio de Janeiro. Taru had sent Akira to the port several times and he had spoken to the shipping company who had sent him Kato's box, but the company said that the KISHIWADA II was privately owned and Georgio Silva did not have an agent or management company but handled his business with the wholesale fish merchants himself. Akira's detective work had produced Georgio's Uncle Souza and assuring Souza that Akira simply wanted to look up an old friend, Souza had told him when Georgio would be back. Souza remembered Georgio's early days at sea had been spent on a Japanese fishing boat and gave Akira Georgio's home telephone number.

It was with some relief that Taru received the telephone call that evening from Akira, from Georgio's house, that contact had been made.

Akira's instructions were to tell Georgio that Taru was Kato's brother in law and as he was staying in Rio at that moment, wanted to meet Georgio and hear about Kato and how he had died. Akira was to explain that his master was in shipping himself and had seen the name of Georgio's boat, but not to speak about anything else, although Akira had been told the full story.

"My other boat is called the KATO" said Georgio proudly as he poured his guest some tea. Akira nodded politely but he was thinking that Georgio must have respected Kato Isami a great deal, to have remembered him in that way.

"We will perhaps go back now?" he asked and Georgio laughed.

"I would not be popular with my family to leave tonight. No, if Mr. Takahashi is staying another few days, perhaps the day after tomorrow?" Georgio was thinking he could take the family with him, Ceyla would like that. But when Georgio took off for Rio two days later, Ceyla and the children stayed at home.

Ceyla was now four months pregnant. She had carried her other five babies without a problem, but this time she was nauseous all day and unusually tired. Two months ago she had stopped being able to feed her youngest child who was now fretful and demanding, clawing at Ceyla's breast each time she picked her up. When she had suspected that she was pregnant again, she had seen a new doctor at the clinic that she hadn't seen before. He had reminded her that she was thirty five and already had five children, as if she didn't know it herself, and had the audacity to hint at the sin of terminating the pregnancy. He also asked her if she or her husband used contraception. When she left the clinic she banged the door behind her and vowed she would never go back again.

"I will be back tomorrow" Georgio had said to her. "I'll stay with Souza tonight."

Ceyla wasn't so happy about that. Georgia's uncle was not married and was often seen driving around town with a highly decorated woman in his truck, but she said nothing and waved as the car drove away.

Chapter 12

Leif was sitting up on deck thinking about their departure and journey back to Gothenburg. He had found it surprisingly easy to run the STELLA and organize his business from the ELISE. Kurt had not only looked after the house but had gone to Leif's office every day to check the mail and telex and pass them on to the STELLA and to Leif on the ELISE. He had more than made up for the problems he had caused with the STELLA, minor problems in the light of what could have happened.

In the relaxed atmosphere of the islands, Leif had started to have a different perspective on most things. Kurt had been trying to compromise but it had got out of hand. The port in Gothenburg was getting back to normal and Leif had sent a statement to the Swedish police through the Consul's office on the islands. He hoped that was the end of it and he wouldn't have to appear in court.

He had just received a telex. Georgio. He would like to see him. They hadn't seen each other for so long now and were bound to have changed but Georgio didn't seem to have changed to judge by the flamboyant style of the message. He was laughing as he read the telex again as Ella came back on board carrying fresh bread for their lunch. "Something funny?" she said leaning over his shoulder and placing her arm around his neck.

"Just the way he writes. It's from Georgio" He folded it up. "Shall we have lunch?"

"Oh, a secret is it?"

"No but something we can talk about while we're eating. That bread smells good."

"You are being evasive" she said in a teasing voice as she went down the steps to the galley. "I'll bring some of our favourite pickles with the ham" she called, and her cheery voice made him sad. They had been so happy, these days in Tenerife, as if they were under a spell. The holiday mood would soon be over. He was partly worried about the tough journey back to Sweden, but more about how life would slip back into the tension of his work, and the effect it had on all of them.

"Never!" said Ella furiously. "I said I would never talk to him again and I meant it, you know that Leif. Why are you even asking me?"

"It's only information Ella. You don't have to talk to him. Just telephone the house and talk to one of the people who work there. I understand he's not even there."

"Don't be ridiculous. You think one of the people at the house are going to give me information about an auction from God knows how many years ago?"

"Of course not. But they will tell you where your father is and we can send that information back. They can contact him themselves. You see? You don't have to talk to him at all."

Ella sat looking down at her plate. "How many letters did I write? How many times did he refuse to come to the telephone?"

"I know. But he is getting old now. He has probably mellowed. It's getting to be a long time ago"

"Don't try to persuade me Leif" She got up from the table. "I'm going for a walk. I have to think about this. Tell Georgio we'll get back to him"

"He doesn't know you and your father haven't spoken for years .."

"I understand that. But Georgio would forgive anyone anything. You know how he is. He wouldn't understand that a father didn't want anything to do with his daughter or the grandchildren he has never seen!" Her voice was shaking and Leif got up to go to her, but she went down the gangway and walked quickly away along the jetty.

Sixteen years ago, Erik Jörgensen was enraged when Ella left her German husband. Later, Erik heard she was living with Leif Hansson and her child, whose name, Jörgen, infuriated him. Items had appeared in the gossip columns, he said on the telephone. It was the last time they had spoken to each other.

"From one common sailor to another" he had fumed, "The whole of society now knows you had a child by a Brazilian sailor. After all I did to protect you! Even to arrange that you were married to a man with a title! I am the victim of this, not you! You have ruined our family reputation!"

Slowly, Ella had replaced the receiver.

When her German divorce came through, and she and Leif were married, she tried to speak to him, and again, when Helen was born, but her father had still refused to come to the telephone.

Georgio and Souza were sitting at the bar of the Jabaru, the club on Rua de Carioca, ignoring the women and the couples dancing on the floor behind them. They had just come from Souza's office. Georgio had telephoned Leif's house and after speaking to Kurt, had sent the telex to Leif on the ELISE and was now telling Souza the story. Souza scratched his chin.

"This man, he is the man who owns the Takahashi Shipping Company? They are big fish, I tell you."

"I can believe that, staying at the Copacabana Palace" Georgio agreed, sipping his beer.

It had been a strange encounter at the hotel. Akira had opened the door to the suite and then disappeared. Georgio had found himself facing a more formidable man who did not smile but simply beckoned him to sit down.

A young Japanese girl sat apart from them at the end of a table, writing, and did not look up. Taru introduced himself, but he did not introduce the girl. A secretary perhaps. Georgio understood he was there to tell his story and so he started at the beginning, when he had run away and joined the KISHIWADA. It was a long story and Georgio was anxious to tell Taru every detail. The man sitting opposite him was impassive, no matter what Georgio said, but he pressed on. Akira appeared at one point with a tray of tea and went away again. When Georgio described Kato's death and how they had been summoned to the captain's cabin and told about the pearls, Taru became animated and sat forward in his chair and spoke for the first time. He told Georgio the history of the pearls and told him that they were never meant to be given away, or sold. Georgio noticed that the girl at the table had now stopped writing and kept drinking from the glass of water on her table. Georgio was at first interested, then concerned and then embarrassed.

"We were not to know this" he protested, "and now, what do we do?" he asked in his mild way.

"We must find them!" exclaimed Taru. "The jeweller, this Erik Jörgensen, he will know who bought them." Georgio's mind was racing. What did this mean for him and for Leif? Were they meant to pay back the money? That would be impossible.

"This is a family situation my boy" Souza was saying, slapping his shoulder "Not your problem"

"I feel, I am concerned... a little."

"A little, yes, but you cannot be involved in this! When you find out where this man is, the one who sold the pearls for you, you quit this problem. You can say, I have done what I can to help, but no more. I know the Japanese people, they are not thinking the way we do and you will get yourself into this before you turn around twice. This is not to say we don't have honour or vendetta here in Brazil as you know" He drained his glass and signalled to the barman for a refill.

Vendetta, Georgio was thinking.

"You cannot come after a man years later and say to him, my brother in law did something wrong and now you have to make it OK. You were a boy! A brave boy who had your own honour. I don't like the sound of this man. I think he is too rich and powerful."

Powerful, thought Georgio.

"I told him Leif's wife was Erik Jörgenson's daughter"

"Aha! He would be interested in that of course. He might see a plot, a connection."

"But he doesn't know how to contact them. They are on the ELISE in the Canary Islands just now."

"This man, who owns one of the biggest shipping companies in the world will not know where to find them? Georgia, wake up. He can find anything, do anything, this man. He found you."

"He will not get an answer before I do. I'm sorry I went to see him. I don't think he cared about Kato at all. He wanted only to find his stupid pearls."

"If you see him again, don't say such thing. You have to respect what he respects."

"Why?"

"You have ambition, no? You like to buy a new boat? You can think another way about this. Maybe if you help him, maybe he will help you."

"I cannot think like this. I am worried about Ceyla. I have no time to play these games."

"Are you going to Ouro Preto tonight?"

"Yes. I will not have more beer. I will phone you tomorrow to see if you have a reply from Leif."

"I cannot believe he is still sailing the ELISE."

"He knows what he's doing. He always did. He has it in his blood. He loves that old ship you know."

"You like to see him?"

"Yes. And I like to see my son."

Chapter 13

Ella walked through the streets of Santa Cruz thinking about her father. He was a master jeweller, a superb craftsman, whose work was sought after and admired, and he became famous within his trade, and among the rich people of the world, but the truth about his beginnings and status among the Swedish nobility would have been painful for him to admit. Perhaps he knew in his heart, but the occasional invitations he received for an event were motivated by Erik's willingness to lend many of the magnificent pieces he had made, to certain ladies who would be attending themselves, and as he became well known, they craved to be the first to wear his new designs. But to those in society whom he thought his friends, he was considered by them to be only a tradesman. Before long, Erik could afford to ignore their snobbery. He became well known internationally, and he became rich.

In those early days, Ella's mother Sara was distressed at the change in him and the social pressures he placed upon her. She was a pianist with a modest talent who was content to perform at local events, church halls and charities, but Erik had forced her to perform out of her range and capability, exaggerating her talent to his hosts to draw attention to himself.

One evening when Sara had had to perform yet again against her will, for a party of rich guests she did not know, and had made many mistakes on the keyboard, she locked herself in her bedroom and shot herself. Ella had been eight years old. Ella was told that her mother had been mentally ill. She knew her mother cried easily and became angry at small things, but she hadn't known why. Later she remembered peaceful times when she and her mother had been alone and she had played the piano, just for her.

It was much later, when Ella was a young woman, and she and her father were on a ship bound for Brazil, that he spoke honestly to her about her mother. It was as if another man was speaking. He had drunk a few glasses of wine, they were in the middle of the ocean, sitting out on the deck. It was peaceful. There were many stars in the sky. He began by telling Ella how they had met. She knew the story, or the facts, but not the emotions, the pleasure, the happiness they had felt in the things that they had shared. Looking up at the sky, Ella heard all of these things for the first time, and from her father of all people, a man with limited emotions. In her memory came the sound of a gun and running footsteps up the stairs, but Erik was speaking with warmth of the time he and Sara were students, attending the same college, studying design, music and the arts. They had shared so much, but when they married, they were very young and poor so he worked in the back of a jewelry shop, repairing watches. It had been Sara who had encouraged him to present the designs he had made when he was a student. Sara found work in a government office, supporting them both while he worked on his presentations. "She placed me in the light and herself in the shadows" he said. "But that was where she preferred to be. I didn't realize that. I didn't bother to understand. I was selfish. Yes, I was selfish. I forced her out into the light, and into a life that she didn't want and wasn't prepared for, and I ignored her distress."

He had put his head in his hands. Ella had got up and stood at the ship's rail and as she had looked out into the night, she heard her father weeping.

Ella could not forgive him completely, but neither could she remember her mother so well. She wished she could meet her, know her, now she was a woman. Her father, with his ambitious nature, was not able to believe anyone else did not feel the same as he did, have the same goals. Ella was experiencing that, even back then, accompanying him on his business trips and acting as hostess at home and abroad. Perhaps it wasn't all her father's fault. She had observed other couples. Ella adjusted her thoughts and memories and became more involved with her father's lifestyle and grew to care for him. Then she had made a mistake. Erik's cold reaction nearly broke her. He forced her to give Jörgen up for adoption and marry someone who suited his ambitions, someone she didn't love, or even know very well. It was Leif who had brought Ella and Jörgen back together, and made it right again.

But the memory of that night on the ship, when her father had shown her his human face, gave Ella the motivation she needed. She would find a telephone.

Georgio was dozing in his car on a steep side street in Ouro Preto, high in the Serra do Espinhaco mountain range. It had taken six hours to drive from Rio. He could not wake anyone at three in the morning. He had pulled the hand brake on as hard as he could and closed his eyes, he didn't want to end up at the bottom of the hill. The sun rose late behind the mountains and it was still dark and misty when he awoke. It was seven o'clock. He got out of the car. The cobblestone streets were slippery and he was cold. He didn't come to see Ceyla's family very often. It was too far away and he never had the time he told himself, but the climate was the other reason. It reminded him of Sweden, everything in order and cold weather. No supermarkets or fast food places here, but historic buildings with terracotta roofs, colorful walls and paintwork against a background of green covered mountains, a beautiful place, but he couldn't live without having the sun every day. He shivered, looking up at the windows for a sign of life. They were not expecting him. He hadn't telephoned. He didn't want to take no for an answer. Better to make his request in person. He hoped Ceyla's sister was at home. He had to meet Ed on the dock in the afternoon for the classification society's periodical inspection. The bank had been on the phone again and there was no putting it off. He had also promised Taru Takahachi that he would meet him again sometime in the evening. It would be another day and a night before he could get home. He hoped Mariana, Ceyla's sister, could take the bus to Ubataba. If she agreed to come back with him now, he could drop her at the bus station in Rio.

It was getting dark by the time Ella came back. Leif had sent Jörgen to look for her, but he had been unable to find her. Leif was in the small cabin he used for an office with the door ajar, trying to work and listen at the same time. He was relieved when he heard someone coming on board and recognized her step as she came along the passageway. He went to meet her and opened the door to their cabin. Ella flopped down on the bed.

"I went to that shipping agency. I decided to phone the house. I wanted to be private so it seemed the best place. They were very pleasant and didn't mind at all, but I had to wait for ages for a line to be free. I paid them for the call by the way". She had a strange look in her eye. Leif waited, he didn't want to ask a lot of questions. He was surprised and pleased. He would be able to send Georgio a telex tonight.

"Like a drink?"

"I would. A large gin and tonic."

When he came back with the drinks, Helen was sitting on the bed talking to her and Jörgen was propped in the doorway.

"Mum phoned our mystery grandpa" Helen said.

"I know" Leif handed Ella her drink and she nearly emptied the glass in one go.

"Bad as that eh?" said Leif.

"Didn't talk to him. I talked to Lennart. You remember Lennart?" said Ella smiling broadly

"I certainly do" said Leif, thinking of Lennart pointing a gun at him in Ella's cabin all those years ago. "So he is still in charge."

"Looking after the security in the house."

"Did you find out where Erik was?"

Ella paused. Leif couldn't read her expression but she wasn't distressed. She seemed amused.

"He got married" Ella announced, enjoying their reaction. "And he is on his honeymoon on some remote island and cannot be reached by telephone."

"Oh, romantic" said Helen.

"That sounds like Lennart being difficult ..."

"No. I don't think so. We had quite a chat. The wife is American, forty two years old and they cannot be reached because she is an oceanographer and it's a working holiday. Her work, not his" Ella smiled.

Leif whistled. "Forty two? The old goat."

"It will be like having a sister, Mum" said Helen

"Don't jump too far ahead. I am still digesting the news. I'll have another gin though. Sorry Leif, you'll have to tell Georgio to wait for any information he needs. Lennart said they are not due back for two months and she is doing research and mustn't be disturbed. There are no phones, hotels or anything like that on the island. Sounds like they're camping or something. Can you imagine my father, camping?"

Chapter 14

It was a bad news day. Georgio and Ed were sitting in a cafe drinking their coffee in silence. It was difficult to find anything to say. The classification people had found so many things that needed to be fixed on the boats that they were overwhelmed. Their report would be at the bank within two days. They feared that the loan they had applied for would be refused. They were not allowed to put to sea and earn anything in any case until all the repairs were made and the boats inspected again. Even if they had the money now it would still take at least three weeks. Then a telex had arrived from Leif saying they would not be able to contact Erik Jörgensen for at least two months. Georgio was not concerned about that himself, but he had to give the news to Taru Takahashi in an hour, and he knew the man enough to know he would not take no for an answer, and would expect him to try something else. What, he had no idea, but it would be something. He seemed obsessed. What was the hurry after all this time?

"Now you can tell that Taru fella to shove it where the sun don't shine" said Ed, looking at the copy of the telex that lay on the table. The idea of saying something like that to Taru made Georgio laugh and almost cheered him up.

The one good thing was that Mariana was on her way to Ubatuba. She had reacted with concern when Georgio had told her about Ceyla and agreed to stay with her as long as it was necessary. They had driven back to Rio that morning and Mariana had even taken over the driving at one point, and Georgio had been able to sleep. She was Ceyla's elder sister and she had no children of her own. Her husband had been killed in the mines and she had been a widow for ten years. She was Aunt Mari, the child minder for all the relatives who lived in and around the town, and would be missed, she said, but she didn't get on with her brother and sister in law who shared the house with her, and was happy to make the change. Georgio didn't want to ask why, but as he was carrying Mariana's suitcases from the house to the car, the sister in law spoke to him under her breath "You'll never get rid of her" she had said, "And we don't want her back here." He was so relieved that Ceyla would have someone to help her and keep her company when he was at sea, he dismissed it as a private quarrel. He gave Mariana most of the money he had left in his pocket and saw her onto the bus to Sao Paulo.

When he telephoned Ceyla to tell her what he thought she would be happy to hear, that Mariana was on her way to stay with her, she wasn't as pleased as he had expected.

"You will have every excuse to stay away at sea even more now" she said and the rest of their conversation was about whether or not he had driven most of the night to Ouro Preto. She seemed to think he had been with Souza and women at the Jabaru. Georgio sighed and simply said "Well you work it out. It takes six hours there and back."

He was angry that she didn't appreciate what he had done. He had only been thinking of her.

Privately he was not happy about the new baby. He had tried to talk to Ceyla about contraception before, but she was shocked that he would even suggest it. Then he had tried to stay away from her more, but as he had neither the time or the money to be with other women, it was difficult.

"You're a goddam saint" Ed would say when he suggested they have a night out together and Georgio shook his head. He suggested it now.

"I don't need more problems. And I have to go and see the Japanese" said Georgio getting up to go. "I'll still be in town tomorrow. We have to talk to the bank so I'll stay with Souza tonight."

"You can stay with me!"

"That's OK. It could be a bit crowded."

Ed was well known at the Jabaru and after dancing with as many women as possible all night, more than one woman would end up at Ed's place.

Georgio made his way to the Copacabana Hotel. As he drove along he thought about the conversation he had had with Souza about Taru Takahashi and it made him smile. When it came to fish, Souza had simple straightforward advice and he was usually right, but first he had told him not to get more involved and in the same conversation had pointed out that Taru was a rich and powerful man, and, he was in the shipping business. "You have ambition, no?"

Leif was reading the International Herald Tribune up on deck. "Strikes and trouble with the unions in Britain." he said, as Ella and Helen arrived back on board "Have to keep abreast of this. It could affect their ports."

"Well, we'll be home in two weeks" said Ella "and you'll be able to find out more."

"Kurt already mentioned it in his last telex. He is doing a great job. I've been wondering if he would like to do a desk job ashore, continue to manage the office" He looked up at her "Nice haircut. It would give us more time together" he added.

"That would be good" She paused and then sat down next to him. "But I am going back to work, Leif. I am going to look for another job in the property business as soon as we get back"

"The Queen of England has her Silver Jubilee this year" he said, continuing to look at the paper.

"You wouldn't be avoiding the subject, would you?" Ella said, and then went to go below. "I am going to do it, just so you know" she called as she went down the steps. The VHF squawked into life with his call sign and he put the newspaper down. "Calling Captain Hansson on the ELISE" the voice continued.

"This is the ELISE, Hansson speaking"

"We have a telephone call for you captain, from Rio de Janeiro. Go ahead caller"

"Hello Leif" Georgio's voice was loud and clear.

"What do you know! How are you doing?"

"Very well." Georgio lied.

"Leif, I am with Taru Takahashi, you know, Kato's brother in law. We are in his hotel room here at the Copacabana"

That would mean Georgio was not paying for the telephone call. Leif relaxed. This was just more about the pearls. "You got my telex?" he asked.

"Sure, sure, but Mr. Takahashi would like to speak to you. We have built our whole lives from the money, haven't we Leif. We have a duty, no?"

"OK" Leif said. He leant back against the wall. This was Georgio preparing him, letting him know the way this man was thinking.

"So here is Mr. Taru, Leif. He talk to you now."

When Taru's voice came over the receiver with all its authority Leif understood that Georgio was under pressure.

"Captain Hansson, I would like you to pursue this matter regarding Erik Jörgensen again. We do not have to wait for two months to get an answer to a simple question surely. I am sure you can find out where he is, unless you know already? There are other ways beside the use of the telephone. He cannot be completely cut off from the world. What other details do you have?

You simply say that he is away, but where is 'away' exactly?"

"Good evening Mr.Takahashi." said Leif, taking the advantage of offering the polite greeting that Taru had omitted. "My wife spoke to the security officer at her father's estate. She was not given any details regarding Jörgensen's present location and as he had asked not to be disturbed, she probably didn't bother to ask for more details."

"Probably?" said Taru. "Perhaps you could ask her?"

"She is not on board at the moment. She is ashore with our daughter" Helen had put her head around the wheelhouse door and Leif held up his finger to his lips.

"Captain Hansson, you must be aware of who I am and my company."

"Yes, I am" said Leif, winking at Helen "I just read in Lloyds List that you are about to retire."

"I am in the position of being able to recommend and guarantee certain business arrangements" Taru said, then waited for a response. Leif remained silent and so Taru continued "For example, a favourable bare boat charter on a new ship. A combination container and reefer for the South American trade, running between here and Europe? We have just built six of these ships.

"If this is a business proposition, I would not be interested. It would be difficult to get cargo with my present limited network."

"Ah, but this would be a package of course. You would have a guaranteed use of our agencies and brokers. It would balance out quite well. You would be more than able to pay for the charter and make a good profit for yourself and my company. You would hire the crew of course as is usual. You have only one ship, the STELLA? She was ten years old when you bought her? So, now, twenty years old?"

Leif was a mixture of emotions. Was this about the pearls or what? He continued to remain silent.

"It would be good for your image to add a new ship to your company at this time, when you have had such misfortune with problems in your home port" Taru continued.

Was there anything this man did not know?

Ella was laying the table for supper in the galley. "Lennart did tell me something. A post office box number, where they are picking up their mail. I wrote it on a piece of paper but I threw it away."

"What did you do that for?" Leif was trying to take the tension out of his voice without success.

"I am not going to write to him if that's what you mean. I might phone him in Sweden when he gets back but I haven't decided yet."

Leif picked up the wrong plates, trying to help, and Ella put them back on the rack.

"We're having pasta tonight" she explained

"Can you remember where the post office was?"

"What is all this about Leif? Is it that auction business with the pearls again? I am not going to try to contact him when he has asked not to be disturbed, not now, after all these years."

Leif picked up her handbag from the bench and gave it to her.

"See if you still have it."

Ella glared at him, but she took the bag and went through the contents. "No, I don't have it."

"Look in your money purse."

"I told you, I don't want to write to him and I don't want you to either!" She found a small piece of paper but held on to it. Leif was tempted to snatch it out of her hand. Ella looked at the paper. "Natal. And the island is called Fernando or something. Leif, I am serious, if you really want to upset me.." but Leif was laughing.

"Natal! I can't believe this!"

"What?"

"Natal. It's a port on the northern coast of Brazil. And I know the islands. Fernando de Noronha. I have passed them many times. Georgio and I even passed that way once with the ELISE. They are on the Atlantic Sailing route, every old sailor knows about them. But it must be true they don't have a telephone. From the sea they look like a pile of tall jagged rocks. The sailors used to call the highest point The Finger of God".

He turned quickly and went back up on deck. Ella followed after him.

"Leif!" she said sharply "What are you planning?"

Jörgen was coiling rope. He looked up at Leif and saw that look in his eye.

Chapter 15

Mariko was bored with everything. She would have been numb with boredom if she wasn't so angry. Bored with the view from the windows, the paintings on the walls, the hotel furniture, the discreet knock on the door each morning as the maid came to clean the rooms, Akira ringing his infuriating little bell to announce that dinner had arrived, (Where had he found the little bell? He must have brought it with him). She had brought some books with her to study, but after ten days in the rooms at the Copacabana Hotel they failed to hold her interest anymore. The first disappointment was that Taru would not let her go out to explore the city, not even with Akira as chaperone as it was considered to be too dangerous, and now they were taking all their meals in the hotel suite. For the first two days, after their arrival, they had eaten in the hotel restaurant, but Taru had complained that one of the waiters in the restaurant had paid too much attention to her, and that she had behaved inappropriately by smiling at him. She was now beginning to wonder if she would be allowed to go back to university when they returned to Kobe. It seemed that Taru had only just woken up to the fact that she was a woman and no longer a little girl.

"A woman" she said to her reflection in the mirror.

"Do you not realise that there are young men who pay me attention at university?" she had said in a rash moment, after Taru announced his decision about the hotel restaurant. "I'm quite used to it. It doesn't mean anything."

Now there had been a telephone call that had apparently meant they were going to stay at the hotel for another two weeks, and the Brazilian fishing boat captain was back, talking to Taru behind closed doors. She knew she had been too outspoken with her grandfather after the last meeting, telling him that she did not like to be sitting in the room and not even be introduced, and why was it necessary for her to be there at all if she wasn't going to take part?

She was just thinking she may as well take her bath and go to bed when there was a knock on the dividing doors "Yes? Come in" she said.

The cable car swung into the station on Pao de Acucar and stopped. "You have to open your eyes now" said Georgio to his companions. He stepped out of the car and held out his hand to Mariko and when she turned to look, she stood very still. Taru and Akira followed, and although Akira was as white as a ghost, he was so astonished at the view that he forgot his fear.

"Magnificent" said Taru. "Many years since I was here but .." he was lost for words. Now they could see how enormous Rio de Janeiro really was. Far below, the city lights spread in every direction, along the line of the great curving bay and twinkling like a thousand stars on the surrounding mountains and foothills. Mariko gasped as she looked up at the brilliant lights shining on the statue of Christ on top of the mountain above them. "Corcovado" said Georgio, "the name of the mountain where you see Christo Redentor. Seven hundred metres above the city he is standing" The wind was warm and with it came the faint sweet smell of a wood fire from far away.

"You are tour guide" It was a statement not a question. Ed was looking at Georgio and shaking his head. "And she is seventeen? You bring her to the Jabaru to dance?"

"Hey. This is business. I am being paid. Good money and as you know, we need money right now."

"How come you got a job looking after a pretty girl and it's business?"

"I am not alone with her! This Akira, he works for the rich guy. He comes along as well. Two weeks, then I can go home."

"What does Ceyla think of this?"

"You think I tell Ceyla? You crazy?"

"You going to take her to the beach?"

"We have to go to museums. Things like that. If I take her to the beach I think I get fired, anyway, she is only two years older than Daniela, I have to take care of her, like a father."

"Yeh, yeh" laughed Ed "So, what's happening with the bank? What's the news?"

"They give us three weeks. Then we decide, or they decide. Maybe something will happen."

"What? What can happen? We sell the boats?"

"This is why I am tour guide, you understand?"

Leif and Jörgen were sitting up on the bow under a sky full of stars. Leif was pointing out the constellations and explaining how he navigated by the stars. Jörgen was interested but he was feeling dreamy and wished they could sit in silence. He wanted to give himself up to this beautiful night. He could not believe there were so many stars in the sky.

"If we didn't have lights in the cities, we could see this all the time" he said.

"As our ancestors did" said Leif "You can understand how much they were in awe of the sky when you see this."

They were motoring across the counter current off the coast of West Africa until they could pick up the south equatorial current. Then they would hoist the sails and the trade winds would take them directly across to Northern Brazil.

It had been a decision made by everyone on board in the end. Leif had recounted the telephone call with Taru Takahashi and what it would mean to him, to the family, and his company. Jörgen had been the first to agree to go to Brazil, without saying why, but Leif believed it was to do with Georgio. Jörgen had been asking questions about him since they had been away. Helen saw it as another adventure and didn't want the holiday to end. She was also interested to meet Erik. Ella had felt trapped, but after Leif had explained that they would wait in Natal and enquire at the post office and not go to the island, she agreed. She saw the ambitious light in Leif's eyes and he had told her the full story about the problems he had had with the STELLA and the port. It was only another two weeks voyage to get to Natal, but Ella was fearful of the long journey back. Leif was not thinking of that, she had said. "If I can produce the information this man wants, I have been promised a deal that will change our lives" Leif explained. "You don't want me to tell Mr. Takahachi where Erik is and have him go to the islands out of the blue do you? He would probably fly in by helicopter or something and then he would tell him where the information came from" They had been in bed in their cabin and Ella was sitting up worrying what to do.

"You would like to see your father again, wouldn't you Ella?" Leif had asked her gently.

Jörgen swung the telescope around the horizon. "Something out there" he said. Leif reached for his binoculars. "Their lights are very dim. It's a good couple of miles away. Probably an old tanker bound for Nigeria. Should change course soon." He put his hand on Jörgen's shoulder."Like a beer?"

Leif went below. Ella and Helen had grown used to the sound of the engine now and were fast asleep. He opened two beers in the galley. He had never felt so in tune, as one, with his family since they had left Gothenburg. He hummed softly to himself as he took the beers up on deck. They sat and drank their beer in silence, looking up at the stars. He would teach Jörgen more another time, Leif decided, there were not many times they could relax together like this when they were underway.

The 50,000 ton oil tanker MAMADOU rose out of the sea and the night like a malevolent black whale. It was riding high, without cargo, and the mate on the bridge had fallen asleep.

When Jörgen looked astern, he could hardly believe what he saw. "Leif!" he cried and clutched at Leif's arm. The black bow of the tanker was only a few hundred meters from their stern, pursuing them as if meant to mow them down. The tanker dipped into the swell, moving slowly, but purposefully. It was so close. Unbelievably close. Leif saw and he knew. He ran to the wheelhouse and switched off the automatic steering and turned the helm hard to starboard. "Get Helen and your mother up on deck with their lifejackets!" he called and Jörgen ran.

Helen appeared in her pyjamas and took in the situation at a glance, her eyes full of fear. She ran to Jörgen, thinking to hoist the sails and they gripped each other's hands, their eyes fixed on the terrible ship, willing it to go away.

Still the MAMADOU came on. Now they could hear a loose derrick on the oil tanker swinging over the manifold, screeching on its rusty bearings like a triumphant animal in pursuit. The lights on board the tanker flickered on and off. It was as if the tanker was about to die.

The ELISE was slow to turn. "Get the flash light" Leif shouted and Jörgen ran. Jörgen flashed the morse light full at the bridge windows of the tanker but there was no reaction. No one came to the windows or ran out onto the deck. It was if the ship was without a crew and running by itself. Leif locked the wheel and grabbed the rifle he kept behind his coat in the wheelhouse. Somehow he remembered and found the tracer bullets. He loaded and fired. Helen and Jörgen watched the bright red bullet streak across the deck of the tanker and disappear into the waves. Leif kept firing. Another, then another. At last a light appeared.

Leif ran back to the helm. As if the ELISE knew the danger she was in, she suddenly responded and turned, slipping away from her pursuer by a few metres as if she did that sort of thing all the time. The wind picked up astern and suddenly, miraculously, they were clear. Ella appeared, clutching her life jacket, her robe around her shoulders. She looked up at the great black ship that loomed above them.

"The MAMADOU" Leif said bitterly, reading the letters on the rusty hull. There were bright lights on the deck now and shadowy figures appeared, looking down on them.

"At least we woke them up" said Leif

"I'll have you know that I have peed in my pyjamas" said Helen "I haven't done that since I was six"

"This is not going to happen again" said Leif. "From now on we will keep proper watch. You see? Now she is changing course. A bit late sailor! Well, they may have nearly killed us, but they were lucky not to have had a real disaster. And Helen, where is your lifejacket?"

"In my cabin."

"A lot of good it would have done you there. No, this was a wake up for us as well. We are going to have a scheduled watch and a lifeboat drill, every day from now on."

Jörgen groaned inwardly. He understood Leif, it had nearly scared them all to death, but he knew what Leif was like when he got that tone in his voice. The holiday mood was certainly over.

Chapter 16

Taru Takahashi was enjoying the time alone in the hotel suite now Akira and Mariko were out every day. He could not remember when he was last left to himself. He ate when he liked, bathed when he liked and sat around in his cotton robe and slippers as long as he liked, only bothering to change when he saw that dinner time was approaching and he knew they would be returning.

He had been pleased with the conversation he had had with Leif Hansson. He found him direct, and Taru was certain his business proposal would ensure that the information about the pearls would be in his hands in a matter of days. Before he had spoken to Leif, Taru's old secretary in Kobe had made enquiries about Hansson and although descriptions like 'headstrong' and 'more a seaman than a shore manager' had been included in the report back, it was the 'trustworthy' and 'experienced seaman' that had influenced Taru.

He was tired of people managing the ships who had university degrees in business and management but had spent no time at sea. The board had even dared to suggest that he was old fashioned, but the reason for the constant problems and misunderstandings between ship and shore was evident. Ship ownership and management was a small part of his company as ship building had taken over, but he had kept it on out of sentiment. It was how he had started the company in the first place. Hand picked captains and crew, managed by captains ashore who had chosen to retire from the sea. Some younger captains had retired to be with their new families, others had an injury that prevented them from going to sea again, and some were simply old, but all knew what was going on out there. The captain on the bridge in the middle of the Pacific could speak to someone ashore who needed few words to understand the situation. Loyalty and years with the company were rewarded and he took a personal interest in everyone, from the ordinary seaman to the captain. When the ship building boom started up it took all his concentration. A great deal of money was involved and it seemed that was the only thing that he had discussed for years, money. He had been thinking that now he was retired, but still had a great deal of power as a majority shareholder, he would interest himself in that side of the Takahashi company again.

Mariko's mood had changed completely since the evening of the surprise trip on the cable car. She felt she had misjudged her grandfather. He had understood what a miserable time she had been having after all, and now she was free every day, well not really free, there was Akira, whose disapproving expression rarely changed all day long. But she was free to look around and she found Georgio a happy companion and attractive too. Old of course, she had noted the flecks of grey in his curly dark hair and the lines at the corners of his eyes, but still, attractive. She flirted a little with him in the rare moments when Akira was looking the other way, or had gone to find the toilet. If they were in a cafe, such moments would worry Georgio, as in that teeming city of millions of people he was sure there would be one who would pass by who knew Ceyla and report back to her.

Georgio did not like his role as a guide, he felt humiliated by it, he was worried about his boats and wondered if this was the kind of job he would be doing in the future. The young girl was nice enough, he had been surprised to discover that she was Taru

Takahashi's granddaughter, and he was amused by Akira who had his own sardonical way of dealing with his life as a servant. He telephoned Ceyla each evening. He had explained about the boats and had said he was working on them himself, which was partly true. He and Ed were down at the port each evening, repairing what they could, but the real mechanical problems required expensive spare parts. Their credit with the marine supply companies had run out several months ago. Now it was cash or nothing else.

Ceyla was not so happy with having her sister in the house. Georgio was starting to dread every conversation.

"She is organizing everything. I cannot find things in my own house anymore."

"But that's good, no? You can rest more."

"She is too bossy. I am to do this, not to do that."

"She is taking care of you."

"Her way. It has to be her way."

"Where is she now?"

"Cleaning the oven. Cleaning, always cleaning."

Georgio remembered what the sister in law had said and groaned.

The robbery took place outside the Museu de Arte Moderna. Georgio had warned Mariko about carrying a handbag and she left it and her expensive watch behind with her grandfather each day, but she had insisted on bringing the camera. So now it was gone. Gone in the second it took for the boy to hook it off her shoulder and for him to vanish with it into the crowd. Mariko had screamed and shouted but Georgio had simply put his hands on his hips and looked at her.

"Go!" Mariko urged him "Go after him! Get it back!"

"No" Georgio said firmly. "It's useless and if I did

find him I am not going to get a knife in the belly for a stupid camera."

Akira did not comment but continued to examine the postcards he had bought.

Mariko completely lost her temper. She continued to shout at Georgio. He moved away from her and walked up the street.

"Come back here!" Mariko yelled, stamping her foot. Georgio stood at a distance and looked back at her.

"No. You can come here to me, before something else happen to you" She looked at Akira who was only looking up at the buildings and taking no notice of her at all. When Mariko started walking towards Georgio, Akira walked beside her without any expression on his face, but he was rather enjoying the confrontation.

"Now" said Georgio "You like to continue today?"

"You take me to the police" said Mariko angrily.

Georgio laughed. "To give them a description of the man who robbed you? Did you see who it was?" Georgio had, a skinny kid of about fourteen with no shoes on his feet. He looked like so many boys passing them on the street, Georgio couldn't have picked him out, even if he had wanted to.

"We can go to one of the favelas and try to find him" Georgio said sarcastically.

"Then we do that" said Mariko.

"I am not serious. You could get killed, Akira here as well, maybe me also. Come, we go in this bar."

"You reminded me of someone, just now" said Georgio as they sipped their cold pineapple juice. "The mother of my son. The son I had before I married Ceyla. She was a rich girl like you. She changed. Maybe there is hope for you one day?" he said smiling. Not many could resist Georgio's smile.

Chapter 17

Natal, a small city and port on the northestern coast of Brazil, became known as the 'Trampoline to Victory' in the second world war, when the allied forces used it as a military base for access across the Atlantic to the war in North Africa.

The archipelago of the volcanic islands of Fernando de Noronha, three hundred and fifty kilometres east of Natal, in the Atlantic ocean, were also in a strategic position. In the eighteenth century they had been used by the Dutch and the French before they were reclaimed by the Portugese. Fernando de Noronha was also used as a military base by the allies in the second world war, then as a prison, a tracking station for guided missiles fired from Cape Canaveral until 1962, and now as a weather station. The population of the islands was always small.

In 1977 there were about a thousand people living around the village of Vila dos Remedios on the largest and only inhabited island, Ilha de Fernando de Noronha. The volcanic peak, Morro do Pico, the highest point on the island, was the amazing rock rising three hundred and twenty one metres above the sea that sailors called 'The Finger of God'.

Nature had won the battle in the end. Whatever disturbance had occurred over the centuries, it was now home to more than twenty species of marine birds and over two hundred species of fish. Dolphins, sharks, stingrays and whales circled the islands in the clear warm waters in a constant temperature of twenty four degrees.

When the rocky peaks of the islands appeared on the horizon, everyone was on deck and had been waiting for the moment. It was their first sight of land for days. The work and the mood had been intense since their near encounter with the oil tanker, days ago, and the sight of the islands broke the tension. They were only passing by. They had to continue to Natal for fuel and supplies.

"Amazing place, isn't it?" said Ella, shielding her eyes against the sun. Amazing too that her father was somewhere on those islands, she was thinking.

"I can see a fair size ship anchored off shore" said Leif "Looks like a research vessel."

"Aha" said Ella "Couldn't imagine him in a tent."

When they had anchored just off the port of Natal, Leif and Helen went ashore in the jolly boat. It was a calm day but Leif asked Jörgen to stay on board in case the anchor started to drag. Jörgen was disappointed not to be the one to go with Leif, but he saw the sense of it. Leif wanted to see the harbour master about taking a berth and also to telephone Georgio. He had called him from the ELISE when they had been closer to the coast but the woman who answered the telephone at Georgia's house could not speak English and slammed the telephone down on him. He decided to try Souza, from the harbour master's office, or if there was a telephone office, from there. Helen was keen to go to the post office to ask about Erik and when he came for the mail, and they found it on Avenida Rio Branca where Helen said she would wait until Leif came back.

The harbour master was a fat smiling man who spoke very little English and constantly interrupted their halting communication by answering the telephone, but with the help of a diagram of the port and a few American dollars, Leif was able to arrange a berth for the ELISE. The telephone call to Rio was much more of a problem. The lines were constantly busy and when he did get through, neither Souza or Georgio were there. Leif decided that it could be for the best. Better to have contacted Erik first and have the information, than to risk that Georgio, in his well meaning way, might tell Taru that Leif was in Brazil. It was over an hour before he was able to return to the post office. There was no sign of Helen.

Helen had quickly discovered that no one in the post office spoke English, but she had pen and paper and wrote down Erik Jörgensen and handed it to them. This produced a lot of shaking of heads and Helen realised they thought she was asking for a person who worked there, so she took the paper back and drew a small post box. This did not work either so she sat down on a bench to wait for Leif, watching the people come and go. There were no tourists among the long line at one of the counters and so it was that Helen focused immediately on a tall thin man, whose lightly tanned face and brushed back grey hair made him stand out from the rest of the people in line.

Helen waited until the man had arrived at the counter and then went to stand to one side of him to hear what he had to say, but the woman behind him poked Helen on the arm and began a loud torrent of Portuguese in protest, thinking that Helen was jumping the line. Helen waved her hands 'No, no no!" she said to the woman who then turned around to the rest of the line and started shouting again and pointing at Helen. The man, undeterred by the uproar behind him, had finished his business at the counter. Helen was moving away from the angry woman, trying to show her she was not waiting in the line at all. The man turned on his heel and bumped right into Helen

"Förlåt" he said in Swedish, and then "Me perdoe" and of course, at that moment, Helen knew.

"I think I knew too" Erik was saying, "I mean not who you were, but that you were Swedish, well not Brazilian anyway. That's why I had apologized in Swedish. It was your blonde hair and blue eyes and you look, well, you are so much a Swedish looking girl." He laughed a little to himself, as if he was a detective who had proved how the villain was found out in the end.

They were sitting at an outside table at the cafe across the street from the post office. Helen was so excited that she kept forgetting to look out for Leif. This was her greatest triumph in life so far, she told herself. No one would believe her at school. She breathed in the sultry smells mixed with cigar smoke coming out from the open door to the cafe. Was she really there, with the grandfather she had never seen, one hour after arriving in Brazil? She could hear that Lisa saying she didn't believe a word she was saying, but it was true.

"Do you know I only come for the mail once every two weeks. It's a long way from the islands where we are staying. It takes at least a day to get here and so I am hardly here every week. Quite a chance, don't you think?"

"You have a lot of mail" said Helen, looking at the overflowing box on the table.

"Oh this is for the other people working on the island, I perhaps have one letter and a few reklam in among all of this. I have little to do on the island you see, so I make myself useful this way." Erik looked up at her.

"You don't look like your mother, perhaps a little but.."

"I look like my father" said Helen proudly "So they say." She looked across the street. "He will be looking for me. Perhaps I should go back."

"I think we will spot him coming along. There are not so many Swedes in town" said Erik. He summoned the waiter. "Would you like something to drink?"

"I would. Something cold and fruity."

"Por favor, dois agua mineral fruitas" The drinks came in tall glasses, piled high with ice and topped with colourful straws. Erik immediately removed the straw from his glass in a fastidious way that amused Helen. "Delicious" she pronounced sucking greedily on hers.

"You are doing well at school?" Erik asked politely

"School is another world right now" said Helen "We have been sailing in our boat. The ELISE. You know about the ELISE? My father's pride and joy?"

Erik shook his head. He was still feeling shocked at the encounter. He supposed it would be another hour before the boatman was ready to leave again. He would still be loading the stores and supplies, but Erik almost wanted to use it as an excuse to leave. He needed time to digest this meeting, this tall friendly girl who had introduced herself as his granddaughter. Yes, no doubt she was his granddaughter, but it was too strange, too sad.

"There he is!" Helen shouted suddenly and galloped across the street, dodging the cars. Leif had come out of the post office for the second time and was standing outside again, looking anxiously up and down. Erik set his glass down on the table and leant back in his chair. Nothing had prepared him for this day and now he supposed this was Leif Hansson striding across the street with Helen bouncing along on his arm, pointing across at Erik and talking excitedly. Erik stood up as they approached. Leif smiled and they shook hands. Helen looked one to the other.

"Erik Jörgensen."

"Leif, as you probably know."

"Is Ella with you?" Erik asked, adjusting his glasses. The question came without thinking about it at all. It made him embarrassed that it had been the first thing he said. He was still standing up.

"She's still on the boat" said Leif "Shall we sit down and talk for a moment?"

As Leif explained why they had come to Brazil and Taru's reasons for his search for the pearls, Erik was remembering the two young sailors standing in Captain Wennström's cabin on board the BUENOS AIRES and he recognised the young man in the older Leif now, but he was sure he would have passed him on the street without knowing who he was. It wasn't that Leif had changed so much, it was that Erik had cut him off in his mind. He was thinking more about that, and Ella, than taking a deep interest in Leif's story and when Leif paused, he interrupted.

"Excuse me, but I would like to send a note with you" said Erik. "Would you wait here for a moment."

Leif and Helen watched him cross the street and enter the post office. He came out some minutes later, crossed the street again and handed Leif an envelope. Leif was so conscious of needing the information about the sale of the pearls that he thought that was what it was, until he saw that the envelope was addressed to Ella.

"I am afraid I have to join my transport back to the island" said Erik, not sitting down again and picking up the box of mail. "They will be waiting for me. Perhaps we will see each other again and I can answer some of your questions then."

Leif and Helen watched him walk away and disappear around the corner.

"Typical of what I can remember of him" said Leif .

"He's kind of upset. Didn't you see that?" said Helen. "He's not what I expected. More normal."

As they walked back to the port, Leif was deep in thought. He had nothing to tell Taru yet, but perhaps he would telephone him and let him know contact had been made.

"Mum's going to be surprised" said Helen. Leif remembered the envelope then and handed it to her. "Perhaps you would like to give her this" he said, "But first I have to make a phone call and arrange the bunkering."

"And buy some fresh bread. I am dying for some bread. Vegetables too, and tomatoes."

"We'll do all of that when we are in port, but we can stop at a bakery on the way."

"Do you hate him?" Helen asked suddenly

"You mean Erik? No, not at all. Too many years have gone by. I'm not sure how I feel about him."

"Well he is my grandfather" said Helen defensively. "And Jörgen's as well" she added.

When they were back on board the ELISE, Leif left Helen to give Ella the news. He busied himself with the bunkering and taking the ship into her berth. He and Jörgen worked well together now. He didn't have to tell him what to do all the time. When he turned around to ask him, Jörgen was usually there, ready. It was dawning on Leif that they had become a team. The four weeks at sea had made it happen. He had needed Jörgen's strength and now he could depend on him. What a difference to a month ago. He looked along the deck at him as they tied up and realized he hadn't mentioned that they had met Erik ashore. 'Jörgen's grandfather as well' Helen had said. Leif couldn't think of it that way. Jörgen was now a man and for almost nineteen years Erik had had no part of his life, had even arranged that he was given away as a baby. What kind of relationship could they possibly have now? But Leif couldn't afford to be bitter about

Erik. There was too much at stake. He wondered what the note had said and went below.

Ella was sitting at the galley table. The envelope was nowhere in sight. "Well we're docked. Got your list ready? You must be longing to step ashore" said Leif heartily. Ella looked sideways at him. Sometimes she didn't understand Leif. He could be so insensitive.

"Surprise eh? Helen was over the moon that she found him so soon" He had passed Helen sitting up on the deck, listening to her walkman. "Shopping?" she had shouted to him and he had given her a thumbs up. "Won't be long" he had called back.

Leif sat down at the table. "Coming ashore?"

"I suppose so" Ella said. She put her hand in her pocket and took out the envelope and gave it to him. Leif took out the card that was inside. Roses on the cover. He opened it up. There were very few words. 'Forgive me' he read, and underneath, 'Come to the island. I would like to see you. 'Very much' had been added at the bottom, almost as an afterthought. He hadn't signed it. Leif put the card back into the envelope. Come to the island it had said. That was encouraging. It was about two days sailing. He looked at Ella to see what she was thinking. Her expression was hard, but there were tears in her eyes.

Chapter 18

Mariko had been told to pack the evening before and to be ready to leave at six the following morning. She was glad to be leaving the hotel at last but Taru had been mysterious about where they were going. She didn't think it was back to Kobe. Taru had been busy on the telephone for two days now, and seemed excited, saying he had a surprise for her.

Now Taru, Mariko and Akira were in a taxi driving down to the port and when they pulled up on the jetty Mariko saw it immediately.

"It's the WHITE WIND!" she cried and got out of the taxi before the driver could open the door for her. She stood on the jetty looking out over the bay at the familiar profile etched against the rising sun. Taru came and stood by her side "You haven't been on board for two years, have you" he said "Neither have I and no one from the company has used her. I kept her in Barbados hoping for a cruise around the Caribbean last year but with my retirement approaching, I could not take the time. I sent for her five days ago and she arrived last night."

"Is that where we're going now?" asked Mariko "The Carribean?"

"No. Not yet" said Taru, happy to speak about his secret now he saw how pleased she was. "We are going to an island a little closer than that. We are going to meet the man who sold the pearls" he announced dramatically.

Mariko's spirits sank. Not that again, she was thinking, but she smiled politely "Maybe after, we can go to the Caribbean?"

"Certainly, after the pearls are returned."

Returned, thought Mariko, and we haven't got as

far as meeting the one who sold them yet. It could be a long time before they got to the Caribbean.

"Where is this island Grandfather?"

"Off the northern coast of Brazil. It will only take us a day or two to get there" Brazil. Mariko groaned inwardly. After bathing her feet each night after a day of museums, art galleries and memorial parks and especially after her camera was stolen, she felt she had seen enough of Brazil. Mariko was not the only one who was annoyed. For all of its luxury, Akira hated to be on board the WHITE WIND. He was not a sailor, and he had already equipped himself with the necessary pills. Also, he was not fond of the steward on board, that is, if it was still the same one.

Georgio had been very happy when he heard Leif and the family were in Northern Brazil and Leif was going to be able to give Taru the information he wanted. He was sure they would get to see each other at some point, but after two weeks escorting Mariko he desperately needed to deal with the bank before he lost his boats, not to speak of Ceyla who was extremely suspicious that he was staying so long in Rio, and almost hysterical about Mariana, the last time he spoke to her. But Taru had insisted that he join him on the WHITE WIND for the trip to Fernando de Noronha and so there he was, waiting on the jetty for the launch to take him out with the others, and questioning his own motives. Is it for honour I am going, or am I hanging on to this rich man's coat so he will help me with his influence and his stupid money, he was thinking as he stood there. Mariko raised her eyebrows when she saw him, but she guessed it was because of the pearls again.

The WHITE WIND was fifty metres long, with a range of three thousand five hundred nautical miles and a running speed of twenty knots. The yacht could accommodate twelve guests and eight crew in the utmost luxury. Georgio was dazzled when he went on board. He had heard yachts like this described as floating palaces, but that was exactly what it was, a palace, with marble columns, mahogany balustrades, enormous mirrors, rich tapestries and sumptuous furniture. It was like being in a dream, a mocking kind of a dream where he was trapped in a kind of heaven while his beloved old fishing boats sank to the bottom of the sea. The captain and crew were all Japanese. They only seemed to speak a few discreet words to each other at one time and always with the utmost politeness. It made Georgio smile to think of Kato's crew on the KISHIWADA, who shouted and yelled, especially when drunk, or pushed each other out of the way when they wanted to pass by, and he laughed to think of them on board the WHITE WIND. The WHITE WIND didn't even smell like a ship. A soft perfume wafted through the rooms along with the tinkling music. The music irritated Georgio after only half an hour of it, but he could not find the source of it in his cabin and decided it was buried in the walls everywhere as a kind of slow torture.

Connie Lewis, or Professor Constance Harriet Lewis, B.M.S.,B.C.S. B.S.P.H., jumped out of the rubber dinghy onto the coral and crossed the small rocky beach. The dinghy immediately roared off, heading back to the research vessel, THE LUCY, that was riding the gentle waves two hundred metres out at sea. Leif, Jörgen and Helen were on the shore in the place they had been told to wait. It would be their first meeting with Erik's new wife. When they saw the boat take off from THE LUCY and head their way, they could not distinguish between the driver and passenger as they were both dressed from head to toe in black wetsuits.

"The Hansson party" said Connie, pulling the tight hood from off her head. She shook hands with them in turn "Helen. Jörgen. And of course Leif" She had a lovely smile and unusual green eyes. "Shall we go up to the house?"

Slim and muscular, she marched off ahead of them, up a narrow path between the rocks. Her light brown hair was cut very short.

"They built this place for me when I was here last year. Kind of a hut more than a house but I have a stove and propane and some good Brazilian coffee. If you need the lavatory I'll show you where it is. It's a real exciting place as you sit with your rear over a hole that leads down to a cave and the waves are crashing in and out all the time. It's a combo WC and bidet you could say."

The path was steep and although she was talking all the time she wasn't in the slightest bit out of breath. "This is it. The old homestead."

She stopped in front of a small wooden barn with a tin roof and opened the door. Windows had been cut out in the walls but they were without glass and the sound of the sea inside the house was as loud as being outside. In the middle of the room was a plastic table and chairs. Connie lit the small gas ring under the kettle and placed four pottery mugs on the table.

"Hate the plastic chairs and table. It's against my principles but we don't have many trees here as you notice."

She went over to a cupboard and took out a wrinkled pair of jeans and a shirt. "Mind turning your backs a minute guys?" she said as she began peeling off the wet suit. "Now I know Swedes are pretty quiet but isn't it about time someone said something? Come on, tell me about yourselves" She was now dressed in the jeans and shirt and making the coffee. They laughed. They had been so curious about her and so intent on staring at her that no one had said a word so far.

The wooden house above the beach was where Connie met visitors, mainly officials from the main land. She was on board THE LUCY most of the time, so it was convenient. Only scientists, divers and crew were allowed on the research vessel, she explained.

"We have to be careful" she said.

"Why? What are you doing?" asked Helen.

"We have a laboratory on board and some of the results we find are not always popular. We check the chemistry of the sea water and identify the dissolved constituents. That's the boring stuff. The more fun part is to identify the fish and the other creatures in the sea, how many, if there is any decline. Snorkeling here is a paradise by the way. I can let you have some equipment if you want to try it."

"How do you count fish that swim around all over the place?" Jörgen said, smiling at the thought.

"Not one by one" Connie laughed."We have methods."

"How did you learn to do all this?" Helen asked

"By going to college for a long time, years of study and exams, but my work experience was working at Marineland, that's the oceanarium on the Pacific coast not far from L.A."

"Isn't that the place where dolphins and those big black and white whales jump out of the water and do tricks?" said Leif.

"Well, that's one side of it. You have to do publicity stuff and entertain the public, sell tee shirts. It helps pay for the research and supports preservation elsewhere. That's what we are really about. Protecting what we have, or what we have left."

"What are you hoping to do here?" asked Leif

"Convince the government, the public, the United Nations, whoever, that these islands should be protected and should be made into a Marine National Park. There are special conditions here and some rare species, so that always helps."

"What's the problem?" said Leif.

"Developers. They want the tourists. There is an airstrip here already you know."

"Doesn't seem to be enough space for tourists."

"Exactly."

"How did you meet my grandfather? Was he swimming in the sea?" asked Helen and everyone laughed.

"He is very involved in the Marine Protection Agency in Sweden and there was a conference. You know organizations love to have conferences but I am not sure what comes out of them, if anything. Erik gave a speech and I didn't agree with everything he said. I was sitting on the same panel and we were supposed to be answering questions from the audience but we got into a heavy discussion with each other. We agreed to have coffee afterwards to continue thrashing out our different points and I fell for him."

"Erik, involved in protecting the seas?" said Leif.

"A lot of other things as well. Birds are big on his list too. He's quite a philanthropist. He's given a lot of money to environmental causes, this one included but I didn't know that at the time. It's not easy for him to be here and live in a tent, but even Erik is not allowed on the vessel."

"Erik is living in a tent?" said Leif amused. "Ella said she couldn't think.. So he is.. that's amazing."

Erik had been standing on the shore when the ELISE appeared over the horizon. Leif had managed to contact the boat agency that supplied the island, so the message had been delivered that they were on their way. Leif had rowed Ella across soon after they had anchored. They had agreed that Ella should have a day alone with Erik before the WHITE WIND arrived. She had been nervous, but when she saw Erik, older, his hair now completely grey, it was her father, yes, it was him, but not as she remembered. The sharp suit had been replaced by slightly baggy khaki shorts and shirt. He was tanned and he was smiling. If she had thought of him over the years, she had never thought of him smiling.

"We can walk" He announced and held out his arm.

There were no awkward moments after all. They didn't discuss the past. To begin with, when they arrived at the place where Erik and Connie lived on the outskirts of the village, she couldn't stop laughing. It was a tent after all, but a tent of such large proportions and luxury. There were several rooms to the construction including a study, two sitting rooms and a porch. "I always thought you wanted to become a Count, but you have become a Sheikh instead" Ella laughed.

Chapter 19

Next morning, when the WHITE WIND came, Georgio was standing on the top deck. They anchored close to the ELISE and Georgio waved to Leif and then disappeared. By the time Jörgen and Helen had joined Leif up on deck Georgio was in the water, swimming. Leif let down the rope ladder and held out his hand.

"My God, Georgio, here you are" said Leif, as Georgio stood dripping water on the deck and looking around at everyone with his famous smile. "Now we will say to each other, you have not changed" said Georgio to Leif and gave him a friendly punch. "You see my grey hairs? It's this fishing business. Next year I will lose my hair"

Helen had gone below for a towel.

"What a nice girl! "Muito obrigada!" said Georgio. rubbing his mop of hair. "You are Helen, yes? You are like your father" He looked across the deck. Jörgen was leaning against the mast and held up a hand to Georgio in a salute.

"And you, that man over there! Come here. You are also like your father. I like to look at you" Jörgen made a step towards him but Georgio went forward and threw his arms around him. Then he kissed him on both cheeks. "I make you wet, but it's good. Cool no? You are no longer a boy. A man!" He gripped his arms. "And strong too. Can you sail the ELISE on your own yet? No I am joking, it's not possible, not even for me."

He sat down on one of the lockers. "I cannot tell you Leif how wonderful it is to be back on a real ship. I have been going crazy on that" He gave a contemptuous nod in the direction of the WHITE WIND. "And still looking good, the ELISE eh?" He looked up at Jörgen "Is Leif boring you with all our old stories?"

"All the time" said Jörgen "But we're making a few of our own now. Would you like a beer?"

"Is the Pope Catholic? I learn that from Ed"

"You didn't like your four days of luxury?" Leif asked him "What was the problem?"

"That is not a ship. That is a hotel. There is a granddaughter, you know about her? Seventeen years old. I was tour guide, can you believe it, for this young girl for the last two weeks. Then I am on the ship and she start to bother me. Georgio, can you bring me my book? Georgio, can you move the sun shade? I tell you. Oh! Here is the beer!"

"Can I have a beer dad?" asked Helen.

Georgio gave her the one he had opened for himself.

"Of course you can have a beer. This is Brazil! Not Sweden! But where is your mother? Maybe she would be angry huh?"

"No. She is not angry" said Ella, coming up from below with plates of shrimp and hot bread. She is still beautiful, thought Georgio, but different and yes, like all of us, a little older. The long hair he remembered was now short, and her eyes were the eyes of a woman in her late thirties and not of the girl of twenty. Ella held out the plate to him and as he took it, he held onto her hand for a moment.

"Welcome on board" she said.

"We have a fine son, eh? We are proud of him no?"

Ella laughed and Leif felt a pang of jealousy that he hadn't felt for years. Ella glanced at him as she passed him a bowl of shrimp.

"Leif, can I stay on board tonight?" Georgio said, eating hungrily.

"What about your clothes?"

"He can borrow some of mine" said Jörgen

"Sure" said Leif, trying not to let the atmosphere change. "But we have to talk to Taru and let him know. I'll get him on the radio later."

"What will happen now, you think? Have you talked to Erik on the island? You see him?"

"Yes, but I don't know anything, yet. Erik wants to tell his story when we have dinner on board the WHITE WIND tomorrow night. Did you know about it?"

Georgio sighed. "Well I cannot be so stupid not to know this is why we are here. I cannot afford this holiday but, here I am."

"Ceyla OK?" Leif asked.

"Not so much. She is going to have number six child and she has a sister staying with her, that I think if I don't get home soon, Ceyla might kill her"

"You have six children?" asked Helen, astonished. She was going to say that he didn't look old enough.

"Five and one half. It's the Pope. He is Catholic" He laughed and reached for another beer.

After their lunch, they sat around, talking and falling asleep in the sun. Leif went to call the WHITE WIND and came back with raised eyebrows.

"We are asked for 'tea' at four. I think we have to go. They will send the launch" Everyone looked up from their comfortable positions and groaned.

Akira met the launch and asked them to accompany him into a side room. They had changed from their more casual clothes. Ella was wearing the summer dress she had bought in Tenerife. It was more a sundress and she didn't feel it was quite appropriate. Helen had found a pair of trousers that were not jeans and a long sleeved blouse that she hated. Georgio had borrowed one of Jörgen's shirts and dried his trousers. Leif was wearing a shirt and tie, the first time in four weeks, he had mused to himself, as he had tied the knot in front of the one small mirror they kept on the ELISE. He found the trousers from his business suit he had been wearing the night they left Sweden, but they were very creased. He tried steaming them in front of the kettle in the galley and was far from happy with the result. Jörgen was wearing the only plain white tee shirt he had and the trousers he was wearing at the party on the ELISE that night. It was strange to put them on. It all seemed so long ago. When they had assembled on deck, waiting for the launch, they had come to the startling conclusion that these were the clothes they would all have to wear for the dinner the next evening.

On the WHITE WIND they looked at themselves in the full length mirrors that lined the passageway and pulled faces of disapproval at each other. They were not the smartest group that had been guests on board. Akira wanted to explain that they had been invited to the Chanoyo, or ceremonial tea serving, and he would now explain how they were meant to participate.

He tried, but they were confused.

"Was it right hand underneath or left?" Helen wanted to know, and they all looked at each other.

"Mr. Takahashi wanted to honour you, welcome you on board in traditional Japanese way" Akira explained "We would have the chanoyo if Mr. Takahashi invited you to his home for the first time. So the WHITE WIND is, for this moment, his home."

What a way to meet a man that I want to impress, Leif was thinking, as they followed Akira through the ship. Looking as if I have slept in my clothes and asked to take part in a ritual I do not understand. It will be easy to do something wrong and cause offense.

After seeing tapestries and shining glass and silver through open doors, they were shown into the main sitting room. Georgio was the most surprised by the transformation, but to the others it was still an unusual contrast to the rest of the ship. Simple wooden screens had been placed around the walls. The western style furniture had been removed. Straw mats covered the heavy thick carpet and a bamboo scroll hung down from the ceiling. The scroll was painted with delicate flowers and cherry blossom branches, the design reflected in the pattern on the large vase placed on a long low table at the end of the room. Three simple branches of leaves and flowers were arranged in the vase. There were no chairs, but small cushions had been arranged on the floor. Akira had given them straw sandals to wear before they entered the room, in exchange for their shoes.

"Please to sit" said Akira and they sat down as well as they could, balancing or kneeling on the cushions. Georgio sat cross legged and Jörgen took the tip and did the same, but in the quiet almost religious setting, Helen and Ella chose to kneel and then lower themselves back on their heels. Leif squatted for a moment and as that didn't seem right, also sat with his legs crossed.

Within a minute, they all had to struggle to their feet again as Taru Takahashi entered the room. Taru was simply dressed in a plain grey robe, white stockings and the same straw sandals.

"Konnichiwa. Welcome" said Taru bowing his head. Everyone bowed their head. Taru removed his sandals before stepping onto the rice straw matting in front of the low table and as it seemed to be expected, everyone else did the same. A tiny stove had been set upon tiles to one side of the table. Small flames flickered inside the stove and water bubbled and steamed in the iron urn suspended on chains over the fire. It was the only sound in the room.

A door opened and Mariko came in, graceful in a pale yellow kimono embroidered with tiny white flowers. A wide sash of grey and silver silk was tied around her slender waist, and her long dark hair was swept up on her head and secured with two bamboo pins inlaid with mother of pearl.

Mariko bowed. She was carrying a wooden stand which she placed beside the table. She went out and came back each time with a decorated tea box, a light wooden ladle and a china resting dish, a medium sized china bowl, a brush and five delicate china tea cups. She folded a small scarlet towel and tucked it into her sash. She went out one more time and returned with five small plates on a tray. She set a plate before each of them.

"Manyu" she said "Bean paste and barley sugar".

Taru frowned at her, that she had broken the silence, and she bowed to him before returning to kneel at the low table. Helen was pleased to know what it was. She didn't like spicy food that was too hot and was worried it was something like the green paste she had eaten by mistake once at a Japanese restaurant.

Mariko now dipped the ladle into the boiling water in the urn and filled the bowl with water. Each teacup was washed, the scarlet towel at her waist unfolded and refolded with three precise motions to dry each one, green tea put into each cup, fresh hot water added and then stirred with the brush that she clicked three times against the side of the cup. Then she rose from her kneeling position in one sinuous movement and came to Taru, lowering herself elegantly almost to the floor and offered him the tea cup. The cup had no handles and was really a small bowl. Taru took the bowl, offered it to Leif on his right. Leif remembered that he had to refuse. Then Taru offered the bowl to Georgio on his left, who having seen Leif, and remembering Akira's instructions, also refused. Then Taru bowed his head again, placed his right hand over the bowl, turned it to show he would not be drinking from the side he had presented and then, at last, drank the tea. Mariko then repeated the ceremony for each guest. It was a bit like that game where you had to remember what had been said or done by someone before, Helen was thinking. Ella was fascinated. She was enjoying the atmosphere of the simple room, and admiring the skill and dignity of the presentation of the tea. Leif was proud. Everyone had managed to get to the point of drinking their tea without making a mistake. Georgio was hoping no one was noticing the hole in his sock, and Jörgen was in a dream. He couldn't take his eyes from the vision of Mariko as she made one perfect movement after another around the room.

Akira had advised, "When you have finished tea, you may give compliment, for flowers, or tea cup but you must not speak of other things. Tea ceremony is for contemplation in friendly atmosphere."

No one seemed to want to break the silence. After a few minutes, Taru stood up and bowed.

"Today we meet. Tomorrow we talk. We talk after dinner."

When they were in the passageway, Taru shook their hands and said their names, one by one. Then he went up the passage and in at one of the doors and closed it behind him.

As they were getting back into the launch, the steward appeared with a large parcel and bowed.

"From Mr. Takahashi" he said, placing the parcel in the boat. He also gave Georgio his travel bag with his clothes. When they returned to the ELISE and opened the parcel, they found five richly embroidered kimonos, three in deep colours, two in delicate pastel shades.

"Well" said Leif "I think we know what we're all going to wear for the dinner tomorrow night."

Helen looked down at her wrinkled shirt and trousers. "Do you think he noticed?"

The following morning, Helen and Ella went ashore in the jolly boat to see Erik and Connie. Leif, Georgio and Jörgen had decided that they were not going to attend the dinner wearing a kimono and Ella packed Leif's suit, Jörgen's party trousers and an outfit Georgio selected from his travel bag and took them with her ashore. She was going to see what she could do at Erik's place or in the village to smarten them up enough to wear to the dinner. "If we all turn up in a Japanese dress we will look like idiots" Leif had said when he woke up that morning and he and Ella had argued about it.

"What does it matter what we wear?" Georgio had asked her, and finding Jörgen opposed as well, Ella had come up with a compromise. It was also an excuse to visit her father again. Leif asked her to check that Erik was still planning to be at the dinner.

"Of course he is coming" Ella had said "He knows we have come all this way for a reason. He understands how important it is."

"Has he said anything to you?" Leif wanted to know.

"Nothing. He just said he had quite a story."

After he had helped Ella and Helen take off, Jörgen found some fishing gear and settled himself on the stern. He had been very quiet at breakfast and Leif had asked him if he was feeling alright.

Left to themselves, Leif and Georgio were able to talk frankly with each other about their lives and present situation. When Erik had sold the pearls for them all those years ago, and they had each received thirty thousand dollars, it had seemed like a fortune that would last them the rest of their lives. Georgio told Leif about the condition of his two fishing boats.

"After tonight, I have to get back to Rio. I feel I

have done enough just to be here now. I felt I was guilty of something when I met Taru but after four days on that ship I ask myself, why? This man, with all his money, he can do what he likes, I have not this luxury. If we had not rescued Kato, these pearls would be at the bottom of the sea. I talked to him one day on the way here, went over the whole story again. I have nothing more to tell him. I think I stay here tonight. Why should I go to this dinner?"

"Could be interesting to hear what Erik has to say" Leif said. He had been about to ask Georgio's opinion about Taru's offer he had made to Leif on the telephone. He would have liked to ask him what he thought about it. Georgio had been there, so he must have heard what Taru said, but after listening to Georgio's problems with his own business, Leif decided against it. Perhaps if he made this deal with Taru and chartered one of his ships he would be in a position to help, but that would not be until sometime in the future.

"We are planning to leave tomorrow" Leif said instead, "and I need to get some extra fuel and stores. Come with us back to Natal. We can sail together again, how about that. You will get a chance to see what Jörgen can do."

Georgio cheered up considerably. "I was hoping for this" he said jumping to his feet and looking around the ship as if they were planning to leave at that moment.

"Well, Taru sent your bag with you last night. Maybe he feels your part in this is over. What was he planning to do with you? Was he going back to Rio? If he is, that could be better. You'd be in Rio a lot sooner."

"I would rather swim."

Chapter 20

It was time for Erik to tell his story. They were all seated at the long mahogany table in the main dining room. A Swedish style dinner had been served as a consideration to the guests and now the coffee cups were being filled. The room was bright with candles. Ella, Helen and Mariko were wearing kimonos. Connie wore a simple black dress, ruby earrings and matching brooch that drew attention. Ella complimented her father, guessing they were his design. Taru and Erik were in black dinner jackets and bow ties, Leif in his newly pressed dark blue suit, white shirt, and bow tie borrowed from Erik; Jörgen in a white shirt and no jacket but sporting a red bow tie, the only other one Erik had, and Georgio, who had decided to come to the dinner after all, stood out from the party looking roguish and handsome in a brilliant shirt of many colours and no tie. Georgio's concession to the occasion were his fitted black trousers. The trousers and the shirt were the outfit he always had in reserve in his travel bag and went with him when he went to sea. When he came ashore he might go to the Jabaru for a special evening, he would say to himself, when he had been away for a few weeks. It was a long time since that had happened, but the shirt and trousers were always in the corner of his bag, reminding him of the possibility.

There had been an atmosphere of celebration from the moment everyone had sat down. Leif was touched by the sight of Ella, laughing and talking to her father. He was happy for her but he was still reserved in his feelings towards Erik. He had caused Ella so much pain with his snobbery and prejudice. Leif wondered how much he had really changed, but he did seem very different to the man he met years ago. Erik was about sixty, he guessed, an age when you were supposed to become wise, and there was the new American wife, she would have influenced him. Relaxed and natural, Connie would not have married the Erik that Leif remembered. Leif guessed that she had worn the jewelry to please Erik, and not for herself, she didn't seem interested in anything outside of her work.

Helen was all fired up about Connie and talked to her all the time at dinner. Connie had taken Helen snorkeling that afternoon, her first experience, and in the clear waters around Fernando de Noronha there was no better place.

"Forty metres Dad" Helen explained "You can see for forty metres down through the coral. Did you know Dad the coral is many colours under the water because it's alive. When you see coral sold in shops its white because it's dead. Isn't that awful? And the small fish, in every colour, electric blue, orange, colours I can't describe and Dad, we saw a stingray, huge, but Connie said to take it easy and he just wandered off. What do you think of that?"

When Erik was not talking to Ella, his eyes went to Helen and Connie. Erik was polite to Jörgen but hadn't engaged him in a conversation so far. He had a cool attitude towards Georgio who didn't care and barely noticed. It was Jörgen, Leif was concerned about. He kept trying to talk to him himself but Jörgen barely answered and seemed irritated with him for trying. Leif was wondering again if he was sickening for something, when he saw how he was looking down the table at Mariko. I know that look, thought Leif and looked across to catch Ella's eye. What? Her expression asked him and Leif slid his eyes to Jörgen and then gave a small nod in Mariko's direction.

Mariko was busy talking to Georgio, something

about a camera, unaware of the constant attention she was getting from a few seats away. Ella raised her eyebrows at Leif and smiled. It was the tea ceremony, Leif was thinking, Jörgen had been struck by the graceful, fragrant and serene young lady whose only task was to serve tea. Leif was listening to the real Mariko, the modern woman, who had her own opinions. Akira, standing to one side, rang his tiny bell and everyone stopped talking and looked along the table to Taru, seated at the end.

"Honoured guests," said Taru, "You all know my story now, the history behind my family pearls that I am seeking, but you have not seen the scroll that was kept with them, so Akira is going to pass a copy around the table. The original is in my safe at home. I would imagine Erik, that if you presented the original scroll with the pearls and known the history it would have increased the value".

"Of course!" Erik agreed, "I have no doubt of that, but for my part, it would have made no difference as I was never paid for them."

Georgio and Leif looked at each other.

"Yes of course I sent the money to you" Erik continued. "There was no reason to suspect that I would not be paid. The auction house was one I had used many times and usually I waited until they had taken their commission and the paper work had been completed, but I knew you were not in a position to wait, something to do with that ship you're still sailing around in?" said Erik, with a half smile, "and Wennström, the Captain you know, kept phoning me, asking me what was going on and had someone bought the pearls. Perhaps he was just curious, but I felt he was questioning my honesty. We exchanged a few strong words as I had already decided to send what I believed at the time, would be the proceeds from the sale. When the theft, you can call it, was discovered, it seemed that I had to live with my decision. It was too difficult to think of asking you to send the money back to me. I imagined a large part of it would have been spent already."

Yes, thought Georgio, on the house for my mother at Ubatuba and Souza's new truck. He looked at Leif, and to buy the ELISE. Yes, a lot was spent quickly.

"I had gone abroad myself, the day after the auction. I arranged for the transfer from where I was staying in Germany. The auction house telephoned me on my return. That was a difficult conversation as I had left the country so soon after the supposed sale, but this slight suspicion of me was to be dispelled later as you will hear. So, the auction house was not paid either. They were embarrassed as you can imagine, reputation and so on. I knew the director of the company, there was no question of wrong doing on their part. They changed a few of their rules after that and certainly never parted with goods again before they were sure of the payment. I have conducted business with them many times since. We made a police report, but the pearls had been taken out of the country. We were certain of that. There was nothing to be done".

Leif's mind was racing. So it was Erik's money that had changed their lives, not the money from the sale of the pearls after all. Georgio was leaning forward, his elbow on the table. He looks as shocked as I am, Leif thought. This explained so many things. Who would not feel hostile to someone you had given thirty thousand dollars to by mistake? Sixty thousand in all, between the two of them. And then finding out that Ella was pregnant with one and then later married to the other against your wishes. Leif looked at Helen. How would he have felt had it been his daughter. He remembered how Erik had given them the cottage to stay in on the estate when he and Georgio first came ashore and how he had helped them to open bank accounts. Why had he thought so badly of him all these years?

"May I ask you, were they not insured?" said Taru.

"For the full evaluation when they were in the vault at the bank. I had a customer for them in the beginning, it would have been a simple transaction for all concerned, but the lady changed her mind. When the pearls were taken to the auction house the insurance was quite different. It was an oversight on my part again. The pearls were underinsured, and eventually, I received ten thousand dollars."

"We shall have some brandy" said Taru, signalling to the steward. "Also a selection of liqueurs. And bring more coffee. I must say Erik this is not the story I expected, nor I suspect, anyone else at this table."

"Up to three days ago, I had not imagined I would be telling it, especially in these circumstances."

"Shall we continue this conversation in the sitting room where we can be more comfortable"? Taru suggested." He signalled to the steward. Akira had returned with the drinks trolley and he wheeled it out again.

It was a relief to leave the dining room. Leif went out on deck to smoke a cigarette and a moment later Georgio joined him.

"This is something eh?" Georgio said "But nothing change since he start to talk. The money? This is nothing to do with it. It was about a man who was dying, saying thank you to us, with the only thing he had. I don't understand all this complication. I don't want to think about something unless it is my own mistake. And this Taru, he is chasing history before he become history himself. Me? I have two fishing boats to fix and a wife and children who are wondering why I am not coming home."

Of the two of them, it had always been Georgio who put things the right way round, Leif thought, as they went back to join the others. He was thinking of Ella now. She and her father had wasted years when they could have seen each other, shared their lives. It was pride, everyone's pride, and he counted himself in on that.

When Leif and Georgio returned, and were shown into the sitting room, they saw that Erik and Taru were looking at the paintings on the walls. The room was so changed from the previous day, when they had taken part in the tea ceremony. It now seemed long ago, almost as if it had happened in a dream. Leif and Georgio asked for brandy almost at the same time and it made Jörgen laugh.

"Shall we sit down" Taru said to Erik. "We would like to hear more, if there is more to tell."

Erik accepted a coffee and sat on a high back chair as if he was about to give a lecture. He was enjoying himself in a way. This whole thing about the pearls had sat with him for years and it was a release to talk about it at last. The story was new to Connie, and he looked at her to see how she was feeling about it all, but she was looking at him expectantly and a little proud as if he was an amusing raconteur and this was like any other party. Ella was looking down at her hands in her lap. This was not so easy for her. He hoped he would have time to talk to her before she left the next day. Perhaps it was too dramatic, now he came to think about it, to let them know about the money in this way, but he had always thought of it as a story against himself, his mistake. At least the rest of what he had to say was merely interesting, and Taru Takahashi would know he could never get the pearls back. He could be released from his quest and turn to other things. He was probably a man who had earned his retirement and a rest from his obligations.

"I suppose the story begins in Alma-Ata in Kazakhstan" said Erik "A man known to me through family in Sweden, was, shall we call him, a diplomat of sorts, and was there under the guise of business. He had gone there before the war started in the late thirties, and was still there when the madness began. It was a place unaffected by the fighting as it was so far from the front. The Soviets relocated a lot of their industry to the area and people from other parts of the Soviet Union were forcibly resettled to work in the new factories. The name, Alma-Ata means 'Father of Apples' as the place was famous for its orchards, still is, I believe. From a small rural town it quickly became a busy and chaotic city with people from all over Russia arriving and also many immigrants. This man, we can call him Lars, used to go to the same cafe each day. One day he noticed a little girl sitting in the doorway who had been there the day before. She was only about four or five years old and seemed to be alone. She was well dressed in traditional Kazak clothes and seemed fit and well. He asked the man who owned the cafe about her. Lars had a son not much older than the little girl the last time he had seen him. The son had returned with his mother to Sweden when the war started, and perhaps Lars was missing his family. The girl was there the next day, and the next. The cafe owner had given her food and so of course she stayed. She was a pretty and talkative child and not at all distressed that she was alone. Although Lars spoke Russian, he had few words in Kazak, so he found someone who could talk to her and he made enquiries himself as much as he could. No one knew who she was or where her parents were. They were probably nomads and had left her behind, officials told him, or she had become separated by mistake. It was 1944 and there were more important matters than concerning themselves with one lost Kazak child. You can guess what happened. Through his connections, he was able to send her home to his wife in Sweden, perhaps through the Red Cross, I don't know, but she arrived and of course, they adopted her. Her elder brother adored her and Lars wife was pleased to have a daughter. They called her Eva. A year went by, the war was over but no more was heard of Lars. He never returned. How do I know this story? He was a distant cousin of mine. When he didn't come back, his wife, Lena, moved to Lidingö and we saw her from time to time. Last year when I received the letter that I shall tell you about, Lena showed me his correspondence from the war, hoping the letters would give us more information. Eva was seventeen when she went missing. Lena was very distressed. She believed that she had been kidnapped. It helped her to think so. I was almost certain Eva had gone of her own free will. There was something very shrewd about her. At the time I remembered thinking that if Eva had not wanted to go somewhere I think she would have got herself out of it."

"I remember her" said Ella. "She was rather wild. Last time I saw her she must have been sixteen, seventeen, I don't know. She was certainly pretty."

"Pretty and wild together was the problem. She tempted the wrong person. After the auction, this man that she met, the pearls and Eva disappeared."

Erik had everyone's attention.

"Lena had asked me to take Eva to the auction. She wanted to see all the jewelry, like any young girl would, and although I didn't really want to be distracted by being responsible for her, you know Ella, I could never resist the opportunity to show off my knowledge." He smiled. "It was only the preview day, after all, the day before the sale, so I said yes, she could come. There were a few of my pieces on display, among other very expensive collections that were also up for auction. I had put a reserve price on the pearls of six hundred thousand kronor but I expected much more."

Erik stopped and reached for his coffee. There was not a sound in the room.

"Now I have to tell you about Kashgari. A strange character. I thought he was Russian. I had met him once at a reception some months before. He was invited to the reception by two very prominent people that I personally didn't like, communists, and possibly spies, I always thought. It was not unusual for a Russian to be in their company, but Kashgari was not Russian, he was from Kazakhstan but of course, the same thing politically. About forty, good looking, very dark, with a full beard, he looked rather sinister until he started to speak. He was like a travelling salesman, talking, drinking a great deal, boasting about things, and I didn't understand the jokes he was trying to make, so it wasn't long before I moved away to talk to someone else and forgot about him. Then, Kashgari appeared at the auction preview. I had met him before and so we spoke to each other. He was quite different this time, serious, not at all the buffoon. Eva was with me and he asked her where she was from. 'Stockholm' she said and of course he laughed and tried Russian and then Kazak. Eva had been only four when she left, but she knew a few words. Kashgari spoke quite good Swedish, so they walked off and toured the room together, leaving me standing there, and it took my mind completely away from my business. Kashgari was taking her arm and talking in a very intimate way to her it seemed to me and Eva was throwing her head back and laughing. I had to have an excuse to interfere. So I showed them the pearls and told them a little of the story about the rescue at sea. How many people have dined out on that story I have no idea, but Captain Wennström for one I am sure."

"I can confirm that" Taru laughed, "but I will tell you later. Do go on."

"Eva was excited by the pearls. I was surprised as they usually appeal to older women. Perhaps she was enthusing for effect, but Kashgari immediately announced that he would buy them for her. I told him that they would be up for auction the next day and what the reserve price was. 'You think I cannot pay for them'? he said, and opened up the heavy leather bag he was carrying. It was full of money. American dollars. When he didn't appear the next day at the auction I was not surprised, but the person who bid for the pearls told me he was there on Kashgari's behalf. Having seen the money, I didn't think there was a problem and told the auctioneer it was probably alright. The auctioneer had seen me with Kashgari and Eva the day before. I left quickly as I was going away early the next morning. When Eva and Kashgari came back the next day for the pearls, they left a money order on a Russian Bank. Of course you would not normally trust such a money order. Who can take money out of Russia? But Eva was there and she probably charmed the poor man. More to the point I had given the transaction my blessing."

"You mentioned a letter" said Taru.

"Six months ago, I received a letter from Eva. Yes Eva, she would be a woman in her thirties now. It was amazing that the letter got through. It was in Swedish, so that probably helped. She wanted to sell the pearls back to me. But, there was a problem, she is in Kazakhstan, she cannot leave, and she is ill. She could not send the pearls as they would be stolen on the way. She wanted me to go there. I refused of course. I heard that her brother was going to try to find her, but it's impossible to get in. He won't get a visa."

"Where?" Taru asked, excited.

"Katon-Karagay. Not only is it the Soviet Union, but Katon-Karagay is on the border of China and Mongolia. I looked into it, briefly. It's one of the most sensitive areas you could choose to travel to, from anywhere. Even if you are a Kazak you need special papers, probably a gun as well."

Taru held up his hand. He looked ill, as if he was about to faint. Mariko went to him.

"What is it grandfather?"

"I know this place. I know this area." said Taru.

He reached for his glass, his hand trembling.

"I was 'detained', you know that Mariko, that I was a prisoner for five years. Three during the war. Then it was two years after that before the Russians let me go. I was put to work, myself and many others, to build a road, a mountain pass up to a lake, Lake Markakol. One thousand five hundred metres up in the mountains. In winter the temperature can drop to minus forty degrees."

"Grandfather, please. You must not think of that now" Mariko said anxiously.

"Why not? Why not? Katon-Karagay is north of Lake Markakol. The Altay Mountains. A beautiful place in the summer. A terrible place to me."

He looked at Erik. "Thank you for coming here" He got to his feet and everyone stood up.

"Thank you, everyone of you" he said quietly. Mariko helped him to the door. He turned back and looked at Erik.

"A strange end to this, is it not Erik? That the pearls are in a place I can never go to again."

Chapter 21

Akira placed the tureen of miso soup into the oven to keep warm. He was content. All was in order for asa-ohan, his favourite time of the day on the WHITE WIND, when he, and not Obuchi Nogi the steward, was in charge. Taru had a separate suite of rooms that included a small kitchen. The kitchen was rarely used, except for breakfast each morning, and this one meal of the day Akira was able to prepare, undisturbed. He began his preparations early so that by the time Taru had woken up and bathed, Akira was ready to participate in the modified form of Kendo that was Taru's morning exercise. The day was already warm at six o'clock. Akira had heard the launch take off for the island and looking out, saw that only Mrs. Jörgensen was being taken ashore. He arranged another place setting, anticipating that Taru might wish to invite Erik Jörgensen for breakfast.

Akira bowed as Taru came into the small sitting room. Taru was not wearing his yakuta but was fully dressed with shirt and tie.

"No exercise today. Mr. Jörgensen has sent a note and he will join me here" Akira congratulated himself on his foresight and went back into the kitchen for the rice and pickles. He reappeared a moment later.

"Will Mr. Jörgensen want a Western breakfast?"

"You can ask him when he comes" said Taru, opening the glass sliding doors and stepping out onto the balcony. Taru's suite was on the upper deck, facing the bow. The balcony curved around the suite and the walkway gave a view in every direction.

"When did the ELISE leave?" Taru asked, calling back into the room. Akira's mind was on ordering eggs from the kitchen and his hand was on the internal house phone. "Quite early, Takahashi san. It was still dark." He gave the order to the kitchen and frowned at the steward's "Forgotten something?" and imagined him smiling on the other end of the telephone.

When there was a knock on the door a few minutes later, Akira opened the door with his most imperious expression but it was Erik Jörgensen and not the steward with the eggs.

Erik had not slept well. He had wanted to speak more to Ella and Leif after Taru had left so abruptly, but they had seemed in a hurry to get back to the ELISE and in the end, they only exchanged a brief farewell on deck. Georgio had to get to Rio as quickly as possible, Leif had explained, and they would be taking him with them as far as Natal, where they would stock up and rest a little before their own long journey home. They planned to leave in the early hours of the morning. Leif had held on to Erik's hand for a few moments at the gangway "We shall see you when we are all back in Sweden" he had said."As soon as we are all back there" he had added. Ella and Helen had kissed him before they stepped down into the launch. Jörgen shook his hand and it made him sad to realize that he had barely spoken to him.

"Extraordinary. Who would have thought it?" Erik had murmured aloud to himself as he shaved, and what about Taru Takahashi and his now futile search for his family pearls, he thought. He could not leave without seeing the man. It was too abrupt. He was concerned at the effect his story had had on everyone. Well he wasn't responsible for how things had turned out, except getting involved in the first place. That had been Wennström's fault in a way. Pity they had fallen out with each other. He and Wennström used to enjoy each other's company, liked to discuss sixteenth century

Swedish history he remembered. He would look him up when he was back in Stockholm. He'd be retired now of course. Everyone he knew and had known seemed to be retired. It was only five thirty. Too early to be rushing about. He had dried his face and went to speak to Connie. She was going directly to work and would be on board THE LUCY all day. He would only be going back to Vila dos Remedios alone.

As Erik had approached Taru's door, he wasn't sure what he would say to him, as apologies did not seem appropriate, but when Taru came across the room to greet him, and Erik saw that he was restored to the vigorous man he had met when they had arrived, there was no need to refer to it.

"You will have breakfast with me?" Taru said, indicating the table laid for two.

"Certainly. Very kind."

There was another knock on the door and Akira opened the door just wide enough to receive the tray from Nogi before closing it again.

"You know traditional Japanese breakfast? We have fish, rice, miso, perhaps you would prefer eggs?" Taru asked as they sat down.

"No thank you. I would like a Japanese breakfast if that is possible."

Akira bowed. Before he returned with the soup, he slipped Nogi's poached eggs into the waste bin.

After breakfast, Erik and Taru went out on the balcony and watched the dazzling blue sea rising and falling around the ship.

"Very interesting, your wife's work. She is an educated woman." said Taru.

"Yes, she is a very educated woman" Erik agreed, wondering what Connie would have made of the note of surprise in Taru's voice.

"I would like to ask you about the brother of Eva" said Taru suddenly. "It would be interesting to know if he had been able to find her."

"I cannot worry his mother. Lena is extremely upset, you can understand, now her son has become determined to find her. She feels she will lose him as well."

"You say he would not be able to get a visa. But was he not born in Kazakhstan?"

Erik hadn't given it a thought. "Well yes, I suppose he was, to Swedish parents. I suppose he was born in Alma-Ata. Well, perhaps he could get a visa into the country, I don't know. But they say if you get into the country, not so easy to get out. I was thinking more of the sensitive border area in the far north when I said it was impossible. Perhaps other places, like Alma-Ata it may be possible, but Kazakhstan is a very big country and Alma-Ata is in the south. Eva said she was writing from their dacha, their country home. She didn't say where they lived the rest of the time, but I understood it wasn't far away from Katon-Karagay. The letter was somewhat naive, if I can say so. It was written in a childish hand and not very coherent. It was certainly written without her husband's knowledge. She made that clear to me as I was supposed to arrive there in some secrecy, stay at the dacha and she would contact me there. I was sorry to know she was ill. She is probably desperate, but the Swedish authorities couldn't do anything. They told Lena that she seems to have left the country of her own free will."

"Would you mind telling me the brother's name?"

"Anders Halenius. He's older than Eva, in his early forties. I told Lena not to worry about him. He is a journalist, and well informed. I don't think he would take too many risks without knowing what he was getting into."

"A journalist" Taru exclaimed. "Then he works for a newspaper."

"Freelance. Not for one newspaper in particular."

Erik didn't think it was wise for Taru to hope for too much again. "If I hear anything, I will certainly let you know. But I must thank you" he continued "I cannot go into my family history, but I haven't spoken to my daughter for many years, that is until a few days ago. Your search for the pearls has brought us together again."

"That is so?" Taru shook his head. "I am pleased to know that. Thank you for telling me."

They looked across the water to the shores of Fernando de Noronha, watching the seabirds wheeling and soaring above the dark rocks.

"And Leif?" Taru asked suddenly.

"The same. I have never known Leif the man. I only knew him when he was young."

"Then you are objective. Your impression is new, like mine. You will not praise him because you have a close relationship with him. That is good."

Not good, Erik was thinking. Not good at all.

"I want to share with you some ideas I have for Leif." Taru continued, "I would like to know what you think, Erik. We are two old men. We cannot change the world so much now, but I would like to return to something I believed in once. Return to it in a small way. No big plans. I have had enough of big plans, big company. This time it is not about the pearls. This time it is about a philosophy."

No one enjoyed the sail back to Natal. Everyone was tired and strained from the previous evening. Jörgen was sullen and uncooperative and Leif had to repeat everything twice to him and lost his temper several times.

"Thought you said he was a good sailor" said Georgio, exhausted from running and up down to make up for Jörgen's mistakes.

"He was. I think he's in love."

"Huh. Lot of good that does anyone when the ship is going over."

"It's Mariko."

"He should spend two weeks taking her around the city. Then I think he is cured."

"He'll get over it. He'll have to. They're on their way to the Caribbean."

Leif took the berth he had before they left and they walked to the harbour office together. "We need to sleep. I'll stay two days, maybe three, before we cross" Leif told the harbour master. "See you" he said to Georgio. They shook hands, slapped backs. "We'll talk when I get back."

Georgio phoned Souza to ask him to pay for an air ticket to Rio.

"You buy yourself, no?"

Georgio sighed. He didn't want to beg for it.

"Ed is hard at work. They start on the KATO yesterday. It's coming along" said Souza conversationally.

"What's that?"

"No one tell you?"

"Tell me what.. I'm away a week, who is what?"

"The bank. They extend your credit three years. The Takahashi Shipping Company gave the bank a guarantee. This Akira, he tell them to give me the information so the work was starting. It's not money, but as good. They finish the other boat already. See? So I say to get your own stinking ticket. I pick you up. Let me know you arrive."

Leif was half way back to the ship. Georgia ran after him.

Chapter 22

The family slept the rest of the day until early the following morning, then Helen woke them up.

"Dad? The WHITE WIND is anchored just off the harbour. Jörgen is already sending a reply. They're sending the launch for you, so get your pants on."

When Leif came back from the WHITE WIND an hour later, he was looking serious. After Georgio had told him about the guarantee, he had expected to be hearing about the new chartered ship, now that Erik had been found and Taru had heard the full story. Leif felt he had more than fulfilled his end of the bargain. Taru did mention the deal and promised he would keep his word, but there was more. Leif wondered how the family would react.

"Jörgen, ask your mother to come up on deck. It's too hot to talk down there. Bring up some cold beer and come back yourself. Helen, you stay too."

"Family conference?" Helen asked.

"You could say so."

Ella appeared, looking tired. She had tried to go back to sleep when Leif had left, but her mind kept jumping from one thing to another. Ella looked at Leif's expression.

"What's up?"

Leif wanted to handle this carefully, but he could see no sense in putting off the real news. "Taru wants me to go with him to Istanbul" he said.

"Where's Istanbul?" asked Helen.

Ella ran her hand through her hair "Turkey, and another step closer to Kazakhstan. Leif, you said no, of course. He wants you to find that woman and the pearls. Who does he think you are? You have a business to run. A family. This has all been too much, just too much, now this! He promised you a deal, didn't he? What happened to that?"

"It's still on the table. This is not only about shipping Ella, there are other things.."

"Oh haha, excuse me" Ella stood up.

"Where are you going?"

"To lie down" She left and they heard a door slam.

"So much for the family conference" said Helen.

"You can just stop these remarks right now!"

"Dad, I'm just trying to be light hearted"

"Did you already agree to go?" Jörgen asked and Leif looked at him. Jörgen wasn't against it. "No, no answer, yet. I said I would talk to you all first. Now your mother has disappeared, it seems we will have to put off the discussion."

"Talk to us. Talk to Mum later" Helen suggested.

"Well, if I went, I'd be away about six weeks probably, maybe less. Taru is going to set up a small company, we would be included. We will work on it on the ship. It would include the charter that he has said is a done deal. Delivery would not be until later this winter in any case. O.K. I'll share my thoughts with you. We leave the ELISE here in Natal, pay the harbour master to look after it. You, your Mum and Jörgen go to stay on Fernando de Noronha with Erik and Connie, they know about this and have agreed. Erik is very happy. He needs time with his daughter. She needs it as well. That's what I wanted to tell her."

Helen was already jumping around "Oh wonderful, wonderful! Dad you know you want me to think of what I am going to do in the future. Well, I know already."

"I am not sitting on an island for six weeks with Erik and Connie" said Jörgen."If I am to wait here, I'd rather wait on the ELISE, here in port"

"I had thought of that."

"But you don't trust me."

"I do. Of course I do. I don't think you would have

wild parties if that's what you mean. Once was enough wasn't it? You would have the radio telephone and the telex. We could keep in touch."

"And Erik comes for the mail. We could come on board and talk to you as well Dad." Helen added.

"What about Kurt?" asked Jörgen "Can he hang in at the office?"

"When he knows the potential."

"You have made up your mind" Helen said, laughing, "Now you have to convince Mum. Not so easy."

"I could take the ELISE to Rio, see Georgio, hang out with his crew" Jörgen said, looking inspired. He waited for Leif's reaction.

"Don't think of it. No one can handle this ship single handed."

"I could get someone to go with me."

"Jörgen, you're making me change my mind. I am not going to leave unless I have your assurance.."

"OK! It was just an idea. What would you have done when you were nineteen in the same situation?"

"I had four or five years of experience by then. You're only starting and I still wouldn't sail the ELISE with myself and one other untried crew."

"Then maybe I should come with you. The wind might get up when the ship is in port and I wouldn't know what to do would I?"Jorgen smiled.

"Would you like to come with me?" Leif said suddenly. You'd get experience on a motor vessel. I could teach you navigation. It would be good to have your company."

"Would you shake on that?" Jörgen laughed, holding out his hand "It's what I wanted all along."

Jörgen knocked gently on the cabin door.

"I'm not asleep. Come in" said Ella. She was looking out of the porthole at the people on the jetty. "I thought it was you."

"How did you know it was me?"

"The way you knocked. Come and sit."

"Brazil" said Jörgen, "They smile all the time."

"Yes. It would be easier to get to know the people here than in a city like Rio de Janeiro."

"Not so many in Natal. People are more relaxed."

"You see that. You notice people don't you? And you are so good looking. Just like your father at his age"

"Is that why you fell for him?"

"Well of course! I was young. It is the first thing you notice. But it was his easy going attitude, and he wasn't impressed with me and I wasn't used to that." She laughed and put her arm around his shoulders "Look at what I got."

"Georgio's OK but I can't think of him as my father. I wanted to, but it doesn't work .."

"That's because Leif has been your father, always will be. And you were brought up as a Swedish boy. If you spend many years away from anyone, you forget who they really are."

"You're thinking of Erik."

"And this whole story. I can't take it in at all. I am so confused and Leif is so occupied with.."

"That's not so true Mum. He wants everyone to be happy, especially you. He's always more difficult with us if he thinks you're upset."

"What a trip this has been. I dread the thought of sailing for another four weeks. I have been thinking to ask Leif if I could fly back. I'm not much help on the boat. Would you mind?"

Leif and Helen were playing cards on deck when Ella and Jörgen carne up from below.

"What are you playing" Ella asked.

"Rummy."

"Mum, don't interrupt. I'm winning" said Helen.

"Well I just came to tell you that it seems we are going to be stuck on an island somewhere .."

Helen jumped to her feet "Oh thank you, thank you. It's what I wanted, so much."

"Well, it's what I would like to do as well" Ella said. "You know, the men at sea, the women ashore, just like the old days."

Conscious that they would be parting soon, they treated the short voyage on the WHITE WIND back to Fernando de Noronha like a holiday but Ella was worried. She asked Leif to join her on the sun deck as soon as the islands came within sight again. "Promise me you won't go ashore in Istanbul" she started to say and Leif laughed.

"Now Ella. You think I'm going to play around?"

"You know what I mean. This search for the woman with the pearls. I am sure Taru is up to something."

"I'm taking over the ship when we get to Gibraltar for bunkering."

"You mean as captain?"

"Taru's idea. The captain here is due for leave. It's part of Taru's plan. He wants to create a company of captains ashore working with captains at sea. He thinks I need a refresher course as I have been ashore so long" He laughed "I probably do. Some of the technology on board this ship is new to me. But I look forward to it. By the time we get to Gibraltar, I'll have the hang of it" He put his arm around her waist. " So you see, I won't be going ashore. I'll be too busy being in charge here"

"What about Jörgen?"

"He'll have to listen to the captain."

"How happy you are. You haven't been really happy all these years ashore, have you?"

"Well I am not going back to sea for good. I have to do my time ashore as well. It's an old fashioned idea. I don't know how it will work, but Taru is prepared to put his money into it. Oil tankers, that's where he sees the future."

"So that's why you're going to Istanbul."

"And probably into the Black Sea. Odessa."

Ella pulled away from him "You see?"

"That's Taru's affair Ella, not ours. If he wants to turn the voyage into a rescue mission, his company has agencies all over the world, including Soviet Russia. I am not involved in the search anymore. I don't plan to do anything illegal or to leave the ship" He pulled her close to him and kissed her. "Anyway, I've never been to Istanbul" he said lightly.

"I thought that boy had grown up."

"What boy?"

"The one who was looking for adventure."

Georgio went home from Rio after the KATO and the KISHIWADA II were repaired and had passed their inspection. He was worried that the situation with Mariana and Ceyla would be such a problem that he would find it difficult to leave again as quickly as he planned. He had told Ed they would put to sea in a week's time, once the old crew had been rounded up and signed on.

When he arrived at the house in Ubatuba he found Ceyla in a good mood. The house was spotless but he didn't comment on that, thinking it would be an unpopular thing to say. Mariana was not there. Ceyla seemed better. She was beginning to show her pregnancy now but had lost the daily nausea. She welcomed him with open arms. She had even put his favourite music on to greet him as he came through the door.

He sat with the one year old on his knee out on the porch and Ceyla brought beer. The other children were at school, so Georgio was able to tell Ceyla the story about Taru and the WHITE WIND and how Taru had helped them with the bank guarantee. He had phoned her many times over the last weeks and tried to explain where he was and what was going on but she had not been in the mood to take it in. Now she was calm and listening to every word. He did not tell her about taking Mariko around the city but he mentioned that Taru had a young granddaughter with him, just in case gossip should find its way to Ubatuba one day.

He was longing to ask about Mariana. He did not like the thought of leaving Ceyla alone with the children again. His question was answered for him when he saw Gilberto's familiar machine coming along the beach. Gilberto swept the beach every day in a home made contraption that was part tractor and part broom and he was a familar sight as he rattled along. Sometimes he would stop and take a beer if Georgio was at home. Georgio raised his arm to wave to him and his hand froze in mid air. It was not Gilberto but Mariana who was driving the tractor. Gilberto was keeping pace, driving along beside her on an old motorbike, pointing out to her where she should go. They both screeched to a halt in front of the porch.

"Mariana has a new romance" Ceyla explained.

Chapter 23

Mariko was more than disappointed that the planned trip had been changed. She showed her anger by only speaking when she was spoken to and when she had to join her grandfather for dinner. Taru was furious with her. He had explained why they were not going to the Caribbean. Had she not be listening at the dinner? Was she not excited? Mariko said nothing, and Taru sent her to her room. From that moment, that was where she chose to remain for most of the day.

They were on their way across the Atlantic now. Leif and Taru had had many meetings together and had agreed how they would proceed. There was little more they could discuss until they arrived in Istanbul and met with the oil company. Taru, feeling bored, with no granddaughter to talk to, came to find Leif and Jörgen who were out on the bridge wing. It was evening and Leif was teaching Jörgen how to take a position from the stars with the sextant.

"You are learning a great deal?" he asked Jörgen.

"Trying."

"I have been thinking that you would also enjoy some recreation. We will not arrive for some days. Akira would like to teach Jörgen in the art of Kendo, the 'way of the sword'. You have seen this? There is no risk of injury. We use bamboo sticks. I practice each morning. Very good discipline and exercise. Akira and I can give you a demonstration."

The image that this brought to mind made Jörgen want to smile.

"Also our steward, Nogi, is very good at ju-jitsu. He is a seventh Dan, very skilled."

When Nogi was cleaning up in the kitchen, he would discard his uniform and wear a sleeveless vest and shorts and Jörgen had noticed his impressive muscular arms and legs.

"In ju-jitsu" Taru continued "You learn to use speed and skill, not force. When you are a master you can be small like Nogi and you can overcome a young man who is tall like you. Nogi is sometimes bodyguard for me, if I feel the need to have one, when I go ashore. I am afraid this does not please Akira, but ju-jitsu is more useful in modern life than Kendo."

Taru wandered around the bridge. Leif and Jörgen waited. He seemed to have something more to say.

"A family matter. Mariko, she is not happy. This is not the holiday I promised her. I was thinking it might be better if she returns home, but it could be that the pearls are returned and she is not here. She is the one who has to receive them. Mariko thinks I am old fashioned but I am not used to this new way that young women are today. I have been thinking that Mariko might enjoy something different to do. This is why I ask you Jörgen, if you like to practice Kendo. Mariko can also take part."

Leif had been hoping that as Jörgen saw so little of Mariko, and when she appeared she was so sullen and unresponsive to everyone, that his attraction to her had faded away. He did not want them to spend time together. She would hurt his feelings, he was sure.

"A rough game for a young girl." Leif said, and Jörgen stared at him.

"You need someone in Kendo to be referee, make score. Also to be in young company is better than to be with an old man all the time. I will arrange this. Or I should say, I will invite her to take part" Taru said with a smile. "I think she will come if she knows you will also be there Jörgen. We have small place on board, like gymnasium. We can meet at six tomorrow morning for the demonstration?"

Jörgen found it difficult to sleep that night and kept looking at the clock. He imagined himself leaping around, brandishing not a bamboo stick, but a sword, while Mariko gazed at him.

At lunchtime Jörgen appeared on the bridge.
"Can we look at the charts after a sandwich? I'm hungry. Sweaty too, I'll take a shower."
"How was the Kendo?"
"Taru and Akira were quite impressive, for old men. I am not so impressive. Mariko is wonderful."
"At keeping score?"
"No. At Kendo. They teach it at her university. She has had a year of practice ahead of me but in a few days I might surprise her. She has decided to be the instructor. Akira is keeping the score."

Chapter 24

Anders Halenius was sitting at a table outside a cafe on the corner of Mametova, drinking shay, a tea made with fermented mare's milk and butter. He had grown used to it after the month he had been in Alma-Ata. Seated opposite him was Muktar, his translator, an eighteen year old student from the university who had been selected for him by the authorities soon after his arrival. Muktar was Kazak and could speak Russian and English. It was because of Muktar that Anders had begun to drink the local tea. At that moment they had just returned from the Ministry for Information and Anders was depressed. He had managed to get a visa, because of his birth place, and more to the point, because he was a journalist. He was supposed to be writing a positive article about Alma-Ata as a prosperous city, thriving under the control and influence of Moscow hundreds of miles away. The article was to be published in various newspapers with left wing views, all over Europe. It was all a guise, but Anders kept poking away at the typewriter in his hotel room, writing what he knew someone would be checking every day when he was out. He had no intention of submitting it to anyone. He had been amused that his idea had got him into Kazakhstan but he found out quickly that he was restricted to Alma-Ata. His passport and papers were heavily stamped and covered with writing that Muktar told him prevented him from leaving the city. "You would be arrested if you travel. They check papers at every station. You can go to the airport but only to use your return ticket" he had told him. "You are followed, of course, and there is also me" he had added cheerfully. "Oh? You would report me if I ran away" Anders had asked jokingly. "Of course" Muktar had replied without any humour.

Anders had started to talk about his adopted sister Eva after he had known Muktar two weeks. He began by telling him about his parents who had lived in the city and then how Eva was adopted and had lived in Sweden since she was four years old, but that she now lived in Kazakhstan. He would have liked to visit her. Did Muktar think they could get permission? He wasn't sure he could trust him not to tell the authorities every word. He may even be recording what I say, he mused, but Anders was used to skimming over anything he didn't want someone to know. They had come to the point where Muktar had offered to come with him to find her address. "You can write to her" he had suggested. Anders had not brought the letter with him to Kazakhstan, thinking he might be searched for some reason. He had committed to memory the name of the dacha and already knew it was near Katon-Karagay. Perhaps it was worth trying to find her main address. He could only give her name as Eva Halenius or Eva Kashgari. Kashgari could have been a name the man called himself when he was in Sweden. His mother had told him that when Eva went missing, no one of that name could be found in Sweden, either on hotel registers or on flights leaving the country. Not surprising. The letter was signed Eva, but that was because she was writing to Erik Jörgensen. It was frustrating that she hadn't put more information in the letter. Perhaps she had been afraid. Perhaps the letter had been a kind of fantasy, something to give her hope. There was so little information to go on and she was sure to have been given a different name. She might think of herself as well known in such a small place. Her beauty would ensure that, but Eva must know that people from outside the Soviet Union could not just turn up in Katon-Karagay and start asking questions. He wasn't surprised at finding nothing, but it was depressing all the same.

"You are getting on well with your article" Muktar asked politely. Anders nodded. He had seen much in the city he would have liked to write about, the effects of the heavy industry that the Soviets had introduced during the war. The mass forced immigration that had fueled the war industry with groups of diverse people who were now left behind, lost, poverty stricken, diseased, unable to leave.

"I could suggest something you can write about" Muktar continued significantly.

"The article is a positive view" Anders said carefully. Was Muktar trying to catch him out?

"This is not about Alma-Ata. If you like to talk more, we can go to the park."

"Alright. Let's go to the park" Anders replied.

He felt like a walk. He saw the regular man, a grey figure in the corner, fold up his newspaper as they left the table. He might enjoy a walk as well.

Panfilov Park was a short walk away but big enough to allow them to keep a good distance from the man with the newspaper. Muktar stopped behind a huge black war memorial and beckoned to Anders.

Muktar opened his jacket. "I want you to see I have nothing to record you" Anders patted his chest. Muktar's thin arms and legs showed through the transparent cotton of his shirt and trousers. He lifted up his sandals one at a time.

It had been an unspoken thing between them then. Muktar had changed his attitude. He was no longer the serious student. He was excited. His eyes were bright with anticipation.

"OK" said Anders "So what do you want to tell me?"

"We will walk slowly now" said Muktar. "Then we will go into the Zenkov and out the other side."

The former Zenkov Cathedral, a many domed wooden building with pink walls, dominated the center of the park. No religious services had taken place since the Soviet time began, it was now a museum and a concert hall, but it would be a place a proud student would think to take a visitor from abroad. It was one of the few remaining buildings from the time of the Tsars. The man in grey saw the direction they were taking and sat down on a bench to read his newspaper again.

Inside, Muktar and Anders walked quickly to a door on the other side, went out and sat down on the grass, out of sight of the man on the bench.

"He will think we take about thirty minutes inside, so we have some time to talk" said Muktar.

"You are going to do the talking" Anders said. Be cautious about this, he reminded himself.

"My family are from Pavlodar, a small industrial town on the Irtysh river, far north of here. Also, some of my family live in villages not far from Kurchatov. You know these places?" Anders shook his head.

"It began in 1949, the first one. Many villages, and how many nomadic people living in the area we do not know, were caught in the radiation, the fallout from the bomb. A great area was contaminated"

"An atom bomb."

"And only the beginning. Since this time there are so many of these explosions, people cannot count how many. They are poisoning my people, my family. Children have been born who cannot speak, who are blind. Many have cancer. Many, many"

Anders stared at him. Was this true?

"They are still testing today?"

"Of course, all the time. They also start to test people to see their blood but these doctors are from the army. They don't tell people why. They don't admit anything. They cannot. There are 40,000 soldiers based in that area."

Anders reached for a map that was folded up in his pocket. He had brought it with him when they went to the Ministry of Information to find Eva's address, along with his father's old travel book.

"Show me where this is."

"You see this place Semipalatinsk. This is the main centre. Many scientists. Now, here is Kurchatov, named for the father of the soviet bomb, so appropriate you say? And here, north of Kurchatov, also on the river, is Pavlodar."

Anders looked at where Muktar was pointing and then a short way across the map, east of the area, to Katon-Karagay, a place he had studied many times even before he came. It was perhaps two hundred miles or less from Semipalatinsk. Supposing Eva lived in the nearest city, what other city would that be? There were not many places big enough to be called a city in the area and if they knew about the tests as everyone would, they would keep a dacha far enough, but not too far away, like in one of the most beautiful places in Northern Kazakhstan. According to the travel book, that was the mountains and lakes around Katon-Karagay.

"How many people would you say are being affected?"

"Hundreds, thousands. You will write about this Anders? If you do not know, you who are a journalist, who does know outside of the USSR? If the politicians in other countries know, then they should be shamed. You must expose this terrible crime."

"I would have to go to the area. I am sure you are telling the truth Muktar but for a piece like this I would need to have real evidence, do interviews, take photographs. How would I get out of Alma-Ata?"

"There is a small movement. Other loyal Kazaks. I am not the only one with family who are ill."

"Good. But first you have to find me a safe telephone. I have to call a major newspaper and get backing. We need money for this."

Chapter 25

"What are you reading?"

Mariko looked up at Jörgen, gave him a small smile and returned to her book. "Snow Country" she said, turning a page.

"No Kendo today?"

"Not today."

"Akira was not there either."

"He has gone ashore with grandfather."

"Is it a good book?"

"He won the Nobel Prize for literature, but it's not so much my style. Grandfather has only what are thought to be classics on board. Something to read."

Jörgen hesitated. He would have liked to sit and talk. "See you later then."

He didn't want to disturb Leif on the bridge so he went out on the stern deck and looked up at the great jagged rock. Leif had taken over the ship that morning and although they were anchored and not leaving until the next day, he knew Leif would be concentrated, checking and going over things now he had the bridge to himself. Jörgen didn't mind being alone. He was struggling every day with his feelings. Half the time he didn't know what it was about. His mind swung backwards and forwards between times of intense lust, tenderness, romantic dreams and anger. Who was she anyway, said one half of his brain, and it doesn't matter, said the other half, I just want to hold her. So there was Gibraltar, a photograph in a geography book come to life. He could see houses on one side and wondered if that was where everyone lived, or perhaps there was a valley that he couldn't see.

There was a rattle of cups and he turned to see Mariko advancing with a tray.

"No one in the kitchen. I don't know where everyone has gone. I made some coffee."

She placed the tray on a small table and sat. Jörgen could smell her delicate perfume, or was it the soap she used. It was very subtle. When she came near to him to teach him how to move when they were practicing Kendo, it was mixed with the musky smell of her perspiration and he would be struggling to control his desire.

"I am curious" said Mariko pouring her own coffee and sitting back in the chair "What are you doing when you are in Sweden? Are you working? Or are you studying something?"

He wanted to say...what could he say? Something interesting, but what? He didn't have to worry. When he didn't answer Mariko started to talk about herself.

"I am studying history" she said with some contempt "This is to please grandfather. But, I was allowed another choice as well, so I am also taking Film School. This is what I want to do all the time. History is so boring."

"Might be useful if you want to make films."

"You're right."

"Think of Kurosawa."

"Of course."

"I thought he had stopped making films but I saw Dersu Uzala not long ago. I found out it won the Oscar two years ago for best foreign film."

"About the Russian surveyor and the Mongolian hunter."

"Japanese and Russian production."

"How many Japanese films have you seen?"

"Not many. Three or four of Kurosawa of course and Tokyo Story, can't think of the director.."

"Yasujiro Ozu. These films are in Sweden?"

"Of course. I belong to a film club. What are thought to be classics, as you would say."

"They are classics. How often do you go?"

"Every week, for the last seven years maybe."

It began as an escape from having to join in after school programmes. The school had insisted he join something. His mother was told he was not making friends so easily and Ella had said he was shy, it was an awkward age, and all the other things that parents and teachers say to each other when a child is unpopular.

"I have a lot of film books"

"Wish we had them here" said Mariko, sighing and stretching out her legs.

"We can still talk about what we know. Maybe make up a competition for each other"

"Such a nice idea" she said, clapping her hands like a child. She gave him a huge smile. It always made her little pointed chin stick out like that, he was thinking.

Leif saw the launch coming with Taru, Akira, and two crew from the ship and told the mate to stand by the gangway. Customs and immigration had been on board earlier that morning and issued passes for those who wanted to go ashore and he was almost alone. Taru came to the bridge immediately, full of energy. Leif expected him to ask how long it would take them to get to Istanbul. He had prepared all the information for him, distance, fuel consumption, time. The chart lines were drawn and the log book was open and ready.

"I have news of Anders Halenius" Taru announced. "I have friend at Japanese Embassy in Stockholm. After I know Halenius name, I telephoned my embassy friend before we left Brazil and asked for his help to look for this newspaper man. My friend is very social, knows many people. He made contact with Swedish newspapers and after time, found a reporter, a Carl Andersson, who knows Anders Halenius, and says Halenius is friend of his. Today I spoke to Carl Andersson from agency office, not half an hour ago! Halenius is in Kazakhstan and has been there for six weeks!"

Taru's eyes were fixed upon Leif "He is in Alma-Ata, but possible he is travelling now. We must not telephone by ship radio telephone or use the VHF Leif, for this in the future. The information must be confidential. I assured Carl Andersson of that, but I do not understand why. Halenius has a visa, he said. He has entered the country legally."

Leif did not want to be a part of Taru's ongoing search. He felt he had fulfilled his obligation, if he ever really had one. It concerned him that Taru seemed to be still including him. He liked Taru the more he knew him and was looking forward to the business relationship they were planning for the future. He liked his sense of justice. He admired his intelligent approach, respected his experience, and discovered he could be humorous on occasion, but when Taru spoke about finding the pearls he became someone else, as if his life depended on it and nothing else mattered. Leif was concerned for him, and worried that it would affect their business in the future.

If Taru decided to take off into Kazakhstan, Leif was not planning to go with him. He would insist on staying with the WHITE WIND. He needed to keep contact with Kurt in the office, and the STELLA. He could not afford the risk of entering Kazakhstan, even if the Russians gave him a visa and a gold watch, he said to himself. It would not be likely that Taru would be able to get a visa either, but when it came to his family honour, who knew what Taru would do. He was rich and he was not without his resources. In every part of the world he knew prominent people in the shipping business, trusted relationships that he had established over many years.

"I told Mr. Andersson that I knew Halenius was looking for his sister, and why I was also interested to find her. I asked agent to tell him who I was, so he would be more confident and listen. I told him of the importance it was for my family. He did not say so much."

Leif could imagine this Carl Andersson in a Stockholm newspaper office listening to Taru's complicated story and saying little in return. Typical of an experienced reporter and typically Swedish.

"He said he would not know more for some time as Halenius could not telephone him, but when Halenius returns to Sweden, he would let me know. He took the ship's telex number, but I plan to telephone him again when we arrive in Istanbul. He is a reporter. He will have found out more about me within a few days. It could be possible he will say more next time I speak to him, when he has found out who I am. Very good news Leif. I have hope. It is good to have hope."

Chapter 26

Anders studied his new beard in the mirror. Muktar had insisted that he grew one and Anders had been worried that it would provoke suspicion from the man in grey, but as he saw him every day, it was a gradual change, and no one had come to question him. It was almost two weeks since the conversation about the nuclear test site. During that time he had had two conversations with Carl in Stockholm about money. He had risked making them from the hotel lobby, knowing international calls would be recorded. They had spoken in a kind of code that had made communication frustrating and had been cut off several times, but Muktar had assured him it was usual, that the lines were always bad. The Swedish could have helped to confuse anyone to begin with, Anders was thinking. They would translate it eventually, but make no more of it than he was asking someone for money. Hardly a crime, but he was always waiting for the knock on the door.

Carl was not hopeful. "A story is not worth an advance until there is some kind of proof that you have a story. That's what they say here. I always told you to become a staff reporter Anders. Then it would have been no problem. This is not for personal reasons is it?" He was alluding to Anders search for Eva. Carl knew why he had gone there. It was Carl who had helped him cook up the story of the report on Alma-Ata that had accompanied his visa application. The second call made him more nervous as Carl said 'an old friend' would contact him and wanted to help. Anders risked asking how this would be done. He had no idea who this old friend was and as he was supposed to know him, couldn't ask directly what his name was, and Carl didn't seem to want to give it to him either. "He'll send regards from me. Best I can do right now. Got to go."

Muktar had told him it would take only a few more days to fix his new papers and passport. He would fly out of Alma-Ata on his present passport and visa and would need the new one after the changeover. Muktar kept saying don't worry, don't worry, as if what he was about to do would not mean he could end up in jail for the rest of his life, even if he was lucky enough to live.

The knock on the door when it came was so soft, that if Anders had not stopped typing and was drinking cold coffee from his thermos at that moment, he may not have heard it. He stared at the door. There it was again. He undid the chain and opened the door a small way. There was a very old man standing in the dimly lit hall. A man in a trilby hat, carrying a cane.

"Carl Andersson." The man said, and Anders undid the chain. The man crossed the room and pointed to a chair. Anders nodded and he sat down. He waited while the man caught his breath.

"You are .." Anders started to say and the man put his finger to his lips and pointed at the ceiling. He withdrew a large thick envelope from the inside pocket of his frayed jacket and gave it to Anders, nodding to him to look inside at the contents. Russian rubles in all denominations, hundreds of notes. Anders had been there long enough to know that it wasn't a great deal of money, but it was money. Probably enough money for him to travel to the north and more. The man reminded him not to speak. He then took an old yellowing photograph from his pocket and showed it to him. It was a picture of two men, one of them in uniform. They were relaxed and smiling and the man in the suit was holding a small boy, about three years old.

His visitor was smiling now. He pointed at the man in uniform and then at himself. Anders knew then who the other man was. It had been so unexpected that when he looked at it, it took awhile to recall the photograph of his father that his mother always kept on the piano at home. The photograph at home had been of a young man, with a smooth face and hair confidently brushed back and oiled in the style of the days. This man was several years older, his hair was not oiled and beginning to turn grey, but the eyes were unmistakable. The child was of course himself.

The man took the photograph back, replaced it in his pocket, and moved slowly to the door. Anders took his arm and silently suggested he share his coffee but the man shook his head. He patted Anders cheek at the door, and walked away down the hall.

Chapter 27

The WHITE WIND was making good headway through the Mediterranean. Leif had spoken to Kurt and all was going well with the STELLA. He was looking at the telex messages he had just received but the noise of laughter and chattering out on the deck kept distracting him. He had been trying to ignore it for the past ten minutes and when Akira came to bring him his midday sandwich he asked him what it was all about. Akira looked resigned, as if he didn't approve.

"They make a game" he said, balancing the tray and wondering where to put it down. Leif looked out at the sundeck. Mariko and Jörgen were sitting at a table with pens and papers. Akira found a place for the tray and setting it down, he bowed and went out.

The Chief Mate came up on the bridge and Leif asked him to take over for an hour. He took his tray and went out on deck. Jörgen and Mariko gave him a glance and went back to their papers.

"No, no, that's not fair. No silent movies" She grabbed the paper Jörgen was writing on and ran off with it. Jörgen jumped up and pursued her. They tussled around, laughing and grabbing the paper.

"OK. I try to make it easy for you" said Jörgen, having retrieved the paper. They returned to their seats and continued their writing.

"I have one you will never get" said Mariko.

"Don't you be so sure."

"We can do this in the sitting room. Too windy here."

"Right."

They gathered up the papers and went inside.

Taru came out on his balcony.

"Mariko is in good humour, but what is it they are

talking about for days? I cannot understand a word of it."

"Films. They are talking about films, movies. Now they are making questions for each other. In Sweden, we call it 'tips promenade'."

"It is suitable for young girls?"

Leif nodded and smiled. We can both do with a lesson not to keep treating them like children, Leif thought, as he bit into his sandwich. For all its size, the ship was a bit claustrophobic at times.

By the time they reached Istanbul, and the profile of minarets and domes had presented themselves as a world so new and exotic to Jörgen, he had thought more about his feelings for Mariko and was content, for the moment. They had become friends, loving friends, he liked to think, not only from their common interest in film, but they had shared their feelings about many things and talked about their families. Their concerns were not so different even if culturally they were so far apart. Jörgen found himself talking to Mariko in a way he had never done before. He was surprised that he had become so outspoken. He confessed to her that he found himself observing everyone else from a distance sometimes when he most wanted to belong. Mariko had looked at him and then said bluntly. "It is what you call being shy. You must not think so much of yourself but of the other people."

"Oh? Is that what you do?" Jörgen had asked.

Mariko had laughed. "No. I am very selfish. But sometimes I try not to be so."

He had asked her about her grandfather's search for the family pearls and she told him the story of her distant ancestor who was given the pearls as an award for an act of bravery.

"If you get them back, you will be the one to keep them."

"Not to keep, but they will be in my care. I will pass them on to my daughter, when I have one. I have begun to understand him. It is not the pearls themselves, is it? They represent something. He has changed since we left home. He is not angry with his brother in law Kato anymore for taking them away from Nagasaki. He has made new friends. He has a new perspective, you say? It matters to him to get them back and now I can say, truly, it matters to me."

And so it began to matter to Jörgen.

Chapter 28

The plan was to take a domestic flight from Alma-Ata to Tashkent on the Kazakhstan/Uzbekistan border, both countries being a part of the Soviet Socialist Republics and subject to the same controls. Anders was to use his Swedish passport and legitimate visa as far as Tashkent, then relinquish them for a new identity to take him back into northern Kazakhstan. The declared journey on his return ticket was a change of planes in Tashkent for an ongoing flight to Moscow and from there to Europe and Stockholm.

Anders had many sleepless nights before the day he was due to leave. He had completed his article and taken a copy to the Ministry for Information, retaining a copy for himself, supposedly to submit to the European publications from a list they had supplied. He was depressed about it. Neither his heart nor his mind had been engaged and the article was dull and poorly written. It was not the quality of the writing that worried him but that his name would appear on a thinly disguised piece of propaganda. He hoped it would be rejected by them all, but with the weight of the Soviet machine behind it, probably not. He understood they would also present it themselves. The request for him to do so and the list was an exercise, or was it a test? It was ironic that he had written articles in the past on subjects he cared about, spent days sweating over his prose, praying that it would be accepted, only to be disappointed.

He packed his flight bag with the few clothes he had brought, stuffed the copy of the article into a side pocket, said goodbye to the ugly room and the wrinkled old lady downstairs who always came to the door whenever he went in and out, and stepped out into the street. He had sewn most of the money the visitor had brought him into the lining of his jacket and he was already sweating. It was thirty six degrees by the gauge on the hotel wall. Muktar was sitting outside in the taxi looking strained. They nodded to each other as Anders climbed in. There was nothing to talk about, they had taken many walks in Panfilov Park. His other constant companion, the man in grey, was driving a very old Lada right behind them.

Anders was forty two years old, of average height and had typical, even Swedish features. He was neither handsome or plain. His pale blue eyes looked out on the world through rimless glasses. His hair, usually light brown, had been bleached a little by the sun, but his beard was dark and gave the unfortunate impression that it might be false. This was the one moment that provided Anders with amusement that day, as when he stood at the counter at the airport, the official was looking at the passport photograph and then at him, all the time stroking his own smooth chin as if he suspected that this was Anders' condition underneath the beard. The serious thing was that if he was delayed and missed the flight, all the other elements would be thrown into chaos.

A surprising champion came to rescue him, the man in grey. He appeared from nowhere and spoke rapidly to the officials and then smiled back at Anders. It was the first time Anders had seen him close up. He had shiny skin pitted with acne scars. Anders held out his hand without thinking and the man in grey gave it a hearty shake "Da svidaniya" he said and watched as the official waved Anders through.

The plane was a small propeller aircraft that held about fifteen passengers. Anders looked out of the window as the pilot removed the cables from the blades. Sweat trickled down his back and he thought of the money and risked removing his jacket to allow it to dry. The plane smelt of stale food and cigarettes. He felt nauseous from the smell and from the fear that clutched at his stomach. He gripped the seat, trying to control his trembling hands. He was not afraid of flying, but at that moment as the blades started to spin, he almost wished the plane would crash.

As he left the plane in Tashkent, a truck carrying luggage blocked his path. He let it pass when suddenly he was grabbed and pushed into the back of a van waiting on the other side. If any of the other passengers had seen it happen, they would have looked the other way. It was a part of their lives, a daily occurrence, and it wasn't happening to them. He had been told to take his bag onto the plane with him. It was his first thought as he sprawled on the floor of the van, but he found that he was still holding on to it. "Your pass and paper" said the tough looking man who was now sitting on sacks in the corner. The van was slowing down. The driver said "Den'gi" and Anders clutched at his jacket. Money.

Chapter 29

The meeting in Istanbul was mildly successful but no decision could be made in Turkey and they would now travel to Novorossiysk in the Soviet Socialist Republic on the eastern shores of the Black Sea. They had been invited for a meeting with the Guryev Shipping Company. It was all about oil. The proposal, that Taru would supply a small fleet of tankers and Leif would operate and manage them from Gothenburg would take months of negotiation, especially dealing with the Russians, but, as Taru said 'There has to be a beginning, and a personal meeting at the start is invaluable'.

Novorossiysk, a major trading port with a deep natural harbour and an oil terminal fed by a network of pipelines that criss crossed the Soviet Union and the Republics, was a major trading port in many other aspects, shipping dry cargo, grain, timber, sugar, fertilizers, ore, and offered other possibilities. It was an excellent port for deep draft tankers except during the winter when the 'bora', north east gales that often became hurricanes, would cover ships in a thick layer of ice, and entry into the port was impossible, although the Black Sea itself did not freeze in the winter. When Novorossiysk port was restricted due to the winds they planned to make Istanbul their major port of call in the Mediterranean.

The invitation from the shipping company would accompany their visa applications and would almost guarantee that they would be granted, but as a private yacht, they would be restricted to a stay of seventy two hours and everyone on board had to apply. Applications could take two weeks and notice had to be given for a berth at the port. Leif was suspicious that someone, somewhere, in a dusty office piled high with papers, would issue the visas with a date that would not allow time for the journey across the Black Sea. He kept emphasising this to the official who had come on board with the photographer for the visa photographs. If they had been a commercial ship, Leif would not have been concerned, as an agent would have been assigned and they would have been given the time that was needed.

"Yes, yes, Captain" the official with the brown teeth assured Leif. "We have done this before. Your seventy two hour period will start when you arrive at the port. The port authority in Novorossiysk will make the stamp in your visa, don't worry." His eyes kept revolving around the bridge. He had never been on a motor yacht as opulent as this before. There were so many curious officials with an excuse to come on board, that Leif had been busy with them for hours, and Akira and Nogi became exhausted, following them around as they toured the ship.

When there was peace at last, Taru invited Leif for sake in the bar off the sitting room.

"You are determined to get me into the Soviet Union" said Leif sliding up on the bar stool.

"Only for seventy two hours Leif and it's not Kazakhstan" Taru laughed. Nogi poured the hot sake into warm cups and then immediately refilled them. After the fourth sake, Mariko and Jörgen appeared.

"We would like to go ashore" Mariko said "We want to see the city"

"Nogi is occupied right now" Taru said

"I can drive the launch" Jörgen said indignantly, "We don't need anyone, just keys."

Mariko laughed "You will drive?"

"You don't have to look so surprised. Everybody

in Sweden can operate a small boat. We have lakes everywhere, don't you know that?"

"Over one hundred thousand" Leif said, his voice sounding thicker than he liked.

"Nogi, can you take Mariko and Jörgen ashore?" Taru asked. "And take care of them in the city."

"Yes sir. I get keys."

"And lifejackets, bring lifejackets" said Leif.

"Lifejackets always in boat captain" said Nogi as he took the stairs leading to the bridge.

"And I am driving the boat, not Nogi" Leif heard Jörgen say as he and Mariko went out on deck.

"I have no news of Anders Halenius" said Taru. "His friend at the newspaper said he has gone undercover. What do you think that will mean?"

"If he tries to get to Katon-Karagay without permission, he could get into serious trouble. We might never hear from him again. When we are ashore for this meeting.."

"You must not worry Leif. This will not interfere with our business". He laughed at Leif's serious face and poured them both another sake "Many things can be possible. Now we sit and wait. We spend time to refine strategy. There is small possibility it will take less time for visas." He looked sideways at Leif.

"I see" said Leif. So someone somewhere could find it worthwhile to have influence over that person in that dusty office.

When Jörgen and Mariko arrived back it was late in the evening. They could hear laughter from the sitting room and looked around the door. Taru and Leif were playing a board game. They were both quite drunk and didn't notice them at all.

"Too much sake!" Mariko whispered, laughing as they slipt away. "I have never seen grandfather drunk."

"Good for them" said Jörgen "Leif needs to get drunk sometimes. He gets too uptight."

"What is 'uptight'? I understand, he worry."

Nogi was passing them, heading for the bar.

"Clean up tomorrow Nogi. They don't need the bar anymore tonight" said Jörgen.

More laughter came from the sitting room and Nogi put his hand across his mouth and headed back in the opposite direction.

When Mariko came to her door and opened it, she turned towards Jörgen and his heart almost stopped. The kiss was like a flower brushing his lips. Then she was gone and the door closed behind her.

Chapter 30

After Anders saw his Swedish passport and visa papers given to someone through the window of the van, he was no longer afraid. They were still close to the airport, but like a helpless kidnap victim he gave himself up to those who were in charge of him, and he fell asleep. The money sewn into his jacket was undisturbed. The twenty American dollars and few rubles he had in his wallet had satisfied the men. So they should be, he had said to himself before he dozed off. The passport must be worth a lot of money to someone.

It was dark when he awoke and the van was lurching along on a rough road. He could see stars and an outline of hills and smelt the dust kicked up by the wheels.

"Drink" said a voice and he felt a plastic cup being pushed into his hand. He nearly spat it out. It was vodka. He swallowed it down. Why not, he thought, and took another mouthful.

"What will happen.." He modified what he was going to say "The plane to Moscow?"

"Someone else take your place."

It was the vodka, but he wanted to laugh. He was imagining someone trying to look and dress like him to suit the passport, wearing a pair of similar glasses, even attempting a few words of Swedish when questioned, but perhaps it didn't work like that. Perhaps that was what the money was for. He hadn't noticed if they had handed over the money he gave them at the same time. His eyes had been focused on his passport as if he was seeing an old friend take off on a journey, doubting that he would ever return.

He drank the rest of the vodka and went back to sleep. He was woken up again hours later by the sound of goats bleating and the hollow clanking of metal bells. The back doors flew open and his companion jumped out and spoke to someone. The driver had switched the van lights off but there was a small lamp being carried around and now he could see the goats. They were tethered at the door of a dome shaped tent. No, not a tent, it was a yurt, but Kazaks called it something else, a kiizuy. His head was aching. Was he meant to get out of the van? A tall bearded figure dressed in a long coat and boots appeared, silhouetted against the stars. "Mr. Anders! Asalam aleykum! Welcome again to Kazakhstan. I am Karim. Please to come."

It was a dramatic moment, but the first thing Anders wanted to do was relieve himself and when he stepped out of the van on wobbly legs he indicated as such. Karim waved a hand out into the dark. When Anders returned he was shown into the yurt and the carved pine door was shut against the night. A fire was burning in the centre, and smoke curled around the latticed walls and up through a hole in the roof. An oil lamp was lit and he was asked to sit. He heard the van start up, saw the headlights spin around the walls in a soft arc and then heard it drive away. He felt a loss, as if the van had been the last connection with the world.

Plates of food were set before him on a low table, rice with thick pieces of fatty mutton and a wooden dish of sausages he knew were made from smoked horsemeat. He wasn't hungry and the food gave him no appetite, but he knew he must eat for fear of insulting his host. He would have liked to take an aspirin, but he didn't want to start hunting through his bag. Karim sat across from him and began to eat, biting into the sausages with strong white teeth and drinking large amounts of kumys, the fermented milk, from a skin that hung overhead. He had a long broad face that was mostly hidden behind his enormous beard. Anders wondered how far the van had travelled from the airport inland, perhaps a hundred, two hundred miles at the most. The journalist in him was starting to wake up to his surroundings. After he had eaten as much as he could bear, he felt stronger and his headache began to fade. He drank a mug of kumys, and prepared himself to ask some questions. Karim seemed to speak good English.

"Thank you for the dinner" he said.

"Would you like an American cigarette?" Karim asked reaching for a packet in the pocket of his long robe. Anders didn't smoke, but he felt he should take everything that was offered. After several puffs and a great deal of coughing, Karim let out a mighty laugh.

"You are not used to smoke!" he shouted, slapping his hand on his thigh. He took the cigarette from Anders and crushed it into the ash tray and then held out his hand to him."Boz Yazenski, from Indiana, USA." It was pure American. The thick Kazak accent was gone. "There's an old biplane out there in the dark behind some rocks. I'm to be your pilot tomorrow."

The next morning when Anders woke up and looked up at the sun shining through the hole in the roof, he didn't know what to make of it or what he was looking at for a moment. He must have gone back to sleep again. He hadn't slept properly for days, but he was surprised at feeling secure enough to sleep so much. They had talked well into the night. Anders had felt irritated at first as if he had been fooled into taking part in a practical joke, but Yazenski had convinced him he was there to help him and disguise would be necessary.

"You will never, and I mean never, get near that place unless you know how to act, talk and eat like a Kazak. Even so, it's a big risk. There are thousands of soldiers, you can imagine the security. You'll need a good Kazak interpreter when you interview the people, and a camera. I can fix that but you also have to look the part so at least you can blend in. You are going to have to live in one of these yurts. They're cool in summer and warm in winter, that's why they're built this way. But look at you. How do you expect to go up there and not get arrested? You have to look convincing. I fooled you didn't I?"

Yes, Anders had thought, but that wouldn't take much. I don't live here. He had thought the goats were going a bit far in the masquerade until he had crept outside at dawn and saw that there were a dozen more yurts spread around the area in the near distance. The people were already up, moving around, tending to their animals. Women sat outside on colourful carpets, preparing food, children ran around. It looked an idyllic scene, but Anders could guess that their life was hard. Some goats, lambs and one or two sheep were tethered. Not a lot to eat, he thought, looking around at the naked desert landscape. The meal he had eaten last night would have been enough for a whole family. One or two of the men stared at him and watched until he went back inside. Boz was still snoring away, stretched out on a pile of sheep skins in the corner.

I must look terrible, Anders thought, putting his hand up to feel his hair. It felt stiff and his scalp itched. He was longing to clean his teeth.

"One of the first things you do is dye your hair" Boz had said, throwing him a small bottle of what looked like dark brown ink. "And rub some on your beard. There's no bathroom and not much water. Don't worry about getting it on your hands. Kazaks use dye for their saddle bags and stuff, just rub it in."

Later, when it got cold, they built up the fire and sat talking. "Just so you know, I'm not the C.I.A. Thought you might be thinking that. I work for an oil company, a Russian oil company. I was born a Russian but I went to the states when I was a baby. That got you? Well it's a funny old world Anders. They know I am disguised, although the beard is real. It was their idea. I am supposed to spy on the Kazaks. They even taught me the language. You can call me a double agent but I ain't no such thing. I'm my own man and I don't like what they're doing up there in the north. A lot of sick people up there."

"How did you know about me?"

"I heard two weeks ago. They gave you a false passport and papers today?"

Anders showed him what they had given him and he looked at it skeptically.

"Yeh, they're amateurs at this stuff but they are skilled at everything else. Real survivors, except surviving nuclear fallout. Who can survive that? I know Muktar's family. They are in a bad way. Muktar, that's who told me about you. See, no Kazak is taken in by me, but the Russians I work for, they believe the Kazak's accept me. They'll know I'm here right now. Think I'm just doing my job. Why do I do it? Kind of for fun. Nothing to do out here. You see I am of a Communist persuasion politically. No way I can go back to the States, or would want to. When I came over, the Russians stuck me out here, flying around for the oil company. I check the pipe lines. I'm their security" he grinned.

"You know I'm looking for my sister."

"Yeh, I heard that. That Chinese, Mongolian border area? You can nearly forget it. I'll start to nose around if you give me what you know about her, but first we have to get you fixed."

"And if you get caught?"

"You mean if we get caught. Hell boy, we'd be shot. What else? You thinking about me being disloyal or something? Wait until you meet some of the people they made sick with these tests they're doing, the children. Then you'll understand loyalty don't come into it. Don't believe everything your country does is right, do you?"

"No. No, of course not" Anders was thinking about Stalin. The writers, musicians, scientists, anyone who disagreed with the regime killed or banished, in exile. How did Boz manage the truth there? Anders no longer saw him as the romantic figure who had appeared out of the desert. What kind of life was it, dressing up and playing this theatrical game by himself. He was probably lonely. Perhaps he had been a spy, was a spy. Perhaps he had been deported. Can I trust him? Is he completely sane? He had to go along with it. It was worrying to realise that this was who Muktar had arranged for him to meet all along, this half deluded madman. There was no one else. If he walked away, where would he go in the middle of the desert.

He still had the money from the old man. He had been touched by his visitor. An old friend of his fathers. A connection. How strange. He wanted to put the jacket on, it made him feel more secure, but it was already unbearably hot. He wondered how Carl had found the old man. He was a bit of a detective, was Carl. He must have looked his father up in the archives somewhere. He had never done that himself. He had been influenced by his mother's fearful reaction whenever he had suggested it, she was easily stressed by any mention of his father. He had often suspected his father had been in intelligence, even a spy. What else did a 'diplomat' do in those days before and during the war? For which country and for what cause? He would see Carl as soon as he got back. He wanted to thank him, and he wanted to find out what he knew.

He had thought about his father many times when he had been in Alma-Ata, imagining him as he had been then, walking along the same streets, sitting at a bar or cafe, finding Eva. Little Eva. She had been four and he eight when she came to Sweden. He was twenty one when she disappeared. How he had cried. He had thought of nothing but her for months after she had gone, always expecting her to come back. After a year he started to accept that she was gone forever, and probably dead. He had married Agneta, they had been happy for awhile, then divorced. He still saw her, they were friends. They had had no children and so little to argue about after the marriage was over. There was the occasional girl friend, but he was out of town a lot and relationships didn't last. It had made it easy to decide what he was going to do when Erik Jörgensen brought the letter. He hadn't discussed it with his mother, she would certainly have been against it, made a scene.

He had ended up leaving a note before he left for the airport.

Eva. He needed more information, the name she was known by now, where she lived. Did she have children? Eva. Why didn't you make it easy to find you? He saw her smiling at his questions and shaking her head. I am in the same country as you Eva and I am going to find you, he said to himself. He got up, feeling inspired. He made tea and gave Boz a shake to wake him up.

Chapter 31

Jörgen could not stop thinking about the kiss. Was it a kiss? Had he imagined it? The next morning they had met for their Kendo practice and Mariko had greeted him in a cheery way with no indication that anything had changed between them. Perhaps nothing had changed.

Leif and Taru didn't appear until lunchtime and Jörgen had gone up to the bridge to check the telex half way through the morning, and stayed there, but there were no messages, and he had left Leif to sleep.

Jörgen laughed when he saw the sunglasses.

"Don't remember you coming home" Leif said, slumping down into a chair with his mug of coffee.

"You had a good time yourself last night."

"At a price."

"Have to relax sometimes."

"Well I don't have a lot to do until we leave again. How was your trip ashore?"

"Great, Nogi kept buzzing around at our heels, suspicious of anyone who came within a metre of us. That was a bit annoying. It's a crowded city. Can't say I liked that. Made me feel I was supposed to be helpless or something. I checked the telex by the way."

Leif removed his sunglasses and rubbed at his bloodshot eyes. "You can take care of yourself. How about the evening before we left?" He smiled. Jörgen folded his arms and leant against the wall.

"When we get home, I'd like to go to the Swedish Film Institute and see about film school. If you think we can afford it."

"I had noticed you and Mariko had that in common."

"Mariko takes a course at her university.. But I'm not saying this because it's what Mariko is doing. I've thought about it before. You know I've been going to the film club for a long time. It's just that you've never asked me about it. I want to learn the technical side, editing or the camera."

"If all goes according to plan here with the new business, I'm sure we can look into it."

"I'm not cut out for the sea Leif. I know you would like me to be interested. It's OK for holidays but it would never interest me as a career" Jörgen couldn't believe the words were coming out of his mouth at last."I have to tell you that. Seems a good time as you don't have a hangover so often."

Leif looked up at him and laughed. "You can do whatever you like, you know that. Good to hear you know what you want. Have to lie down again. See you later?"

Leif made his way to his cabin. It's been my fault he hasn't started anything since he left school. Nothing has interested him? No, he's been stuck with my dream of working together, hinted at constantly but never expressed enough so that Jörgen had been able to be honest with me before. He had confused Jörgen with himself and the memory of his own ambition to go to sea. He did want to lie down, but he had left before he said something he didn't want to say, something bitter. He was disappointed. Good for him, he thought as he poured himself a glass of water. He finally knows what he wants to do. I have no business to feel hurt about it. Get over it, he said to himself and stretched out on the bed, but he was sad, and couldn't get rid of the feeling for some time.

In the afternoon, Jörgen went to find Taru and found him cheerful and alert reading business papers in the dining room.

"Would you like some tea?"

"No thanks. I wanted to talk to you. About the Nagasaki pearls."

"The Nagasaki pearls you say. Yes I suppose you could call them that but they are the Yumiko Suzuki Takahashi pearls. Did you see the scroll?"

Taru went out and came back with the scroll and handed it to him to read. Jörgen had only glanced at it at the dinner, his mind had been elsewhere. Taru was delighted to have someone to talk to about it. He knew the subject was not popular with Leif.

"Your father is ambitious. He thinks my search for the pearls is too much of a distraction from business" he said, but his tone was kind, humorous.

"Leif is only interested in ships and the sea, well, not only. He likes us. He's interested in us."

"The family. Ah, yes, important. Leif adopted you did he not? But you are like his own son to him"

Jörgen shifted uncomfortably. "Well, I think of him as my father."

"But you call him Leif."

"That's because of, well, it's family history."

"Family history, yes. Would you like to hear more about the pearls I am looking for"?

In the twenty four hours it took to cross the Black Sea, Leif had little time to reflect as he navigated the busy shipping lanes, but Jörgen kept coming into his mind. It had been reassuring to receive the telex from THE LUCY off the coast of Fernando de Noronha, a happy message that he kept pinned up on the bridge near the coffee station, so that when he took a break, he could read it again. It was not only from Ella and Helen. Erik and Connie had put their names to it as well. They would all be flying back to Sweden within the next two weeks.

Leif hoped he and Jörgen would be home by then but he couldn't be impatient for that. Who knew what Taru had in mind to do next? Another destination? He must ask Taru when he could expect the relief captain to make it clear that he did not expect or wish to be the captain on the WHITE WIND for much longer. He still had his business to attend to at home, although Kurt seemed to be growing in strength since he had been left alone to run things by himself.

It was this thought that made him think of Jörgen again. Too protective, too domineering, and what had it led to? I have not been listening to him. I have not allowed him to grow, Leif was thinking. He hoped he had left that behind. They had been kicking their heels for a week in Istanbul and during that time he had felt it was better that he left Jörgen to himself and not to mention his future, but he had changed his mind on the last evening before they left. After dinner, Leif had been listening to a discussion on the merits of different film directors between Mariko and Jörgen and had been impressed by Jörgen's knowledge and the way he had expressed himself. "Jörgen is going to the Swedish Film Institute" he found himself saying to Mariko. "Film School" he added, realising as he said it that he didn't know what he was talking about, but they only broke off their discussion for a moment before resuming, but not before Jörgen had looked at Leif with such a light in his eyes that it had stayed with him, and as Leif looked out across the sea, he kept remembering it.

Jörgen was not thinking about Film School at that moment or even Mariko. He was thinking about the visitor who would be arriving the next day. Taru had told him in confidence several days ago, that he was trying to contact someone from his past, someone he knew when he was a prisoner, when he was one of many nationalities helping to build the mountain road near Katon-Karagay during the war.

The man was a Russian soldier, but he and Taru had become friends over time as there was little difference between the conditions suffered by the prisoners and those who were guarding them, especially during the long months of winter. It had begun when Taru had stepped in to act as a translator for one of the German prisoners. Taru knew a few words in German and only a little more in English at that time, but it had been enough. Later, he was able to save many situations from becoming more serious. Alexi Simonov had been his counterpart, the one soldier among the many there who also knew some German and English. Alexi had been a teacher before the war and had taught Taru Russian. With regret, I have forgotten most of it now, Taru had added. Taru had understood that for someone like Alexi to be enlisted and sent to that place was a form of punishment. Alexi told him that there was a musician and two political prisoners among the soldiers guarding them, men who were not trained and not suited to be soldiers. The Commandant was a trained soldier and why he had been sent there wasn't known, but he took every opportunity to take out his bitterness on both prisoners and the soldiers under his command. "The harsh treatment we shared from the commandant made many comrades. Alexi was intelligent man. The Commandant not so. We fool him, as you say, many times. We called it 'the game'. It was only the game and Alexi that kept many from giving up. After war was over, they use me and Alexi for translator for Japanese prisoners. This was also very bad time for me. After war was over, I was not released for two years. Last time I see Alexi was 1947, waiting for train on the South Siberian railway."

The story had stayed with Jörgen. He was realising that he knew little about the world. It sent him searching for books in the ship's library.

The evening they were due to arrive Taru sent Akira to find Jörgen and ask him to come to his rooms.

"We speak in confidence?" Taru asked him and Akira scuttled away to stand behind the kitchen door.

"I think I find Alexi Simonov." he continued. "I am with hope it is same man. Strange, but he continued his life as soldier. He is Colonel if I can believe it is him. This was why it was not difficult for my agency to find him. I speak with shipping agency boss in Odessa on radio telephone from Istanbul and now agency call back, today. Like me this Alexi is about to retire, like me he is probably a little fat and losing his hair" Taru's eyes were full of laughter and tears. He took Jörgen's arm.

"Jörgen, you must help me.. Alexi is coming here late tomorrow morning. Your father and I have our meeting. I do not wish to disturb Leif with this. I want you to welcome my old friend" He looked at the open kitchen door. "Akira! Come! Come, I know you are listening. Akira you will make a welcome lunch here for my Russian guest and Jörgen will entertain him until I return. I fear the meeting ashore may take all day, but I will come when I can. Can you do this Jörgen? It is not suitable for Mariko."

"Of course. But what do you want me to do? Can I ask him questions? See if he is the right man?"

"You can speak as you find Jörgen. I know you will do well with this. I think you will soon discover who he is. If you are sure, tell him I am looking for someone who has knowledge of my family and where we believe she is living. Do not mention the pearls. I trust the old friend that I knew, but people change. They change.

You will find that is true. We keep the pearls a secret for the moment."

"And what if he isn't your friend?"

"If he is wrong man, you must give him my apology. Tell him there has been a mistake."

"Why would another man pretend to be your friend?"

"When you have money and position Jörgen, people do many things. The agency speak with him. They would tell him of my company and I am here to consider trade with the Soviet Union. He could see opportunity, perhaps position.. If it is the Alexi I know you will find out" Taru walked to the window and looked out at the sea. "I do not want to listen to someone who comes because of ambition."

People change, Jörgen was thinking. The memory of this friend was important to Taru and he wanted to protect him from being hurt. If it is Taru's friend he might also be coming because of ambition, now that Taru was no longer a helpless prisoner but a rich and powerful man.

Taru opened a drawer and took out a small jewelry box. Among the cuff links and tie pins was a small metal plaque inscribed with Cyrillic letters and numbers and attached to a thin piece of leather. Taru slipped it onto his wrist and pulled the leather string to fit, then he set it loose and gave it to Jörgen. "My friend would know what this is."

Chapter 32

Boz was getting tired. Anders saw that his eyelids were drooping and he kept talking to him to keep him awake. They had been flying now for at least six hours, landing once to refuel from the tank that was kept on board. By then Anders had got used to the heavy drone from the old Tiger Moth and slept a bit himself. They were not flying very high and the wide barren land stretched out before them, mile upon mile. Sometimes a small settlement could be seen with animals dotted around but they were avoiding the few towns that lay on their journey north. It was getting dark and rocky hills were ahead, a new feature on the horizon. All at once the plane started to dip down.

"Are we landing here?" Anders asked "I don't see a town anywhere. Where do the people live?"

"Well, west of us are the labour camps. Coal mining at Karaganda. Thousands live in that area, lot of military too. Prison camps for enemies of the state. Not a good place for us. If they spot the plane flying over, chances are they'll think I've come to spy and shoot us down. We're landing in the foothills over there. Near a place called Kaynar. From Kaynar the road goes to Semipalatinsk, that's a major city and the center for the test site programme, about two hundred miles north east from here. This is kind of in the middle of things and just south of where they're doing all these tests. Better start watching out for military planes. I'm not authorised to be in this area" Anders was looking at his map when, as if in reply, the radio crackled into life and over the static, voices were speaking in Russian.

"What are they saying?" Anders said, scanning the skies around them.

"Just a lot of bullshit to each other. They ain't spotted us yet. Before they do, we better get down."

The last time they had landed Anders had thought they were going to crash and had struggled with himself not to vomit in his lap. The method of landing on rocky uncleared land with no proper landing site, seemed to be, to almost stall the engine and glide along about a hundred feet from the surface, until Boz felt it was OK to commit them to a spot where they could land without destroying the aircraft.

After they had juddered to a halt, the night came quickly and they slept. In the cold early dawn they took their bags and started hiking up a track between the hills. They walked for two hours, almost in silence. It was good to walk after sitting cramped up in the plane.

They were now in a more mountainous area and as they turned into a ravine a freezing dusty wind began to blow. They covered their faces and it was through a gap in his scarf that Anders saw the man on the rocky craig above their heads, a man in a fur hat and long coat, holding aloft a huge golden eagle. Boz and Anders stopped walking and stared up at him. The man ignored them. He was concentrating on the bird that was balanced on his gloved hand. The bird's feathers ruffled in the wind as it rocked to and fro. Then it gave a cry, spread its immense wings and took off, swooping over their heads and continuing far down the hillside towards the valley floor. The man whistled and a shaggy horse appeared. He jumped onto the horse's back and raced away down the mountain in the direction the eagle had flown.

"He likes to get there 'fore she damages the prey" said Boz, moving on again.

"He was hunting."

"Sure. He's an eagle hunter. They're all females

those eagles they hunt with. They, think they're more aggressive".

"What a size."

"Wing span seven feet tip to tip. If there's anything to be caught in the valley, she'll see it first. They have ten times better eyesight than you or me. Hunting with golden eagles is a Kazakh tradition hundreds of years old. Don't see it so often these days. Well, seeing him, means we must be close to being there. He probably came along with the others for the ride."

They walked for another half an hour until they reached a depression in the hills and a place where three yurts were standing.

"This is it" said Boz and waved to one of the men. "You'll be staying with Ibrahim. He speaks English and he's supposed to have brought a camera, it'll be Russian I guess. Hope he remembered to bring film. Ibrahim's kind of the chief guy of those fierce looking guys over there by the horses. They got a stream not far from here. Don't know how the water is. Wouldn't drink too much of it, but they may have some bottled water" He gave a shout and other people began to appear. They moved slowly until they were standing directly in front of them. There were eight men and three women. The women had dull eyes and sores on their faces and hands. One man stood back, holding up his hands to show his bent fingers. Others hobbled towards him and pointed at their swollen stomachs or opened their mouths to point at their throats.

"All these people are ill?" said Anders." Every one of them?"

"They came by horseback, many miles. They come from one small place, but this is no exaggeration boy. There are hundreds, maybe thousands of people like this. Problem is, we can't get you to them. So here you can at least meet some of the people and get their story. You got twenty four hours and then I have to get you out of here."

Boz started to walk away and Anders followed, taking the map out of his pocket as he walked. He held it out to him.

"I need to get to this place Boz, Katon-Karagay. When you come back, you can take me there. This place. Can you take me here?"

Boz didn't even look at the map.

"Tell you what Anders. You are in hiding here, that don't mean someone won't come snooping around to check on these people. That's why you have to look like a Kazakh. It'll give you a fighting chance. Now, you have to know that I am taking an even bigger chance to bring you here, and to take you back. But that is it. I can't take you any other place Anders. You get it?"

"You did say you would try.."

"I'm sorry buddy. I'm sticking my neck out far enough as it is. I'll be back at the same time tomorrow." He went to walk away and then turned back "Your sister is just one, one person. You can help thousands of people if you let the world know what's happening here. Think of that."

Anders watched Boz disappear back down the track. This far and no further. How could he go back now without trying to find Eva? It was the reason he came. He would think of another way. The horses. He could go with the people when they left, but where would he go? People were gathering around him again, trying to talk to him and a tall smiling man in a turban was advancing.

"Ibrahim" said the man, pointing at himself. What am I doing here? thought Anders suddenly.

"Asalam aleykum Mr. Anders" said Ibrahim "They say, thank you.. All are thanking you for coming."

Boz didn't come back the next day, or the day after. Anders had completed his interviews with Ibrahim's help and taken the photographs. He had wept and then he had become angry, not for himself, not even at his frustration at ever being able to find Eva, but for the kind people who fed him and brought him whatever they had, in spite of their suffering. He was determined that he would tell their story. The women had told him of the many children who were born blind or disfigured, if they were born alive, as many were stillborn. There were entire communities where the population suffered from one form of cancer or another. There were those among the older generation who had never developed and remained as children, always dependent and unable to work. If they left their homes where were they to go they asked Anders, who had no answer to that either. Surely in this vast land they could live somewhere else, he asked himself. Some of the people who were ill were taken to the military hospital, but many agreed it was only to study them, not to cure them. Perhaps that was it then, Anders thought, they are useful in that way, so they don't bother to move them out of the area. The idea was so inhuman he could not bring himself to believe it, but what other reason was there?

They told him of people who lived further away from the test sites who still knew when there was a nuclear explosion, even if it was underground. The ground shook and walls were cracked up to fifty miles away. Rocks fell from the hills and fissures opened up in the land. They knew lakes where the water was contaminated as their animals became sick, but no one in authority would listen. If you complained too much you would be considered unpatriotic, or worse, an enemy of the state.

The most terrifying were the nuclear tests in the air. They would hear the heavy drone of the plane and hide in their houses in fear until the brilliant light on the horizon had faded away. Believing the worst was over, Anders thought bitterly. He asked them if they understood that the wind could carry the poisonous air many miles over the land and they considered what he had said. One man spoke up "But we cannot control the wind" he said, puzzled that Anders seemed to think that they could. It's true, Anders thought, why even mention it. They couldn't give him dates or many details but they did speak about their parents who had described seeing terrible explosions when they were children and Anders realised that the tests had been going on for many years.

Why was this not known in the world? He knew it was possible to detect and identify distant nuclear explosions. Many countries must know these tests were going on. There had been a nuclear test ban treaty signed by the USA, the UK and the USSR in 1963. What had that meant if anything at all? How much notice had he taken of it himself? Politics. The so called Cold War. These people were considered expendable. What did the rest of the world know about the Kazaks and this remote place? How much would they care if they knew? The least he could do was make sure that their story was told. He understood now what Boz had meant. He could not risk looking for Eva now. He must get away, get out of the Soviet Union as soon as possible so he could publish the story.

In the early morning of the third day Anders walked back down the mountain with Ibrahim, taking the track he had walked with Boz when they had seen the man with the golden eagle. They stared across the valley, hoping to see the plane appear over the horizon, but nothing came.

"Something has happened to him" Anders said. "I think he was a good man. Something has happened"

Ibrahim turned away. "You will come with us. We will take care of you."

That day Anders helped to take down the yurts and pack their few belongings on to the horses to begin the trek down the other side of the mountain. He hid his notebook and the reels of film in the lining of his jacket and was thankful to feel the packet of money. He would need it more than ever now. It would be a long journey across the deserted plane to Sarjal, south of Semipalatinsk, where the people lived.

When they came to the road Anders embraced each one of them as they said goodbye. There were many miles still to go, but Ibrahim and Anders would take two of the horses and journey the long way round along a desert track. There was a great deal of military traffic on the road and although the trucks sped by without a glance at the group of Kazak people and their horses, Ibrahim said anyone of them could decide to stop and question them and Anders would be discovered and taken away. "They could even shoot you and leave you by the roadside" he said.

When they were some distance from the road, Anders took his notebook, tied it up in cloth, and slipped it down the side of his boot. If they shot him perhaps they would leave his boots on, and the right person could find it one day. "Cowboys in the American west" he said to Ibrahim "They were supposed to be buried with their boots on" but Ibrahim didn't understand his joke.

Chapter 33

Jörgen had dressed himself as formally as his limited wardrobe would allow and was now standing waiting on Taru's private balcony. He could hear Akira setting the table in the room behind him. Taru and Leif had left early for their meeting and Jörgen had felt a twinge of conscience that Leif knew nothing of the visitor who was expected later and Mariko had been particularly annoyed with him when he didn't arrive for their practice.

"Akira is busy today and I have to prepare for a meeting on behalf of your grandfather" he had told her when she came looking for him.

Mariko had raised her eyebrows "What meeting?"

"Something private" Jörgen had replied and she had walked off with her nose in the air.

That had made him feel better than he expected. He had begun to realise that he made himself too available and too anxious to please. The trust that Taru had placed in him had given Jörgen a new confidence. He wasn't feeling nervous, he was looking forward to it.

It was almost twelve when the military car pulled up on the dock. The two soldiers who were on duty at the gangway saluted as a tall slim figure in uniform emerged from the car. Jörgen had got tired with waiting in Taru's rooms and was up on the bridge. He asked the chief officer to go to the top of the gangway to meet and escort him and he took the back way himself. When Akira opened the door, and Alexi Simonov walked in, Jörgen was there ready to greet him.

"Colonel Simonov" said Jörgen and held out his hand.

The Russian nodded and shook the hand that was offered but he was obviously puzzled.

"Mr. Takahashi sends his apologies and hopes to be here as soon as his meeting is over" said Jörgen "Would you like a beer or a glass of wine while you are waiting?" he added, remembering how Leif would welcome guests who came to the house.

"No thank you, but some tea?"

Akira went to the kitchen and returned with tea for both of them that he placed on a tray on the side table. Alexi was walking around the room looking at the paintings on the walls, ignoring Jörgen. So, he thinks I am one of the servants, Jörgen said to himself. Alexi had a lean face with a thin nose. He removed his cap and placed it on the sideboard revealing very short white hair, cut evenly all over his head. He looked like a schoolmaster you would never dare to cross, not the overweight and kindly friend that had been the person Jörgen had expected.

"My father and Mr. Takahashi had an important meeting ashore this morning. He would have let you know but had no telephone number" said Jörgen, sitting down himself in front of the tea tray. After a moment of hesitation Alexi joined him and Akira poured tea for them both.

"They are not allowed to give my number" Alexi explained in his rich Russian accent, then, "I will smoke?" he said. He was taking a cigarette case out of his pocket as he spoke, as if he didn't expect to be refused. He didn't offer Jörgen a cigarette. Jörgen didn't smoke anyway, but he caught the slight, and it didn't help to warm his feelings towards his visitor. He is a professional soldier, a Colonel, Jörgen reminded himself, calming his irritation. He was thinking of films he had seen, 'Patton' with George Scott or 'MacArthur' with Gregory Peck. There was always a private man, but how do you communicate with that man when you have so little time to do it.

"I'm Jörgen. Jörgen Hansson. I am half Swedish and half Brazilian" he said, thinking it would help to explain who he was. "My father is a sea captain. He has a shipping company in Sweden and he and Mr. Takahashi are going to make a company together."

"Half Brazilian eh? Like your new queen in Sweden. Do you know her?" He laughed. "Very beautiful woman. So this is why you are tall like a Swede but look like a Brazilian" He reached into his breast pocket and took out his wallet. "This is Yuri" he said, showing him a picture of someone in uniform about Jörgen's age.

"Your son?"

"You flattering me! Grandson. A good boy. He is also soldier. He is in Berlin right now or he would come to play football with you. He is very good at the football"

"You knew Mr. Takahashi a long time ago"

"Many years ago" Alexi replaced the photograph. "Strange to get his message. I had to come, had to come. He is doing well I see."

"He has talked about you. He asked me to show you this" Jörgen took the metal tag from his pocket and placed it on the table.

"He has kept that".

"When did you know each other?"

Alexi sighed. He picked up the tag and looked at it. "In the war, and after, also, for a time"

"Was it here, in Russia?"

"Kazakhstan. The Soviet Socialist Republic of Kazakhstan, close to the Chinese border. You know how we were working, what we are doing there? Digging a road to nowhere in the ice and snow."

So he was the Alexi Simonov that Taru had known.

"Taru wanted me to invite you for lunch, if he wasn't back by now."

"Taru is it? No more Mr. Takahashi? You are friend

also?" He was no longer the threatening schoolmaster but a man who liked to tease. Akira had come into the room as the word lunch had been mentioned. He smiled in approval at Jörgen and bowed his head.

"Yes" Jörgen replied "I think I am."

After lunch, and Akira had prudently placed a bottle of the best Russian vodka in front of him, Alexi became more relaxed and talked a lot, mostly about his grandson Yuri that he hadn't seen for two years. Jörgen told him about the ELISE and their adventure across the Atlantic to Brazil. They were sitting out on the balcony and it was the middle of the afternoon.

"Taru will be disappointed not to see you. Can you stay longer?" Jörgen asked him.

"Today, yes, yes I can. Tomorrow I am very busy. I have many of my soldiers standing by, waiting to go north. They are replacement and I will go with them the day after tomorrow."

"Where are you going?"

Alexi laughed. "You cannot ask a military man these questions Jörgen, but I am going to Kurchatov"

"Is that near a place called Katon-Karagay"?

"Where we were in the war? No. Long way from there but northern Kazakhstan. It is northern Kazakhstan."

Jörgen decided to tell him about Eva.

"I can't explain, but it's the most important thing in his life, to find this woman. She is connected to his family history and the last anyone knows is that she was living there, in Katon-Karagay, but I think that was only a holiday place".

"A dacha"

"And we don't know her name. Only the name she had when she lived in Sweden. Eva Halenius"

"She is Swedish?"

"She is from Kazakhstan but she was adopted and

lived in Sweden until she was, I don't know, I think she was seventeen, eighteen when she left and went back to Kazakhstan"

Alexi poured himself another vodka. "I can find anybody, but this? Not so easy. Is she an old girl friend you think?"

"No" Jörgen said laughing "More important than that"

"I will talk to people when I am in Kurchatov. We keep this between us Jörgen. It is not so possible that anything can be done. She would be how old today?" "Thirty eight, almost forty" Alexi took out a small note book. "Eva Halenius Swedish/Kazak. Thirty eight" he wrote. Jörgen was tempted to tell him about the pearls but he remembered how Taru had cautioned him not to mention them.

After a few minutes Alexi fell asleep in the chair. Jörgen went back into the dining room and signalled to Akira that he was leaving for a few minutes. He was also feeling tired although he hadn't drunk any vodka, but he wanted to go to the ship's library and see where Kurchatov was on the map.

Chapter 34

They had heard the airplane for the last half an hour. At first Anders hoped it was Boz, coming to look for him, as it kept circling around, but this was not a light aircraft. He could see it now, a large grey plane, flying about two thousand feet above the featureless land, about a mile away.

They stopped walking and sat beside the horses. "Are they looking for us"? Anders asked, but Ibrahim only shook his head and Anders saw that he was afraid. The horses were restless and Ibrahim stood up to tighten their harness. It was the last thing Anders saw, Ibrahim's hands working the leather straps, before the world around them was obliterated in a blinding flash.

When he became conscious again, Anders couldn't move, something heavy was pressing him to the ground. There was a searing pain behind his eyes and he tried to open them. At first he could only see bright lights. When his vision cleared and he was able to see, he thought that he had gone blind. There was nothing to see but dust, great clouds of dust and smoke, rolling all around him. He could feel a wind on his face and thought, why doesn't the wind blow away all this smoke. In the centre of his vision, a long way off, he could see a ball of fire. Then there was a gap in the smoke and he saw blue overhead and a glimpse of the sun, and away on the horizon, a billowing mushroom cloud rising up into the sky.

When the eagle hunter saw the smoke rising hundreds of feet into the sky he spurred his horse back in the direction he had come. He was many miles away but his heart was full of foreboding and when he had travelled some way towards the smoke he found her sprawled on the ground. He had seen other birds lying dead in the dust as he rode along, he knew how it would be, but he wept as he folded her great wings and tied her onto the saddle. He had been looking for her for hours that day and knew she had gone far. He had been angry then, but now there was only sorrow.

He travelled some hours before he came to the road and he found it deserted. Nothing moved in any direction, no traffic, no people, but there was something. A man in the distance, stumbling out of the desert. When he came to him he didn't recognise who it was, although he knew him well. Then he saw it was Ibrahim. His face was burnt and his clothes hung in shreds. He screamed when the eagle hunter tried to lift him onto his horse and so he set him back down again by the road.

"Leave me" said Ibrahim."But you must take this and go quickly" He held out a package wrapped in cloth.

"But where do I take it?" the hunter asked

Ibrahim turned the package over and showed him the address written on the other side, but the hunter could not understand the writing. He knew the man who had come to help them was from a place far away and he struggled to remember as he continued north. He could have asked the pilot American man but he was dead. He had seen the wreckage of his plane in the mountains with the buzzards circling around it three days ago and had ridden away, fearing that his eagle would get into a fight with the Buzzards and be damaged.

When he came to Sarjal he looked for the people who had travelled to the meeting place and he found one of the men. The man was trying to mend an old rusty bicycle in the yard of his tumbled down house and he took the hunter inside to find the only book he possessed that was not written in the Cyrillic alphabet, an atlas. They turned the pages back and forth, trying to match the word that was written in large letters at the bottom of the address and when they found it, they agreed that if it was sent by post, it would be opened and destroyed and so the hunter would take it to the only person they could think of, the wife of Karazin, the one they called the Swedish woman.

Chapter 35

Leif and Taru came back in the early evening exhausted from their meeting and by that time Alexi had left. Jörgen went to Taru and told him that Alexi had taken the ship's details and would call on the radio telephone or send a telex the next day but he would be too busy to come to the ship again. Jörgen didn't mention the conversation about looking for Eva. Taru accepted the news that he would not be able to see his old friend, he seemed too tired to think of anything but going to bed.

"We will be returning here another time I think .. I hope to see him then" he said "Thank you Jörgen. But what did you think of him?" he asked as an afterthought.

"Good company."

"Yes, he was always good company. Well, I say goodnight Jörgen. We can talk tomorrow."

Jörgen went to look for Leif in his cabin and found him in a bad mood. "I am not sure we can deal with these people" Leif confided "That was the most confusing meeting I have ever had in my life"

"Can I get you a drink?" Jörgen said, leaning in the doorway.

"You're looking very smart" Leif observed "Is this for Mariko? You know you cannot get involved there, don't you?"

"Why? Because of your business deals?"

"Because of everything you know already!" Leif thundered "Because you are from different cultures and family and it would never work. Taru would not allow it and neither would I."

"I see. But I am not from only one culture as you put it, am I? Anyone I end up with is going to be different from me and it's not your business by the way" Jörgen shouted. He slammed the door as he left and almost ran into Mariko in the passageway, coming along in the opposite direction. She walked by without looking at him. So what, Jörgen said to himself and went to the bar. He poured himself a large whisky and took it to his cabin.

In the morning Jörgen woke up late with a headache and went to the sun deck to lie down, but the cranes working at the ships on either side were making too much noise, so he went up to the bridge. Nogi was there, polishing around. He pointed at the freshly made coffee and gave Jörgen a cheerful mock salute."They go ashore already" he told him, "Mr. Takahashi and Captain, go ashore again. I take Miss Mariko ashore shopping this afternoon. You come? This soldier on dock, he have to come too" he continued conversationally.

"I don't think so." said Jörgen pouring himself a mug. He remembered that Alexi might telephone.

"Second mate on duty" Nogi continued "He coming in two minute" Good, thought Jörgen. He wasn't sure how the radio telephone worked.

"Can you ask him to call me if he gets a telephone call for Mr. Takahashi?"

Nogi hesitated "For Mr. Takahashi? You will take call?" His tone was disapproving.

"It will be from the man I had lunch with yesterday" said Jörgen giving him a look.

Nogi bowed his head. "I will tell second mate."

In the middle of the afternoon Alexi telephoned. He didn't ask to speak to Taru but to Jörgen, so the second mate was comfortable to call Jörgen to come up to the bridge.

"I have found Eva Helenius. Her name is Tania Karazin. She and her husband live outside Sarjal"

"How did you find her?"

"It was not so difficult. I have very good secretary in the ministry in Kurchatov. Tania Karazin will be in the military diagnostic centre in Semipalatinsk tomorrow, and will be taken very good care of. She is on a list of people for examination. So you see, you don't have to worry about her anymore"

"Good to hear that" Jörgen answered cautiously

"Now I call you for something else. Yuri would like you to see our university in Semipalatinsk so you can think seriously about your application. He is applying himself as you know, next year. I am flying up tonight and we will be stopping there on our way to Kurchatov. I will arrange your pick up at the ship and your return tomorrow. Is that suitable Jörgen?"

It took Jörgen a moment to understand, then he remembered that the radio telephone could be overheard by every ship in the area, not to speak of the port control and the police. He was excited, but he wasn't going to allow his excitement to prevent him from playing along with the game.

The military transport plane was the biggest airplane Jörgen had ever seen. It dwarfed the trucks and equipment that were in position at the ramp and the lines of soldier getting ready to board. The officer who had driven Jörgen to the military base east of the port of Novorossiysk had issued Jörgen with a jacket and cap and checked his passport and visa before placing him in the line. He had told Jörgen the journey would be about seven hours as the plane was loaded and would be flying at about three hundred miles an hour. He gave him a bottle of water and a tin that contained some bread and cheese. Jörgen put them into the small rucksack he had brought and slipped the passport and visa back into his jeans pocket.

Boarding the plane was like entering a warehouse in

the dead of winter and he was glad of the extra jacket. It was not going to be a comfortable ride. The metal seats had no backs and were attached by clips to the wall of the aircraft with a simple strap to hold you on. The priority was to cram as much equipment and men inside as possible. When the ramp doors were finally slammed shut it began to warm up a little as soldiers were piled around on all sides of him. The seats were apparently a luxury as many of the soldiers were sprawled on the metal floor. Then the noise began. With insulation at a minimum, to maximize the space, the heavy roar of the engines seemed as loud inside the aircraft as outside. When they reached altitude and leveled off it dropped to a less abrasive tone but Jörgen's excitement at the journey was fading. This was going to be rough and he would have to endure the whole thing again going back.

The soldiers shouted across to each other and one offered Jörgen a stick of gum but after half an hour nearly all of them were asleep, except Jörgen, who was now wondering what was being said on the WHITE WIND, hundreds of feet below them. The landscape and the port vanished out of sight as they disappeared into the clouds.

It was frosty and snowing slightly when they landed at Semipalatinsk at dawn. Jörgen was relieved to see Alexi waiting in a car on the runway, there had been no sign of him on the plane.

"Snowing? In August?" Jörgen said as he got in. It was mercifully warm inside the jeep.

"This is warm weather!" Alexi laughed "Can be minus forty in two months."

"Then I'm glad I made it a summer visit" said Jörgen, looking out at the bleak buildings emerging in the half light.

"Dostoevsky wrote The Brothers Karamazov when he was detained here, so you see, it can be an inspiring place. I can admit, it does not look inspiring"

"Detained?"

"He was in the military service but the choice was not his."

"Why did you continue in the military after the war Alexi?"

He didn't answer him for awhile.

"Can we say, I think, I try, to make a difference?"

They were stopping in a car park in front of a line of grey concrete buildings. A soldier stepped out from under the dim light bulb over the entrance. He saluted Alexi and snapped to attention.

"I will have to hand you over to the soldier on duty, but he has been informed. He will take you to the lady. You will have a few minutes to talk. Jörgen, I advise you not to talk in any way that is, shall we say, controversial? Nothing political, you understand?" He leant across to open Jörgen's door. "Good luck. I hope you find out what you have come for. I come back for you this afternoon"

Jörgen followed the soldier along the corridors. It was a cheerless place, smelling of damp and disinfectant. Is this a hospital? Jörgen wanted to ask. One of the doors was open and Jörgen glimpsed wires and machinery inside before the door was slammed shut as they passed by. He was shown into an airless room that had been painted green. There was a single bunk bed and two chairs in the room. The bed was made up, but the blankets were not clean. The window panes were papered over and a little light was softly creeping in. There were no curtains and no heating that Jörgen could detect. He looked around for a light switch but when he found it, nothing happened. He looked up at the bulb inside the paper lampshade and decided not to try it. He was terribly tired and in spite of the cold, the discomfort, and the slightly menacing atmosphere, his head dropped to his chest and he fell asleep.

Jörgen didn't know that two hours had gone by while he slept. The opening of the door woke him up. The soldier who had brought him there had been replaced by another and he came into the room swinging his rifle around his shoulder and looking into every corner. He went out again and returned with a woman and Jörgen's heart began to pound. The woman was wearing a long heavily embroidered dress covered by a loose woolen coat of the same length. A thick shawl was wound around her head and as she put her hand up to straighten it, bangles clattered at her wrists, but the woman was old. The scarf that framed her face exposed her forehead and Jörgen could see that her hair was grey. Dark shadows surrounded her eyes and her cheeks were lined and pale. Jörgen judged her to be about fifty years old, and his heart sank. She stared at Jörgen suspiciously and stood by the door until the soldier ordered her to sit down. Jörgen had stood up when they came into the room and he now sat down on the other chair. The woman avoided his eyes and sat with her hands clasped, looking into her lap. The soldier leant against the door and lit a cigarette. This immediately brought forth a stream of angry words from the woman. She waved her hands in the air. She was almost screaming at him. The soldier shrugged his shoulders and opened the door wide, but she continued to shout at him until he went out into the corridor, but he left the door ajar. Then she became quiet again and resumed her position, with eyes downcast and her hands in her lap.

Jörgen sighed. This was a mistake. The soldiers had changed guard and now they had brought him the wrong person.

"Tania Karazin?" he said quietly, hoping at least the woman would know who he meant. She gave a start and looked at him.

"Eva Halenius" he said without thinking and her eyes filled with tears. Could it be? He spoke in Swedish "Are you Eva Halenius?" he said, his hopes rising. "Were you Eva Halenius once and are now Tania Karazin?"

He could hear the guard out in the corridor who had now met a friend and was conducting a loud conversation.

"Yes I am." the woman answered in Swedish.

Jörgen fought back the tears in his own eyes.. "I am Erik Jörgensen's grandson. I am half Swedish. My mother is Ella. Do you remember Ella?"

She looked fearfully towards the door, but the soldier was still talking along the corridor.

"Quickly" she said softly "I have something to give you" She reached under her skirt and took out a small package wrapped in cloth. "Put this in your bag" she whispered. "Don't let them see it"

Jörgen thrust the package into his rucksack. It had felt like a book.

"I wish I could talk to you. I have so much to tell" she whispered.

"I have much to tell you as well. The soldier cannot understand Swedish. Why can't we talk?" She raised her eyes to the ceiling and pointed at the light bulb.

"Eva, there are many people who would like to help you.." He stopped, as she looked so afraid. "I mean we would like to help you get well."

"Too late" she said shaking her head.

"You need money?" Jörgen whispered.

"They would only take it. I am going to be operated on this afternoon. So you must take this as well" She reached into the plastic shopping bag she had been carrying and took out a small embroidered bag, suspended on a cord. Jörgen could hardly breathe. He stretched out his hand, but as he went to place it in the rucksack he felt someone was looking at him. A man was standing in the doorway, a large man with a full beard and a gold watch chain that he was dangling from his fingers. Jörgen had now placed the little bag deep inside the rucksack. He drew the cord on the rucksack tight but the man's glittering eyes were fixed on him the whole time and now he gave a shout down the corridor for the soldier.

"My husband. Be careful" said Eva quickly in Swedish and to Jörgen's horror the man stepped forward and struck her once across the mouth. "I must not speak Swedish" Eva said and the man struck her again.

"But I can speak to you in Swedish. Eva, you don't have to look at me, look away as if you can't hear me. Put your hands over your ears, but listen to what I say."

The soldier and Karazin were now shouting at each other at the same time.

"I came here with Colonel Alexi Simonov" Jörgen continued. "I am here with his permission. The soldier must contact him and ask him to come here. You can tell them that. Perhaps it will stop him from striking you again."

Eva was looking away from him, her hands over her ears but she answered him by slowly shaking her head as if to say it was hopeless.

Karazin lunged across the room, his arm raised, ready to strike, but Jörgen, more trained than he had realised until that moment, quickly deflected the arm away with a sharp blow. Karazin was just recovering from his surprise and thinking to try again when Eva started shouting and Jörgen heard Alexi's name. At that, the soldier stiffened and decided to change his attitude. He spoke harshly to Karazin and made him step outside into the corridor, but Karazin wouldn't leave without his wife. He grabbed Eva's wrist and pulled her outside with him.

The argument continued out in the corridor. Jörgen was thinking for one wild moment that he would take a chair and smash the window and escape that way, but he knew that was stupid. He had to rely on Alexi.

Chapter 36

Alexi didn't arrive for another two hours. The soldier had indicated that Jörgen must sit where he could see him in the entrance hall. Karazin had left but came back soon after Alexi arrived, summoned no doubt by a phone call. Eva had now gone to the operating theatre. She had been able to whisper to Jörgen in Swedish in the few minutes they had together after Karazin left and before the nurse arrived.

"The packet I gave you wrapped in cloth. Don't let them have the packet. You will never leave here if they see that packet. Your Colonel will not be able to save you. Promise me. People have died to get it to me. There is an address on it in Sweden. You must deliver it yourself. You cannot know how happy I am that you came when you did. They gave it to me only yesterday. I did not know what I was going to do and today you came. Today I may die but now they will not find it" Her eyes had become luminous, passionate, her lips moist, and for a moment Jörgen saw the beautiful girl who was once called Eva.

When she was leaving with the nurse she looked back at him and said again" Don't give it to anyone!"

"Don't worry" Jörgen had called after her. He had stood and watched as she walked away. He held up his hand when she got to the end of the corridor, but she turned the corner without looking back again.

Alexi was not happy. He had been forced to leave in the middle of his meeting in Kurchatov and had had to drive over fifty miles back to Semipalatinsk, earlier than he had planned.

"What is this man's complaint?" he barked at the soldier as soon as he arrived. Karazin stepped forward and started to shout.

"Be quite!" Alexi said sharply and to Jörgen's surprise, Karazin sat down again while the soldier explained. Alexi turned to Jörgen.

"He says his wife gave you something" he said angrily "You better give it back to him"

"It doesn't belong to him" Jörgen protested.

"Jörgen, you are dealing with a man whose very wife and everything she is and she owns is in his possession. Just give it to him"

Jörgen stared into his face. He could only speak to Alexi in English, perhaps this Karazin would understand what he was saying. What should he give him? He cursed the packet Eva had given him. He would have to explain to Taru. He was bitterly disappointed himself, but he had promised her. He had to give him something. He reached into his rucksack and withdrew the small embroidered bag. Karazin snatched it from his hand immediately and tore it open. It had been fastened with a button which now flew across the room followed by something else, but what was it? Jörgen looked at what had fallen. Something like wheat. That was it, something the colour of ripe wheat and another thing, like the head of a flower. Karazin turned the bag inside out. It was flowers. The little bag was full of dried flowers. Jörgen caught their musky smell as Karazin scattered them onto the table.

"You have brought me here for this!" Alexi roared at him. Karazin threw the bag onto the floor. He glared at everyone then he turned on his heel and slammed out of the door. Jörgen bent down and picked up the bag. "Why didn't you tell me what it was?" said Alexi "Why couldn't you give that to him before?"

"I didn't know what it was myself." said Jörgen.

He scooped up the flowers and poured them back into the bag. At least he could give Mariko this. It was beautifully made. It reminded him of something, yes it was Eva's dress. It was the same blend of colours as

---

her dress. It really was an exquisite little bag. He was suddenly dizzy and sat down.

"I think you need to eat eh?" said Alexi, calming down. He placed his hand on Jörgen's shoulder. "There is no point I go back to my meeting. You have to be at the airport in two hours."

"Airport?" said Jörgen. For an ordinary commercial flight he hoped.

"Many soldiers go back tonight" said Alexi as they crossed the car park.

"Did you manage to speak to this woman at all? I hope you have found out what you came for and have something to tell my friend."

Alexi had given Jörgen a present before he boarded the plane. It was a fur hat with ear flaps and it had helped him to sleep on the journey. At first he had imagined himself arriving at the gangway wearing it, but it seemed too flamboyant for the mood he was in. He knew Leif would be angry. He had left a simple note to say he was travelling north with Colonel Alexi Simonov and would be back the following day. He hoped Taru would explain and be able to smooth things over, but on top of it all, he had suddenly realised that the ship had been given only seventy two hours to be in port. The deadline was eight o'clock that evening and he would not arrive back until after midnight. His visa as well as those of everyone else on board would have expired.

It filled him with a profound sense of failure. What had he achieved? He had only created a huge problem for everyone. In the last hour before they landed, he was wide awake with worry. He thought of the packet and opened the rucksack to look at it. Carl Andersson. It was addressed to Carl Andersson at a post box number for a newspaper in Stockholm. Where had he heard that name before? Had Taru mentioned it? There were a lot of Carl Anderssons in Sweden. And there was Eva's bag. He was still feeling stressed by their meeting. He would have liked to rescue her, take her back to Sweden. Something heroic like that would have meant something, more than bringing home a small bag full of dried flowers. Why had she given it to him? Perhaps they were flowers she had kept from the time she was in Sweden. What had she said? 'I am going to be operated on this afternoon, so you must take this as well'. You must take this. You must. He looked down at the bag. It was decorated around the edges with a thick band of intertwined silk ribbon. He ran his fingers over it. Was it wishful thinking? He pressed his thumbs all around the edge. He could feel something. Evenly spaced and of the same size. It was. It had to be. Two of the soldiers sitting close by were looking at him and made a joke. He was longing to take a knife and see, just to be sure, but he would have to wait. He couldn't help his spirits soaring. What did it matter about the visa. There was every chance he was coming back in triumph.

The military car dropped him off before the entrance to the dry cargo port and before he had walked a few yards he could see that the WHITE WIND had left. He continued walking anyway, where else did he have to go? As he approached the edge of the dock, he saw the soldier out of the corner of his eye and then there he was, suddenly standing in front of him, sardonic and all powerful with his gun slung over his arm, a knowing ease in the way he stood there confronting him, with his lazy but menacing smile. He held his hand out, snapping his fingers. Passport, papers, visa, Jörgen knew what he wanted. He looked out across the entrance to the port, towards the wide open sea.

The soldier moved closer to him and said something, obviously asking for his identity. What was he doing there? He answered him in Swedish to confuse him.

"I am waiting for my ship" he said.

The soldier snapped his fingers again and pointed at Jörgen's rucksack.

There was a movement to one side, at the edge of the stern of the bulk carrier moored to the left and a figure came moving swiftly out of the dark, walked up to Jörgen and slapped him across the face. He hit him with such a force that Jörgen had to hang on to his rucksack or it would have flown out of his arms and over the side of the dock. The soldier took a step forward, unsure what to do.

"Why are you coming back here so late?! What the hell are you doing here now?!" It was Leif. Jörgen saw everything at once in his eyes. He was acting, but he was very worried that things were going to turn the wrong way.

Leif confronted the soldier. "I am the captain of the WHITE WIND. This man is our cook and we have been waiting for him for hours. We have been docked here for three days. You must remember me, surely you remember me, Captain Hansson?" he said taking the soldiers arm in a not too friendly grip. The soldier was not sure what to do. He understood certain words, cook, captain, the name of the ship.

"Get into the launch!" Leif shouted to Jörgen, giving him another blow to the head. Jörgen saw that Leif had tied the launch to the anchor chain on the bulk carrier. He jumped, thinking all the time that any moment he would hear a bullet whistling past his ear.

On the dock, Leif squeezed a few dollar bills into the soldier's hand. It was very fast. He didn't linger over the transaction but turned and followed Jörgen by jumping down into the launch himself.

"Cast off" Leif shouted. It was a sweet sound, the

rasp of the outboard motor as it sprang to life. They roared away from the dock and headed out to sea.

"You didn't have to hit me so hard" Jörgen said, rubbing his cheek.

"Didn't I?" said Leif at the helm "You're lucky I didn't knock you into the dock"

The lights of the WHITE WIND appeared on the horizon.

"We've been using a lot of fuel, sailing up and down, waiting for you to turn up. You had better have a good story after all this."

The first person he saw as he climbed on board was Mariko. Mariko, with tears in her eyes, coming towards him. Then she was putting her arms around him and pressing her face against his jacket. Jörgen looked around. There was Akira and Nogi up on the sun deck, waving to him.

"You come to the sitting room" said Leif. "Taru wants to know what this is all about."

"Can we make it the dining room?" said Jörgen, feeling light headed. "I'm really hungry. Akira!" he called, looking up at him "Can you bring me something to eat?"

Leif marched him into the sitting room and Taru looked up with a smile. "Your father found you I see. I heard the launch. It is good you are safe" He stood up and shook his hand.

"Sorry about the time."

"A resourceful man, your father."

Jörgen could see himself in the mirror. He looked like hell.

"I asked Akira to get some food."

"You are hungry, of course. We will go to the dining room" said Taru, leading the way.

Leif reached for the house phone. "Bridge?" he said "Full steam ahead."

Jörgen ate as fast as he could while Leif, Taru and Mariko watched and waited. Then Jörgen began to tell his story. At the end, he turned to Akira.

"Akira. Can you bring me some sharp scissors?" Within a minute, they were in his hand. Please let it be true, Jörgen prayed as he took the embroidered bag out of his rucksack. So far he had left this part out of his story. Jörgen opened the bag and tipped the dried flowers onto the table "These are from Eva" he said. Then to everyone's surprise, he took the scissors and very carefully, cut the ribbon away from all four sides. The soft wool stuffing started to spring out, and the first pearl rolled across the table. Jörgen picked it up, reached across the table for Mariko and placed the pearl in the palm of her hand. Everyone stared in silence. Something magical, unbelievable was happening.

"Number one" said Jörgen. He looked at Taru. "I hope there are fifty" he said with a smile.

Chapter 37

Jörgen slept on and off for two days and when at last he woke up, he lay with his hands behind his head, thinking of the scene in the dining room. Would he ever have such a moment in his life again. Everyone had joined in with counting the pearls and when they had agreed that all fifty pearls were lying there, on the table in front of them, Taru had opened two bottles of his best champagne.

Jörgen got up, showered, dressed, and then stood looking down at his rucksack lying in the corner. Then he went to find Leif, who was, as usual, on the bridge.

"We are in the Mediterranean" said Leif, holding the binoculars up to his eyes. "Now what is that stupid little boat doing now" he muttered and Jörgen smiled and went to leave.

"No, don't run away now. O.K. he's decided at last to turn to starboard" He shook his head. "The problem with this ship is that too many people get curious and want a closer look."

"I have to eat something anyway" said Jörgen, picking up a biscuit from the coffee station. He looked at the telex, still pinned to the wall.

"Heard from Mum and Helen again yet?"

"They're probably on their way to Rio by now, getting ready to take a flight home."

Home, Jörgen thought. The thought of home had never felt so good.

"But this came in the night" Leif pointed at the telex lying on the shelf under the windows.

WHAT YOU DO ABOUT ELISE?
HARBOUR MASTER NATAL CONTACT ME. SENT HIM MORE MONEY. LUCKY FOR YOU JUST HAD RECORD CATCH. NO HURRY ON THIS. SAY HELLO TO EVERYONE ESPECIALLY JÖRGEN
REGARDS GEORGIO

The ELISE, of course. Jörgen didn't ask Leif what he was going to do. He knew he didn't have an answer to that right now.

"We're going to bunker again off Gibraltar."

"Where are we heading?"

"Gothenburg."

"We are?"

What else could make today more perfect than it was already, Jörgen was thinking, but there was a note of sadness creeping in. He would be saying goodbye to Mariko, Taru as well, and Akira and Nogi. They had become a family on board the WHITE WIND, used to seeing each other every day. This is what Leif had with Georgio. Jörgen understood more about the bond they had between them, now he had experienced these long weeks at sea.

But something was worrying him "I want to talk to you when you have time" he said, and Leif gave him a look.

"Is this about Mariko?"

"No. But we need to be alone somewhere, any suggestion?"

"I'll come to your cabin when the next watch takes over. Get yourself some breakfast. See you soon."

Jörgen wandered into the dining room. The table where they had sat was cleared away and polished but there was a thread of silk on the carpet under the table. Jörgen picked it up just as Nogi came in and bowed to him. Jörgen bowed back and laughed.

"You like fish or ham sir?"

"Anything. Is it OK to eat in here? What is everyone else doing?"

"Mr. Takahashi eating lunch in room. Miss Mariko also in her room, busy."

"Busy?" Jörgen knew he was overstepping the boundaries. He shouldn't press Nogi to give him information, but his mood was so high.

"She is.. " said Nogi, his eyes shifting about. Then he pointed to the thread of silk Jörgen was still holding between his fingers and he made a sewing motion.

"I understand. So, fish or ham OK. Thank you Nogi, and tea. A large pot of tea" said Jörgen, sitting down at the table.

Perhaps Mariko was repairing Eva's embroidered bag. He wouldn't ask her about it, he decided, he would wait and let her surprise him.

The package lay on the table between them. "Do you know where this came from?" asked Leif, but it was a rhetorical question. "Carl Andersson is the reporter friend of Anders Halenius. I think this is from Anders Halenius, Eva's brother.

"From her brother? The one who is in Kazakhstan looking for her? She knew that, that's why she was so worried about it."

"I'm not sure she would know it was from him, unless the person who gave it to her told her. And why would she not tell you that? It would have been so significant. It could have made you more concerned to hang on to it. You see how tightly it's bound up and these burn marks. I don't see any sign that anyone has opened it. There's no return address. The letters are printed not written, but I doubt she would have recognised his handwriting. She hadn't seen him for twenty years."

"Why do you think she was so afraid someone would find it?"

"Could be drugs" said Leif "You were lucky that soldier didn't get to search you" He picked up the package and turned it over in his hands. "Feels like a book, but it wouldn't be the first time drugs had been hidden in a book."

"That would mean that Carl Andersson is either a drug addict or a drug dealer" said Jörgen and they both laughed.

"Maybe a report of some kind, for the newsapaper. They're pretty sensitive about their politics."

"But I can mail it to him when we get to Sweden"

"I don't know. This is Taru's ship. I think we should ask him first, just in case the Swedish customs want to make a thorough search when we get to Gothenburg. I can't think it contains drugs, but if Taru thinks we should open it to check, then we'll do that. We can always throw it into the sea before we get into port if we find something."

Later in the afternoon Leif asked Jörgen to join them in Taru's rooms. When Jörgen came in, he saw the open package and a notebook on the table. Jörgen wondered what it contained. Leif was tense and the atmosphere in the room was very sombre.

"Well Jörgen, we have opened it as you can see, and it is a report from Anders Halenius as I suspected. We also know that he had not found his sister at the time it was written. He says at the end of the report something about it, I'll read it to you. 'Very doubtful I can risk looking for Eva anymore and will try to send or bring this to you if I can manage to leave. I am in the middle of nowhere right now but I am making this report the new priority' It's dated five days ago."

Taru was standing out on the balcony with his back to them, staring out to sea.

"What's the matter Leif? Something wrong?" Jörgen asked quietly.

"You can take this away and read it for yourself, but Taru and I believe it to be an accurate and truthful report."

Jörgen picked up the book and turned to the opening page 'Scandal of the Ongoing Nuclear Tests in the Soviet Socialist Republic of Kazakhstan' Jörgen read aloud 'A First Hand Eye Witness report by Anders Halenius. The people of Kazakhstan who live within the area of the Semipalatinsk Nuclear Test Range'.. but this is where.."

"Yes. You were there, in that city"

"This is why Eva is so ill" Jörgen said, then continued to read "The inhuman and far reaching consequences of.."

"You can take it with you Jörgen. I have translated and read it to Taru, so we know the contents. You can see that it gets delivered into Carl Andersson's hands when we get back to Sweden. But I wouldn't handle it more than you have to, and we could seal it inside a new envelope."

"Are you worried about me?"

"A little. But we can have regular checks in good hospitals, not like the people you will read about in that report. Now Taru and I are going to have a meeting here, so you will have to excuse us."

"What's up?"

"When you read it, you will know what this report will mean politically in the world and to anyone with a conscience, and especially to Japanese people. We are cancelling our plans to do any business with the Soviet Union. It's OK Jörgen, don't look so serious, neither Taru or I have been happy with the way it was going. This has made our mind up for us."

Leif opened the door to show him out and stepped out into the passageway with him. "We are planning to go back to the small company idea as before, just two or three ships and general cargo, maybe container ships, but no oil tankers."

"I'm not sorry" said Jörgen "We would never have seen you. You would have been so busy there would have been no time for us, even to go sailing on the ELISE in the summer."

Leif did something he hadn't done since Jörgen was a boy, he kissed him on the cheek "You're a good lad, but you are going to be busy in Film School, right?"

"Right" said Jörgen. "But I'll be home in the holidays. We'll go sailing then."

Chapter 38

When the WHITE WIND arrived in Gothenburg, everyone was on the dock to meet the ship. Ella was wearing a new hat and hanging on to it in the stiff breeze. Helen was all in white to show off her tan. Leif and Jörgen were out on deck looking down at them as the crew eased the ship alongside. The surprise was to see Erik and Connie as well. Kurt joked to Leif that if they needed any new crew, he would be glad to volunteer.

They gathered in the sitting room to say goodbye. Taru was going to make a speech, but Mariko and Jörgen were not there.

"Out on deck" Helen said to Leif, looking through the windows "Shall I give them a shout?"

"No. You can leave them."

Leif watched Jörgen and Mariko walk away along the deck. He slipped his arm around Ella's waist and thought of himself when he was nineteen and so in love with Ella. Sometimes when he looked back he couldn't believe that they had come together in the end. How painful it was to be in love with someone you thought you may never see again. He would have liked to find something to say to comfort him, but he had been too harsh about it before, and now there was nothing left to say.

Jörgen and Mariko leant against the rail. Ships were passing up and down on their way to Frihamnen, the commercial port across the river. The WHITE WIND was tied up at the berth at Lundbykajen, usually occupied by the ELISE. Jörgen was thinking of the ELISE, so far away, left behind in the harbour at Natal.

"How long in Stockholm?" Mariko was asking, although they had discussed it many times.

"Two years, maybe more, depends on a lot of things. How brilliant or not I turn out to be. Right now I want to stand here like this and not go anywhere"

Mariko looked across the water. They would be leaving that way, and very soon, down the river to the sea, on their way home to Japan.

"You are my very best friend" she said quietly.

"You also."

"We can see each other again? I must think that we will see each other or I cannot leave Jörgen"

She looked up at him and he wanted so much to kiss her, to hold her, but he could imagine how startled everyone would be. He reached for her hand.

"We can and we will."

"I will keep this with me always and think of you" she said, reaching for Eva's embroidered bag that was hanging on her shoulder, the woven silk ribbon now repaired with silver braid.

There was a discreet cough behind them. It was Akira, with a tray and two glasses of champagne.

Chapter 39

Jörgen had taken an early train to Stockholm, hours before he was due to be at the Film Institute for his interview. He was going to call at the newspaper and see Carl Andersson at last. Jörgen had sent the notebook to him four weeks ago by registered mail and had checked twice that it had been received, although he didn't get to speak to Carl himself. He understood perfectly now that Carl was avoiding him. Jörgen and Leif kept scanning the newspapers but so far nothing had appeared. Jörgen had been quite ruthless when he reached him on the telephone at last. "I don't think anyone has heard from your friend Anders" Jörgen had said, "You think he may have given his life to get that article to you?" and it had won him an appointment.

Carl Andersson was a short fat man with a permanent cigarette in his mouth. Jörgen found him behind a divided office wall in the corner of an enormous room, full of other people in other divided work stations who were either typing or talking on the telephone. Carl swung about in his chair and surveyed Jörgen with a shrewd expression, wrinkling up his eyes against the drifting smoke from his cigarette as if he was playing the part of a reporter in a film.

"Sit down Jörgen. I am going to tell you a bit about the facts of life" he said.

Jörgen stopped pacing around the streets and went into a coffee shop and sat down. He had to calm himself for the interview. He had prepared himself for this moment. He didn't want to arrive with anger seeping out of every pore. He found that he was glaring at everyone as if he hated them. He closed his eyes and thought of Mariko, far away at her university. He would write to her when he got home that evening and share his outrage. No he wouldn't. Why should he make her feel as cynical as he was feeling? He would write it down though. It had always helped him to write things down. The thing that was nagging him the most was that he hadn't thought to make a copy of Anders Halenius' notebook before sending it to the newspaper. If he had, he would have distributed copies all over the city; maybe contact other newspapers who were not so concerned about upsetting the Soviet Union.

This was why he was so very angry. Not only that they were not going to publish it for political reasons, or that Carl talked down to him as if he was a naive child, but that Jörgen himself had not been careful enough with such precious material and thought to make a copy. He had asked Carl for the notebook back as they were not going to publish it. "Well, I think it was meant for me not you" Carl had said, dusting the ash from his lapel as he spoke. "And something you don't know but I actually advanced him money. We kind of bought whatever he was going to produce. Can't help it if the people upstairs don't want to print it. That's life."

Or death, Jörgen had wanted to say and wished he had. The final blow was when Carl produced a piece of copy entitled 'Prosperity in Alma-Ata' that had Anders Halenius name under the title. "Just got this through the wire. We're putting this in this week. So he's getting something printed. You can look out for it."

Author's Footnote

Between 1949 and 1989, the Soviet Union exploded an estimated 480 nuclear bombs in north eastern Kazakhstan, 117 above the ground, in an area covering 18,000 square kilometres. The contaminated land that was affected by the tests, caused by changes in the wind, was 300,000 square kilometres, an area that would cover two thirds of the land in Sweden. There were two million people living in that area. The illnesses, deformities and still births mentioned in the book were a fact that was covered up for years. It was not until the Nevada-Semipalatinsk environmental movement was established in 1989 by Olzhas Suleymenov, a Kazak poet and politician, and huge protests were made on the streets and a million signatures collected, that the Kazakhstan Communist Party and the government in Moscow called a halt to the tests. The area was then declared an environmental disaster zone, this after forty years of an average of one nuclear explosion every month. Many people in Kazakhstan are still suffering from this terrible legacy.

Photo: Anna-Karin Lund, AW-fotoateljé, Lidköping

Jill Vedebrand was born in London, England. She worked in the film business as a production manager in the United States for many years and then moved to Scotland where she and her Swedish sea captain husband had a small farm. She has also travelled all over the world with Tomas on board his cargo ships. They now live in Sweden.